Loving War

The Sterling Shore Series,

Book 4

C.M. Owens

Loving War
The Sterling Shore Series

LOVING WAR

They say there's a thin line between love and hate. With Kode Sterling, that line is very, very thin.

Chapter 1

Kode

Maverick and Corbin are completely wasted, and while I'm entertained, I'm also incredibly annoyed. They'll end up in jail tonight. No doubt about it.

I laugh as one of the girls rolls her eyes and walks away from Maverick after whatever he whispers in her ear. He holds his hands up innocently, seeming genuinely confused by her walk-off response.

He recovers quickly and finds a new girl to stalk, so I return to sipping my beer and scanning the scene. I came out tonight to have fun, and all I've done is think about Rain being with Dane. I know he's the one she wants, but it doesn't make it any easier to fucking swallow.

We drove all the way to come to a bar where the women didn't know the two idiots I call cousins. Their reputations are steadily growing. If they keep screwing over the women in Sterling Shore, not even Rain will be able to save them anymore.

Rain. Fuck. I have to stop thinking about her, and everything I think about is somehow tied to her. There's nothing I can say, do, or even think that doesn't trigger some sort of connection to the girl I chased for too many years. I need to get drunk. And I need a distraction—a female distraction. Someone who doesn't look the least little bit like the girl who refuses to leave my dreams.

As the beers keep coming, I get a little drunker. The drunker, the better. It'll numb my mind.

My distraction serves itself up on a mouthwatering platter. Dark hair touches a small waist, crossed tan legs are beautifully exposed, and a tight little short dress catches my eyes.

That'll fucking do.

She looks to be alone, which is perfect. That means I won't need a wingman to distract her friend, and I won't have to deal with some guy she might be with.

She's all the way at the bar, and I'm in the far back. This booth is perfect, because I can view her sexy profile. I can't see her face from this angle because her hair is in the way, but judging by the way every guy in here keeps glancing her way, trying to gather the courage to approach her, I'm confident she's going to be just as hot from the front as she is from the side.

She dismisses the first guy who finally has the balls to take a shot, and I grin. She's not going to be easy prey. All the better.

The bartender slides a drink in front of her—from one of her admirers most likely, because she shakes her head to refuse it, and he carries it over to a sulking man. My grin only grows.

This is going to be fun.

Tria

Why did I come here? I don't know. I guess I just wanted to be out of Sterling Shore and away from everyone who knows me. It's fun to be someone mysterious instead of the girl everyone associates with Dane and Rain.

I love my sister, and I'm so thankful we're getting along—finally—

3

but I'd like for someone to talk to me about something other than the beautiful couple. I get it. I really do. They are a dream match, and she wrote an entire book about him. Several, actually. I doubt there's ever been a romance she wrote where Dane wasn't the lead role in her mind. But still... It would be nice if someone was genuinely interested in *just* me.

"Is this seat taken?" a deep voice asks from beside me.

I barely turn to see the guy who doesn't even come close to being my type. Is that... makeup? There is definitely mascara on his lashes. He looks like he spends more time getting ready than I do.

"It will be when I find someone I want to talk to," I mutter, refusing to grant him any more of my attention.

"That's rude," he scoffs.

"It'd be ruder to lead you on, let you waste your money on drinks for me, and then leave with someone I would rather be with. Don't you think?" I ask, feeling somewhat bitchy. Old habits die hard. I've been the Ice Queen for too long, but damn... How can I play nice with wolves?

He walks away—after several attempts to try a new angle—and I'm left in peace once more. I want someone to be interested in me, not just what I look like naked. Of course... this dress and this bar probably weren't the best ways to get that sort of interest. In all fairness, I'm probably judging too harshly.

"I need another Corona with lime on the Sterling tab," a waitress says, making my breath catch in my throat and my heart stop in its tracks.

No. Surely not.

"Which one? I have three. Maverick, Corbin, and... Kode Sterling," the bartender says, unaware of the three devils' names he just spoke aloud.

How in the hell did this happen? How did I come this far away and still end up in the line of fire? No. It has to be a mistake.

"Kode Sterling. Can you get Missy to take it to him? He's in the corner booth near the back. It's time for my break."

I cut my eyes in the direction they've warned me about, and I peek out around my hair just barely. Sure enough, the devil is there, and he's staring this way.

I whip back around, desperately trying to think of a way to get out of here without any of them seeing me. I spot Corbin and Maverick when I turn the other way. They are hounding girls on the dance floor, which is perfect, because I won't have to worry about either of them noticing me while they're prowling.

I wish they'd hurry and get Kode his drink so he'd quit staring this way. With my new, darker locks, he most likely has no clue who I am. I can still get out unscathed.

Think, Tria. Think escape.

I stand, but a warm body is suddenly very close behind me, and I stiffen. Please don't let it be—

"You can't possibly be leaving so soon," a deceptively seductive voice murmurs close to my ear, making me all the more tense as his warm breath fans my cheek and leaves unbidden chills in its wake. Shit. He knows it's me. "Because it'd be a shame if you left before meeting me."

Oh. My. God. You've got to be kidding me. Kode Sterling is hitting on me? How much has he had to drink?

I clear my throat, but I refuse to turn around. "I'm pretty sure I'm not your type," I say, but my voice sounds off, a little higher than I want it to be.

"And how would you know that?" he asks, pressing his front closer to my back.

Oh damn. He's turned on—turned on because of me. This would be hilarious if I didn't know him well enough to be certain he'll punish me for this.

I turn around, giving him a second to study me, and his eyes widen in horror as his drink sputters from his choking mouth.

"Probably because you've hated me for eleven years," I say evenly, letting not one droplet of emotion taint my deadpan delivery.

My eyebrow cocks up as he stumbles backwards, making a fool of himself. I'm definitely going to pay for this. He's a ruthless son of a bitch. I should enjoy it while it lasts, because the upper hand I have will soon turn into the foundation of a stronger sense hatred.

"Tria?" he says through a cough, sounding as though he's disgusted and shocked in the same breath.

I can't help it; I stifle my laughter, but my mocking smile creeps into place.

"No," he says, shaking his head as if he's seeing things, hating himself in this moment.

A humiliated and dumbfounded Kode Sterling—love it.

"Yes," I say, relishing my ounce of power before he jerks it away.

"Fuck," he hisses, staring at his bottle of beer as though it's the enemy. Then those murderous eyes cut back toward me, and I almost shrivel up. "What the hell are you doing here?"

No. I won't cower down to him. You stand up to bullies, right? I won't cry in the corner tonight. I'll fight back, damn it.

"Probably the same thing you're doing. Having fun in a place where no one was supposed to know me."

"Mr. Sterling, your beer," a waitress says, interrupting us.

He waves it off, acting as though he's terrified of what might be in it. "I changed my mind," he mumbles, setting his almost-finished bottle on the bar.

I have to get away while I still can.

"Tria?" a familiar voice says, but unlike the last familiar voice, this one is welcome.

"Raya," I say, smiling, so damn grateful she's here. Kode won't dare do anything to me in front of her, because he'd be terrified it'd get back to his precious obsession—Rain.

She looks from me to Kode as if she's confused. No doubt she's become painfully aware of our horrible history by now.

"You two together?" she asks incredulously.

I laugh, but Kode still seems to be in utter shock.

"No. You here alone?" I ask, not elaborating on the screwed-up situation.

"Yeah... but Kade is on his way. He had a meeting with a restaurant that wants to start distributing some of his wines. I told him

I'd meet him here."

I loop my arm through hers, savoring the saving grace she does not know she's offering, and start walking away. "I'll keep you company."

Kode

Un-fucking-believable. Why am I still watching her? What is wrong with me? Why is my damn dick still hard?

Ah, hell. Are they really going to play pool?

Raya seems to be instructing Tria, and I watch with guilty pleasure as Tria leans over the table, offering me a peek closer to her perfectly sculpted ass.

No. No. Hell no. I cannot be attracted to Tria Noles. Nope. Not happening.

I glance down at my betraying appendage and curse it for refusing to lose its arousal. Several muffled swears and threats spill through my lips, but the damn thing is still at full attention.

"Pep talk?" Maverick jokes as he steps beside me, looking at me as though I've lost my mind.

I have lost my mind.

"No. It's exactly the opposite," I growl, wishing it wouldn't hurt if I punched my own crotch.

"O...kay... So, I finally found a group of girls who aren't total prudes. You coming?"

I glance over at the table full of sexy women that Corbin is already working over, but my eyes involuntarily gravitate toward Tria again.

Damn... those legs. Does she have to hold that stick like that?

I groan and actually slap my own face, which earns an eyebrow raise from Mav.

"Dude, did you do drugs or something? Because you look like you're tweaking."

I scrub my face and make a silent oath to never drink again. Yeah right. I need something hella-strong right now.

"Whiskey—straight up," I say to the bartender.

"Whiskey? Really? The hard stuff makes you a little... crazy."

Maverick is grating on my nerves. I have serious problems right now. Whiskey can't make me any crazier than I apparently already am if I'm losing my mind over Tria Noles.

The bartender hands me the whiskey and I toss it back in one sip.

"Keep them coming."

"Dude," Maverick grumbles, "what the hell happened?"

Again, my damn traitorous eyes find the brunette I don't want to want, and my pants get even tighter, which I didn't think could be possible. She's leaning over that table again, and all I can picture is fucking her on that damn thing.

"I've lost my damn mind. *That's* what happened."

He laughs, as though any of this is funny. He wouldn't be laughing if he was hard as a rock for Tria. He'd be as freaked out as I am.

"Hey. Didn't expect to see you two here," a friendly voice says, and I groan inwardly before making a calculated turn—keeping my erection hidden—and face Kade Colton.

"Well, I'll be damned," Maverick says, grinning. "Did the woman

9

let you off the leash for a night?"

I pretend I have no knowledge of the fact Raya is here... with Tria.

"First of all, she doesn't keep me on a leash, and secondly, I'm actually meeting her here," he says, letting his smile lift at the very thought of her.

Like a nasty habit, I glance back over to the pool table, and my jaw clenches when I see a few guys talking to Raya and Tria. Did that fucker really just touch her? I'll break his damn hand if he does it again.

What. The hell. Is wrong with me?

"Damn. I better go get my girl before someone falls in love," Kade says, grinning bigger when he spots her shooing away the unwanted attention. Tria isn't shooing away her groper. Why is she even speaking to that son of a bitch?

"You guys can join us if you want to," Kade says while walking away.

"No, we've got—"

"I'll come," I say, interrupting Maverick.

I don't know what I'm doing, but I can't just sit back and watch this douche rub his hands all over Tria.

"Dude!" Maverick calls loudly.

"Catch up with you later," I call over my shoulder, rushing my steps.

Kade tries making idle conversation with me as we close the short distance between us and the girls, but I tune him out. My attention is on one thing, and that's the jerk whose hands are all over Tria. He doesn't even know her.

"Sorry, boys," Kade says loudly, "this one is mine."

Raya's smile could brighten a room when Kade makes a show of kissing her, but it only briefly distracts me.

"Kode," Tria sighs, seeming annoyed with my presence.

I try to act casual as a waitress brings me a fresh glass of whiskey. "Care to introduce me to your new friend?" I ask, motioning to the animal who is groping her ass now.

She flinches when he moves in behind her. She doesn't want him touching her. So why isn't she just slapping him away? Why the fuck is this eating me alive? I can't stand to see his hands on her.

Tria

The only reason I haven't punched this guy in the nose for his brazen gropes is because Kode Sterling is seconds away from unleashing his wrath. Why else would he come over here?

"I got us a booth. This place is supposed to have phenomenal burgers," Raya says, tugging Kade's hand. "You guys sitting with us?"

She looks from me to Kode several times, and then she looks at the jerk who is sliding his hand around my waist. I roll my eyes, and Kade pulls Raya toward the booth, deciding not to wait on a response.

"Okay, that's enough," I grumble. That's all I can take.

He doesn't let go. Instead, he tugs me to him tighter. "Let's get out of here," he whispers, acting as though he completely missed what I just said.

"She said enough," Kode says, keeping his tone strong and a little threatening. "It wasn't an invitation for more."

11

Oh boy. If he's helping me out, then it's only to execute some master plan of humiliation later.

Considering Kode is easily 6'3, and this guy is a mere 5'10 tops, he backs down from the sandy blonde with a fight in his eyes. At least Kode is scary to everyone—not just me.

"Thanks," I mutter when the guy walks off.

"You shouldn't be letting them hang all over you if you don't want them expecting more," he says through a bored tone, but his jaw clenches as if he's pissed.

That makes no sense.

"I was trying to keep you from possibly humiliating me. It seemed best if I had a guy around. I should have picked someone a little soberer," I mumble, frowning.

His right eyebrow raises questioningly, and then his panty-dropping smile comes up as he leans down to get right in my face. "You thought that douche could stop me from doing anything I want to you?"

Was that... seduction? Surely not. He's not trying to seduce me. It's Kode. This is a game.

I swallow hard, denying my body the right to shiver under his heated gaze. There's no way he's looking at me this way. He's fucking with me. He probably knows I once had a crush, but that was years ago—before he tortured me to damn death and grew an unhealthy obsession for my sister.

"Let's play," he says, making me go on guard.

A warning? Kode Sterling doesn't usually warn his victims of his impending attack, and I don't feel like playing his games.

"I knew you were going to—"

"Pool," he says while setting his glass down on the rim of the pool table, interrupting my would-be rant.

My mouth opens and closes a few times as he starts chalking one of the pool cues. What is going on?

"I'd rather not," I say, backing up. I'm almost worried he's going to jerk my dress up while I'm bent over the table, just so he can embarrass the hell out of me in front of everyone here. It would be like high school all over again when he pulled my skirt up in the hallway after an argument I had with Rain. People still make fun of my Hello Kitty underwear.

He smiles a little as his eyes meet mine.

"It's not a trick, Tria. It's just a game of pool."

He has to be shit-face drunk right now to even think I'd fall for something like that.

"What're you drinking?" he asks.

I glance down at the fourth glass of vodka I've had. I hit the strong stuff once I realized Kode was here.

"Vodka."

He motions for a waitress and orders us two more glasses of our drinks before he walks over to me, making me falter for my footing. I wish he'd stop looking at me like that. Is this my punishment? What game is he playing?

"Hitting the good stuff, Tria?" he asks, but he doesn't wait on my response before coming to stand behind me. He places a pool stick

13

directly in front of my body before saying, "One game."

I shiver when my body refuses to be as strong against him as my mind.

"I'll even let you go first," he adds, making it sound so much dirtier than necessary as his breath coats my ear with a teasing touch.

Damn him.

"Fine." I take the stick away from him, and ignore his hard as hell length against my back before stepping away. "One game. And if you do anything to embarrass me, I'll break this stick on your balls. Got it?"

Why am I doing this? Any sane girl who knows Kode as well as I do would run away before he can execute whatever terrible plan of torture he has in mind.

"Got it," he says, grinning like he has already won.

I warily step to the other side of the table, and I do my best to focus on breaking the balls. I strike the white ball hard, but it slowly rolls right instead of into the triangle.

Crap.

"Here," he says, walking around the table to come stand behind me again. Damn. Why is he so hard? "You're doing it wrong. Let me show you."

His body rests over mine as he leans against my back and wraps his arms around me to adjust my hold on the stick. "Like this," he says against my ear, pressing harder against me. "And then one easy stroke with just the right amount of force will be perfect."

I swallow hard. I really don't like this game.

The waitress returns with a glass of vodka for me, and I almost run out of the intimate position we're in before I guzzle it down. I should leave. But I can't. My twisted mind keeps wanting him to play with me a little more.

I really need to get laid if I'm fantasizing what it would be like to be bent over a pool table by Kode Sterling.

Chapter 2

Kode

I'm about to explode. Every time I help her line up her next shot, I press my cock as hard against her as I possibly can. Surely she's felt it by now. She has to be turned on. Doesn't she?

I need a CAT scan.

Maverick and Corbin are still clueless about who I'm with. Apparently they don't recognize her any better than I did, but they're staying on the far side of the bar, completely engulfed by the women around them. I've ignored the curious looks from Raya and Kade. If I don't find a way to fuck Tria and get this over with, I might commit myself to the asylum.

Surely if I fuck her, then I'll be fine. It'll be out of my system.

Tria was always pretty enough, but it was hard to see her as anything other than the enemy because of Rain. Now... I fucked up by not knowing it was her. Had I known right away it was her, then I wouldn't have fallen into this nonsensical infatuation.

"Eight ball, corner pocket," she says, bending over right in front of me.

I groan as her dress slides up just enough to make me want to slam into her from behind. I want to be buried inside her right now. I can't do it. It's Tria. She's hotter than I've ever fucking noticed before, but it's Tria, damn it.

"Never gonna happen," I mutter, reminding myself this is off-limits.

"Watch me," she says, thinking I was referring to her shot.

I step closer, my feet moving of their own accord, and I run my hand over her ass before I realize what I'm doing. I shouldn't have had so much liquor. It makes me too hands-on.

She stiffens under my touch, and I give her ass a squeeze, feeling my dick almost try to detach after the extended amount of time it's been fully erect. I honestly don't know if I've ever needed to fuck someone so badly in all my life.

My emotions and thoughts keep contradicting themselves, making it hard to decipher what the hell I'm actually going to do.

"I need to go," she says, putting the pool stick down on the table without attempting her shot.

She staggers slightly, and I wrap my arms around her to steady her... Or at least that's what I'm telling myself.

"You're drunk," I say, waving at the waitress to bring over my tab. "You can't drive."

"I have a hotel room," she mumbles. "Across the street. I planned ahead."

She had to mention a hotel. Damn. And what was she planning for?

"Don't tell me you came here to get laid," I almost growl.

"Don't tell me you didn't. I need to go. Mission *not* accomplished."

Really? She's not the least bit turned on by me? After all that?

"I'll walk you." I'm a little pissed that she was going to fuck some stranger but not me. At least she knows me.

I roll my eyes when the voice in my head starts sounding like an annoying bitch instead of a badass guy.

"I can walk myself," she says, pushing away from me.

Fine. If she doesn't even want me to walk her out, then who am I to argue? She's a grown woman.

When she staggers all the way to the door, my jaw clenches. She's not fit to cross a street alone. Some guy winks at a group of his buddies when he spots her, and he ducks out the door behind her, making his intentions clear.

Oh hell no.

I take quick strides, ignoring Maverick when he yells for me, and I burst through the doors to see the guy laughing as he steadies her.

"I've got you, sweetheart," he says, chuckling. "Where're you headed? I'll help you."

Like hell.

"I've got her," I interrupt, knocking his hands off her as I wrap my arm around her waist.

"The fuck you do," he snarls, acting like I'm stealing easy prey from his jaws.

"Kode," Tria purrs, smiling as she pulls at my shirt. "Take me to my room."

From the pool table to here, she's finally making sense. Good.

The guy rolls his eyes, but he walks away, sulking. I start crossing the street with her safely tucked under my arm, but I'm staggering almost as badly as she is.

We both laugh when we take a diagonal route by mistake, and she clutches me tighter once we reach the sidewalk. I smirk when she takes off her heels and holds them in one hand.

"So much better," she groans, and then she tugs at my jacket. "Come in with me."

I smile as she tugs me harder. "I'll walk you to your room."

Her vixen's grin only makes my already aching cock hurt that much more. But I can't fuck her now. Not now that she's this drunk. It's as though walking outside made the alcohol catch up with her. Hate it when that shit happens.

We step into the elevator, and she presses the button for the fifth floor. I notice she doesn't have a purse. It's not like her dress has pockets. Where's her key?

She staggers into me, and in my already drunken state, I stumble into the wall. "Mmm," she says, making me laugh as she rubs up against me.

The doors open, and I start steering her off the elevator. "Which room?" I ask, trying not to act affected when she continues to tug at my shirt and backs against a door.

"This one."

I tilt my head, ready to ask where her key is, when she reaches into her bra with her free hand. My eyes dart down—of course—and I get a peek at her erect nipples behind the lacy bra. That's like putting a steak in front of a starving man.

I groan as I lose all my ability to hold back, and I lower my head while pushing her dress and bra down in unison to allow way for my

19

mouth to close over the hard little nub.

She moans when she feels it, and she pulls me to her, tangling her fingers in my hair when she drops her shoes to the floor. That thin thread of sanity I had snaps, my morality collapses into a pile of rubble, and I lift her into the air before pressing her hard against the door.

I jerk the key out of her hand and blindly fumble with it, never moving my mouth away from her breast until the door opens. After I kick her shoes inside, we stumble into the room, and I lose my hold on her nipple, but her mouth is on mine before I can go for it again.

Her greedy tongue sweeps in and my knees try to buckle. I've been kissed by many girls, but this is more than a kiss. It's as though Tria is unleashing years of pent-up desire on me, and imprinting herself on me with each hungry stroke of her tongue.

The door slowly shuts on its own as we start tearing the place apart. She actually rips my shirt off as her legs clamp around my waist, and I start unzipping the back of the dress that has been fucking with my head all night.

Everything around me becomes forgotten. The sounds echoing through the room are raw and desperate, both of us seeking all we can get from the other before the illusion is shattered and we have to return to reality.

"You'd better have a condom," she says against my lips, making me smile.

If she's sober enough to think about protection, then she's sober enough for us to do this. God knows I can't stop now.

"I've got plenty."

Her kiss resumes—an almost violent and punishing kiss that has my eyes trying to roll back in my head. I hold her to me for a second longer before I put her down, quickly removing and discarding her dress.

Fuck me. Tria in lace isn't something I was prepared for. A thong? I'm never going to last. Not after being hard for this long.

She reaches her hand in my pants, and delicate fingers take a firm grip on my cock, stroke it, and make me stumble again when my knees falter. Damn. She's going to make me fuck up and come too early if she keeps this up.

I lift her to be on the dining table in her massive suite. Her girly panting makes me hurry my motions as I fumble for a condom. She gets to work pushing my pants down while I tear open the condom, and I roll her thong down, desperate to be buried inside her the way I've fantasized about being all night long.

I rip the pack open with my teeth, but she takes the condom from me and rolls it on like I'm taking too long. The slightest touch of her hands on my cock has me counting to ten, trying my damnedest not to embarrass myself.

The second it's secure, she spreads her legs and jerks me to her. A low growl comes from my throat as I grip her to me, my eyes roll back as I sink in, and I almost come then and there when she moans in delight.

I was really hoping she wouldn't feel this damn good. Fuck. It's like a hot, wet, velvet heaven is encasing me, squeezing me like a gentle vice.

21

I start moving slowly, doing what I can to last long enough for her to find her release first, but it's never going to happen. Not after the way she's had me worked up all night.

"Kode," she murmurs, pushing back.

Fuck. She's changing her mind now? Damn it.

"Yeah?" I mutter, going down to kiss her neck, praying she doesn't stop me just yet.

"We hate each other," she says, tilting her head to give me a better angle, and I take advantage. I also push back inside her, making her breath catch when our bases meet and rub together.

"So?" I ask, knowing where she's going with this, but praying I'm wrong.

"So fuck me like you hate me, already."

Damn. If I didn't hate her, I think that would have made me fall in love. That's really not going to help me last long.

I pull out of her and flip her over, pressing her against the table, and I slam into her from behind before she has time to register my actions.

"So much better," she moans as I ram into her again, and that's all I can take.

Fucking three strokes later and I've humiliated myself by getting off so damn quickly.

"No," she groans, pressing back on me, begging me to keep going.

"Five minutes is all I need, and then I'll fuck you like I hate you all night," I say against her ear, enjoying the chills that rise on her soft skin.

"You'd better."

Chapter 3

Tria

Shit. It wasn't a dream. Kode Sterling is still in my bed, proving all my wild fantasies from the night before weren't just incredible dreams. Even the devil sleeps, apparently.

His arms are closed around me—a parody of a lover's embrace—and his blonde hair looks even blonder in the room full of early-morning sunshine. His evenly tanned skin, along with that hair, gives him the appearance of a laidback surfer, instead of a Sterling mogul. And that body… No man should have a body like that to match a face like his. It's just not fair to the rest of the world.

He looks so peaceful, and if everything I remember is real, then he's probably exhausted.

No. No. No. This can't be happening.

Groaning internally, I rush to the bathroom to pull on my robe. After stepping over all the carnage, I quietly slip into the bathroom in search of a few answers. I gasp when I see the trashcan. One, two, three, four… five condoms? Oh damn. This is bad. So, so bad.

How do I face him now? Maybe he was too drunk to remember it was me. Surely he was.

Since I'm in a straight panic and have no idea what to say or do, I decide to shower. Maybe he'll just leave while I'm in there. Perhaps he'll think it was some random girl and not the object of his hatred. I have nothing in there that would tell him it was me… unless he finds my purse.

The water blasts free from the showerhead, and I stay under it, praying it cleanses me completely from the devil's touch that I can't seem to stop thinking about. He's my enemy—has been for years. One night of amazingly hot sex doesn't change that fact.

I swear it's the longest shower I've ever taken, and if he's still in my bed, I might just scream. I steady my breath, clutch my towel, and push through the door to find an empty room.

Thank God.

But what happens now?

Tria

"You're late. You are coming tonight, right?" Rain asks over the phone.

"I'm coming."

I'm not really too thrilled about it. I'll have to see Kode, and after waking up in a hotel with him yesterday... this could be awkward. No, awkward is too kind of a word for how this will probably play out.

"Great. How far away are you?"

I glance up at the enormous house right next to the ocean, staring at the front door that promises a night of problems, especially considering the fact that Kode's favorite Audi is already here.

The devil awaits.

"I'm here now."

I hang up as I take my first wary step, moving away from the safety of my car that promises to whisk me away from this certain hell.

I knew I'd have to face him sooner or later.

Each step I take forces more knots to form in my stomach. By the time I make it to the door, I'm ready to double over from the weight of the dread that is festering inside me. But I'm a big girl, so I force myself to act composed and confident, and I walk in, ready to face the worst. That's a lie; I'm not ready. But I can fake it like a pro.

Maverick is the first one I see, and he motions toward the living room. "Everyone's in there. You've missed most of the fun."

He still hates me. I can see it in his eyes. There was a time when my sister and I had... issues. I never did anything half as vicious as they thought I did, but it's apparently not good enough. Dane is the only Sterling boy who doesn't envision my head on a stake.

I don't say anything. Maverick leads, I follow, and we make our way toward the living room in heavy, uncomfortable silence. I almost get sick when I see the familiar strands of sandy blonde.

Kode.

In his designer suit that fits him too damn well, he looks like royalty. It was a lot easier to not drool before I knew how good he was in bed. Now... shit. I hate this.

I feel shallow and stupid for even having this twisted attraction to him. He's the spawn of evil, and I fucked him all too willingly because of his outer-coating. I wish he looked half as hideous on the outside as he is on the inside.

He looks up from his conversation with Dane, but he merely glances my way before returning his attention to his brother. I'm surprised by the pang of disappointment that strikes.

That's exactly what I wanted. So why do I feel like he just slapped me in the face?

"Finally," Rain says as she comes to hug me. "I was starting to worry that you weren't going to make it at all. We're not far from doing the last toast, and then we're going to discuss Vegas for next week."

Vegas. Crap. I forgot about Vegas. Dane's engagement gift to Rain is a trip to Vegas with all her friends. I *really* wish I could go back in time and refuse that offer.

Kode

I'm actually sweating. Dane is talking, but I can't hear a damn word coming out of his mouth. It was supposed to be a one-night get-it-out-of-my-system fuck, and now I'm fighting incredibly hard not to look her way.

Christ. Does she have to wear such short dresses?

My eyes ride up her legs, scandalously peeling off her clothes as I think back to what she looks like in lace and nothing else. She's oblivious to my appraisal since her attention is focused on Rain.

"So you're still good with Vegas?" Dane asks, finally breaking through my thoughts.

"Vegas," I murmur, smiling then frowning in a fluent motion. I should be thinking about gambling, drinking, or half-dressed women throwing themselves at me, but all I can think about is having a week where I'm just down the hall from Tria. "Vegas is good." Vegas is going to be *so* damn bad.

When Tria's eyes meet mine, I try to force a smile of some sort, but my lips don't cooperate. I'm so fucking confused right now, and it's pissing me off.

No. Tria is off-limits. It was one night of insanely hot sex. One night. I can't go back there. I don't want to go back there.

I break the eye contact when she does manage to force a smile. This is the woman I've hated for years. She's Rain's evil sister. I don't care if they've made up. She was still a bitch to Rain, and Rain is my best friend. End of story. Tria is too good at being a bitch to stay nice for too long. She'll fuck up with Rain, and my hatred will return.

I really fucking hope it returns.

When Tria walks away, joining Tag and Ash, I take a moment to watch her ass—every perfect curve of it. I hate her for a whole new reason right now.

Chapter 4

Tria

So far so good. Kode and I have been in the same room with each other numerous times now since our one night of temporary insanity, and nothing terrible has happened. If he's not ignoring me, then he takes the chance to say something snide or witty in an effort to be a dick. And I just ignore the hell out of him when he does.

Everything is back to normal.

I'm almost positive he has no clue that he slept with me. It's relieving and irritating at the same time.

Now we're in Vegas, and everything is running smoothly. I feel like the outcast of the group, considering how close the guys are with Rain. The rooftop party going on behind me sounds as though it has gathered more people, but I stare ahead at the city lights, ignoring everything and everyone. I just want to go home.

I wish Kade and Raya had come. I really get along with Raya.

Tag and Ash had to stay behind because they didn't want Trip to have to travel so far. It's not that far. They're just overprotective parents.

"Hey," a smooth voice says from behind me, prompting me to turn away from the railing and face him.

Yep. The party has quadrupled in size since I last paid it any attention. The rooftop pool is packed with unfamiliar faces. How does Dane Sterling draw this many people in everywhere he goes?

29

The guy who has demanded my attention has soft brown hair that shags a little long for my taste. He's tall—not as tall as Kode. Though he's attractive enough, he's not really doing anything for me. I really wish he was.

"Hey," I say softly, forcing a smile. At least I don't look like the loner anymore.

"Don't know anyone?" he asks, smiling as he grabs two champagne glasses from a passing tray.

He proffers me one of the glasses, and I willingly take it, ready to drown out as much of the next three days as possible.

"I know the two that assembled this party. You?"

He smiles as his eyes flick toward Rain. She must radiate some pheromone that draws attention from everyone.

"I know Rain Noles," he says while turning back to me. "I've worked on her marketing team for a while. I asked her out a few times, but she was always unavailable—according to her. I guess she's really unavailable now. So, what's your name?"

So glad I'm his second option, I think dryly. Nothing new.

It takes a great amount of willpower not to roll my eyes.

"Tria. Rain's sister."

His eyes grow wide with amusement, and I sigh in boredom. If I'm forced to feel alone, I'd rather feel alone in my house.

I look over to see a girl wearing a skimpy red dress and strutting up to Kode, putting her hand on his arm. He smiles down at her, and she leans in closer, using her body as a weapon of mass seduction.

Bitch.

Jealousy? No. I can't be jealous of Kode. That's beyond crazy.

I have to stop looking at him. I need this jerk who is still talking to me to move on so I can put my back to the party again.

All in all, I really need to get out of here.

Kode

"Who's that guy talking to Tria?" I growl, staring at the shaggy haired idiot who's practically drooling as Tria's eyes move to the city once again.

"I dunno," Maverick says, distracted as he watches the ass on a girl wearing a bikini.

"You and I need to find somewhere a little more private to talk," the girl hanging on my arm says.

It was funny at first; now it's annoying. I can only be nice for so long before I act like a dick. I've reached my limit.

"Or you could go find someone who wants to *talk* to you."

She leans back and gives me a glare that promises she believes I've lost my mind. "Excuse me?"

"I have no excuse for you," I quip, walking away from her and Maverick on my way toward the bar.

I need more to drink. Tria's ass in her trademark short dress is about to drive me crazy.

"Corona," I say to the bartender, moving my eyes back over to Tria as she smiles up at the loser who can't seem to stop looking toward Rain every five seconds.

Surely Tria realizes this guy is a tool.

31

"Kode Sterling," a familiar voice purrs.

Fucking Courtney Hughes—Kade Colton's ex-girlfriend. Should have known she'd crash this party. This girl is always driving someone to the brink of madness, and not in a good way.

"Not now, Court. I've got something on my mind."

Tria starts laughing at whatever the douche has said, and my teeth grind together as his hand slides up to touch her shoulder. It shouldn't piss me off, but my blood feels like lava as it pumps through my veins at a furious pace.

"Where are you—"

Before Courtney can finish, I walk toward Tria and the jerk, trying to think of something clever to say. I'll need a good entry line to make this seem... less like I've lost my motherfucking mind.

Tria lets him take her hand, moving toward the pool with him, and something inside me finally snaps. Seeing her touching him is the final straw, and reality checks out as fury drives me on.

I don't stop or even make an attempt to show any rationality. With barely any exerted effort, I shove her into the pool with one hand, while using my other to turn my beer up for a much needed sip.

I hear the gasp, the splash, and the scream, but I don't turn around as I casually keep striding, pretending as though nothing just happened. I make it two more steps before Rain is pummeling my arm with her fists. She looks like the energizer bunny on cocaine right now. It actually forces a laugh out of me.

But quickly my eyes widen, and I narrowly dodge her attempt to knee my balls. She always goes for the fucking jewels shot. I'm losing

32

my edge, because she almost got me.

"Why the hell did you do that?" she barks.

A few snickers erupt, drawing my attention. I glance over my shoulder, and nausea strikes me in the form of the bitch called... I don't know what it's called, but everyone is looking at Tria as she walks out of the pool, her pale blue dress now almost see-through. And it's really pissing me off to the point my jaw ticks.

No fucking bra.

The thin material clings to her as Dane walks over and hands her his suit jacket, and she takes it quickly before wrapping it around her. Several whistles emerge, and I fight real damn hard not to go put my fist through something—or someone.

I really didn't think this through. Now everyone has had an eyeful of the girl I didn't want anyone looking at. It was supposed to make everyone point and laugh, embarrass the hell out of her, and send her to her room to pout. It was *not* supposed to draw every fucking guy's attention.

"Are you listening to me?" Rain harps, slapping me on the arm.

Her pathetic assault doesn't even register pain, but I finally curse as I turn back toward her, barely even managing to tear my eyes away from Tria.

"What?" I growl.

She narrows her eyes threateningly, and points her small little finger at me like it's supposed to be intimidating. "Go apologize. Tria is already on edge anytime she's around any of you. I swore to her you'd all start treating her better, and here you are pushing her into the pool for no damn reason. She hasn't said or done anything to you!"

No, she hasn't. That's the fucking problem.

I know I'm not imagining the things we did, the sounds she made, or the fact her walls clenched around me countless times. My mouth has touched every part of her body, yet she has gone on as though that night never existed. Does she even know it was me?

She'd better fucking know it was me.

"I'll go apologize," I say tightly, planning on getting some answers as well.

That damn girl has my head all screwed up, and I need things to be right again. It doesn't make sense. None of this.

"Where'd Tria go?" I ask Corbin. Dane might chew me out right now, so I'd rather avoid him for a while.

Corbin snickers while motioning to the rooftop elevator.

"She just headed down. Some guy went with her to make sure she made it to her room safely."

I'm going to have a brain aneurism.

"What guy?" I snarl, and he tilts his head, confused or amused—I'm not sure which.

"I don't know him. Why?"

Sucking in a painful breath, I manage to rein in my temper long enough to get through this asinine conversation. "Rain is making me apologize, and I don't want too many people that know me to witness it."

It's a shitty lie, but he buys it, shrugging as I walk toward the elevator. I stab the button over and over until the doors open, and then

I press the button for her floor just as furiously.

How can she just walk off with *some* guy?

The elevator takes its sweet time descending, but after an excruciating twenty seconds, the doors finally open to Tria's floor. I'm glad no one asked me why I didn't need to know her room number. I didn't think about that posing questions.

I only asked the flirty desk clerk what room Tria was in because I wanted to make sure to avoid that room. That's it. I had no intentions of using such knowledge for any other reason. Nope. No other reason at all.

My palms start sweating like I'm a nervous kid at a middle-school dance the second I reach her door, and I loosen my tie while nervously clearing my throat. Like a fucking idiot, I lean my ear against the door and listen for voices.

It's quiet, though. No sounds at all.

After shrugging off the unprecedented nerves, I finally summon the necessary courage to knock. The sound of feet shuffling toward the door catches my attention, and then I hear more silence before a few muttered curses behind the door.

I probably should have covered the peephole.

"Go away," she says.

"I came to apologize. Open the door." I can't help but give her my best grin, even though the effect probably isn't as strong through the distorting lens of the peephole.

"You don't need me to open the door for that."

Shit. Why did I get myself into this mess?

"Just open the door. Rain will come down here any minute to find out if we're—"

The door swings open, and I swallow the rest of my words when Tria stands before me in nothing but a towel. Her wet hair is hanging down in sexy locks, letting trickles of the chlorine water ride the swells of her breasts and gather in her cleavage.

My jaw goes slack, my eyes become transfixed, and all my blood drains south.

"I really don't give a damn if Rain comes down here. You wanted her attention, apparently. Now you have it. Glad I could play your pawn."

Her bitter words snap me out of my trance, and I look up to meet her eyes again. My eyes narrow as I force my way into the room, trying not to enjoy the way she stumbles backwards when I get too close.

When the door shuts, her eyes look at it like she's plotting her escape.

"I wasn't trying to get Rain's attention. You were pissing me off."

Her eyebrows go up in surprise, and then she gives me the sexiest glare I've ever seen, even though I'm sure it is supposed to be warding me off instead of enticing me.

"I wasn't doing a damn thing to you. I've stayed out of the way since we got here, just like I always do."

I take another step forward, and she quickly takes one backward to compensate for the reduced distance, expanding it once again.

"You were talking to some douche, laughing with him, and letting him touch you."

She stares at me for a moment—lost, I think. Then she laughs humorlessly while shaking her head and turning her back on me.

"I can't believe this. You've acted like we didn't spend a night together since you left my hotel room, and *now* you're pissed because someone else is interested?"

She turns back to face me, clearly amused by the fact I'm making an ass out of myself.

"Don't kid yourself, Tria. That prick couldn't keep his eyes off Rain. You were just going to be the consolation prize."

Her amusement falls, and I silently curse myself when all the life falls from her face.

Her voice is soft and tired when she finally speaks to me, her gaze on the floor now. "Go, Kode. I wasn't planning on being his consolation prize. And I'm sure as hell not going to be yours while I'm sober."

Yep. I'm going to strangle her. And then I'm chopping my dick off for being such a pain in the ass.

"So now you merely fucked me because you were drunk? That's what you're saying? Because you knew my name, and you asked me to fuck you like I hated you. And you sure as hell had no problem with begging for more each time I—"

"Are you going to recap every detail?" she groans, her face red and her eyes screwing shut as she turns away again.

"I was starting to wonder if you even remembered, since you've treated me as though I don't exist."

She laughs bitterly, keeping her back to me. My eyes start trailing down to where the towel barely covers her ass. Fortunately I haven't had much liquor tonight, so I'm not crowding her with my hands or tongue… yet. The night is still young.

"Kode, you've treated me just the same. I assumed it was a mutual kiss-and-don't-tell moment."

I step in behind her, unable to keep looking without touching, even though I'm not the least bit drunk. My hands slide around her waist, tugging her back against me, and she shivers while trying to escape. Holding her to me tightly, I run my nose up against her hair and cheek, carelessly letting her wet hair soak my shirt. She smells like exotic fruit and chlorine. It shouldn't be such an intoxicating medley.

"We did a hell of a lot more than kiss."

She stops fighting, but she's so stiff that I'm worried she might break in two if I move wrong.

"We fucked, Kode. One night. Don't tell me you want more, because I won't believe you."

Her towel is the only thing stopping me from having her naked. It's all physical. Logically I know we have zero things in common. It's not like I want a relationship with her, but apparently my dick wants to be in charge, and Tria is all I can think about right now.

Never had this problem before.

"We did more than fuck, Tria. My mouth has touched you in ways that had you praising me."

I feel her smile, but I can't see it because I've started working on nipping at her neck, enjoying the way she immediately arches against me. Apparently she's no more in control of her body than I am.

"I don't remember that part."

That pisses me off. I did some of my best work that night.

"You're serious?"

She nods, angling her neck with a small sigh as she gives me access again. "You should go. This is… so screwed up. And you just pushed me into a pool."

"Because you were talking to that douche," I remind her. It's not my fault she's making me crazy. She has to shoulder that on her own.

"I assumed you were too distracted by the girl hanging on your arm to notice anyone talking to me."

This time I grin. "So you were jealous, too? What do we do about this, Tria? One night didn't get it out of my system, and apparently you're still just as into me as I am you."

She pushes away from me, but I pull her back, spinning her to face me, and my lips crash against hers in a rough kiss that reminds her how she likes it. Her hands go from pushing me away, to clawing at me to get closer.

There's nothing romantic or graceful about it. It's raw and carnal, just like this thing between us. Her towel falls away, and I drop her to the bed, nudging her legs apart so I can settle in between them.

She suckles my tongue, and my hips thrust forward, my cock straining against the fabric of my pants. But when I start fumbling when my belt buckle, she shoves me hard, breaking away from the kiss.

Before I can protest, a loud banging interrupts us, and Tria's eyes go wide. She quickly starts slapping me and shushing me when I grunt, and I climb off her with a begrudged motion while she goes to scramble for her towel.

"Tria? It's Rain. Open up. I swear I'm going to kill him."

I grin over at Tria who rolls her eyes at me. "I'm coming."

She grabs my hand, putting her finger over her lips, but I knock her hand away and pull her to me for a hard kiss that has her pushing and pulling at me again. Finally, pushing wins out, and I stumble into the room's bathroom.

She points a warning finger at me while Rain pounds harder against the door, and then she closes the door to the bathroom, where I decide to stay. No need in pissing my brother off by telling him I'm trying to fuck Tria. I'm barely staying on his good side these days, and he has started viewing Tria like a little sister he has to protect.

The problem is, there's no protecting her from me until I stop obsessing over her.

Tria

What the unholy hell just happened? Am I seriously that big of a masochist that I let Kode run his greedy hands all over my bare body after humiliating me in front of the entire party? I know damn well my daddy issues aren't that bad.

I have to get the hell out of here. Thank God for Rain right now.

"Hey," I say, clutching the towel back around me as I open the door for Rain.

Her platinum blonde hair is in disarray, like she and Dane just had a moment where they snuck away from the party. Leave it to Rain to get the nicest, most perfect person in the world for her. I refuse to envy her because it'll only make being her sister that much harder.

"Can I come in?" she asks.

My eyes reflexively go to the bathroom door where Kode is playing nice. But if he wants to get Rain's attention, he'll be storming out at any moment, trying to use me to make her jealous. And it wouldn't be the first time I was a pawn. Or the second. Or even the third.

Gah, I sound pathetic right now.

Stepping aside, I let Rain in, preparing for Kode to walk out in his boxers or something.

"Get dressed. We're going back up there, and you're going to stay with Dane and me for the rest of the night."

Great. I'm not the only one that knows I'm pathetic.

"I'm fine, Rain. Really. I was just about to go hit the gym instead, and then shower for bed."

She pouts adorably, and I turn to grab a pair of shorts and a tank top just to go along with the ruse. As I start pulling the shorts on, bypassing panties, I glance toward the door to the bathroom again. Kode is being completely silent.

"I don't like this," Rain groans as I pull on my sports bra. "I can't believe Kode did that. And I don't know where the hell he went. He told me he was coming to apologize, but obviously he's not here and hasn't been here."

Swallowing on a choking wad of air, my eyes flick to the rumpled bed, and I curse myself for letting him get me naked and worked up. I was ready to push him away, but I'm sure I would have just given back

41

in.

He's like a walking magnet, and I'm the polar opposite that can't stay the hell away. Everything was fine until he saw me at that bar. Am I so weak that I can just dismiss the man he really is because of his sex appeal?

Yes. Yes I am. I have to get out of here. Out of Vegas. Anywhere far away from Kode.

Rain talks about introducing me to more people tomorrow as I work on braiding my hair into twin pigtails. Apparently she's not going away, so I might actually have to go work out. Fine by me. Maybe I can find my dignity and sanity on the treadmill, while trying to run Kode out of my system. It'll also give him time to leave instead of us continuing this stupid conversation.

Kode is still in the bathroom when I finish pulling on my sneakers, and Rain follows me out of my room. She keeps promising to talk to Kode, and I glance over my shoulder as we head down the hallway.

"I'm just going to take the stairs," I say with a wave when she presses the elevator button.

"You're sure you don't want to just go back up there? I swear Kode will behave around Dane."

I doubt Kode would behave in front of the pope. In fact, I'm almost certain he could tempt a saint to attempt murder.

"I'm positive," I say before heading down the stairs.

After swiping my hotel key card through the slot in front of the workout room, I push through the door and find the first open machine. Should have grabbed my phone, because I hate working out without music.

After running on the treadmill for an hour, the boredom gets to me, and I hop off to grab a towel from the rack. Unfortunately, that run did nothing to clear my head. Kode is still very much cluttering it up.

Sluggishly, I make it back to my room, push through my door, and... stumble to a halt while gasping.

"Good workout?" Kode asks from my bed, casually lounging on it in nothing but his navy boxer-briefs.

He flicks the channel on the TV, acting as though there's nothing at all wrong with this entire scene.

"What the hell are you doing?" I ask in disbelief.

He gives me a shrug, flipping the channel again. "Trying to find something worth watching."

His eyes don't even meet mine, and I continue staring, torn between being speechless and confused. Confusion wins, prompting my lips to move.

"Why are you in my bed?"

"The bathroom wasn't very comfortable."

I'm going to kill him.

"Kode," I groan, pinching the bridge of my nose, "why are you in my bed?"

"Better question," he says, flipping the channel once again. "Why are you in a regular room instead of a suite?"

That's not a better question. It's a stupid question.

"I took a regular room to make sure everyone else coming for this week had a nice suite. The hotel only had a limited number left when I checked for availability, so I booked this room since I'm less high maintenance."

He snorts as though that's a ludicrous claim. "*You're* less high maintenance? You were driving a top-of-the-line Benz when you turned sixteen. Your wardrobe costs more than most people's homes. And you have enough makeup in that bathroom to take care of Broadway's needs. Seriously, who brings that much makeup? You have like thirty of everything, and there's three bags of the stuff in there."

I frown, realizing he's been snooping. I suppose he didn't just sit in the bathroom and stare at the back of the door while I was trying to get Rain out.

"That's for something I'm doing while I'm here. I arranged a lunch meeting for tomorrow."

That seems to get his attention because he leans up from the bed and flips off the TV.

"You're selling makeup?" he asks with an eyebrow raised.

It's not surprising that no one knows or cares what I've been doing with my life. It shouldn't bother me that Kode has no clue, but it does. I know every business he owns or invests in.

Christ, I sound like a stalker.

"I'm launching my own line. The lady I'm meeting tomorrow has a chain of department stores. They're small and admittedly low-end, but it's a start. I don't expect to be an overnight sensation. But if the meeting goes well, I'll get a second meeting in the afternoon, and I'll need to have that makeup with me."

His grin slides up as his eyes do something funny. He's amused. The bastard is amused. I should have kept my mouth shut.

"Get out of my room if you're going to sit there and make fun of me. I've put a lot of work into this."

I turn and head toward the bathroom, but the sound of the bed shifting and feet moving hurriedly have me turning around. I almost bump into him when he tries to match my abrupt stop.

"I wasn't making fun," he says with a cheeky grin that betrays him. "I swear. I was just surprised that you're doing this the hard way. You're the niece of Paul Colton—fashion master of the universe. Call him. He'd put your line in his stores, and it would take off with ease."

Rolling my eyes, I head into the bathroom, groaning when he follows behind me and shuts the door. I'm not claustrophobic, but right now, with Kode sharing this small space with me, I'm finding it hard to breathe. I focus—or try to focus—on the conversation at hand, as opposed to the gloriously nearly naked man.

"I don't want to do it the easy way. I want to earn my spot so that no one can take success away from me if I make it. I still have money from my trust, and every dime is going into this. It means a lot to me."

His grin only grows as he leans back against the counter of the small bathroom, watching me with guileless amusement. His exposed body is very distracting despite my attempts to ignore it, and that only pisses me off more. He shouldn't be so frigging sexy when I'm pissed. And he really shouldn't be hard right now.

"Stop looking at me like that," I say in a clipped tone. "I realize it seems laughable to you because you own a chunk of Sterling Shore businesses, and you have investments in large New York companies, but this is a really important part of my life. Don't spoil it by mocking me. Please go away."

Again, his smile only grows. "You seem to know a lot about me for someone who hates me."

He crosses his arms over his chest, watching me with that stupid grin. He needs to put on clothes before I do something stupid like kiss the bastard again. And he needs to get out of the bathroom. This space is too intimate, and my mouth is running before my mind can censor the words. I have to stop accidentally revealing too much.

"Know your enemies," I mumble.

"You're going to go that route? I'm not stupid, Tria. Be honest."

Honesty is not an option. I can't tell him how mildly obsessed I've been with him. Not when he's only ever looked at me like an annoyance.

I need a therapist.

"I'm not as self-absorbed as you are. So yes, I know what others do with their lives. Go. Away." Insulting him instead of fueling his ego is a much better route than honesty.

He shrugs while pushing off the counter, and heads out of the bathroom. That was easier than I thought it was going to be. Trying not to think about him putting his clothes back on, I strip and climb into the shower.

The water shoots out, icing me down before warming up. I take my time getting the sweat and pool water to wash away. I really hate Kode Sterling right now. I might have been lonely and lost before sleeping with him, but now I'm lonely, lost, and confused.

Cursing him, I cut the shower off and wrap up in a fresh towel. After using my last clean towel to wrap my hair up in, I head out of the bathroom… and again I'm stumbling to a halt while my eyes gape in disbelief.

"You're still here?" I groan.

The blonde-haired devil on my bed gives me a lopsided grin that has my heart betraying me with a racing rhythm. He pats the bed beside him, winking at me, and I mutter a curse before walking over to my temporary dresser. Why is he still practically naked?

"I think your room is actually better than my suite. It's cozier."

"Then I'll trade with you if it will get you to leave me alone," I mumble absently while searching for something to put on.

"You're welcome to head up to my room. I'll give you a five minute head start."

I toss a glare at him over my shoulder, and head back to the bathroom to dress in a pair of skimpy shorts and a midriff-showing tank top. If he wants to play this game, then let's play. I'll torture him the way he's torturing me.

After once again braiding my damp hair into twin pigtails and dressing, I head back in. When his eyes turn on me, his gaze heats, and I instantly regret the choice in wardrobe.

"Come sit down. I don't bite, Tria. Well, that's a lie. But you like it when I bite."

My whole body turns about five shades of red, but I finally go to stand beside the bed.

"Why are you doing this? You know this thing between us is twisted. Possibly psychotic. You're an asshole. And you hate me."

I expect him to announce his master plan to use me for whatever sick reason. It'd be better than this guessing game.

His dark smile sends shivers down my spine, and he tugs my hand until I'm falling on the bed very ungracefully. I quickly shuffle around to get away from that hard bulge he is shamelessly leaving on display, and I sit down on the bed at a semi-safe distance away from him, crossing my legs.

"You hate me, too, but you still want me. So why the hell are you being such a pain in the ass about it?"

That earns him an eye-roll. "Gee, keep talking like that, and I'll throw myself at your feet," I mutter dryly.

He snickers softly before reaching over and running a finger down my leg. "I'm not exactly the sweet guy with Hallmark lines coming out my ass, Tria. Nothing new. But you didn't mind it that night. Was it really just the alcohol?"

Blowing out a harsh breath, I shake my head. "I wish. It had nothing to do with alcohol. But it doesn't mean I want it to happen again."

That finger of his runs the line of my calf, slowly trailing down my ankle to my foot, before he runs it across the tips of my hot pink toenails.

"Why not? Just tell me what is making you so damned stubborn about this."

Stubborn? That's not the word I would use to describe me at all.

Borderline crazy would be a better assessment, because I should not be sitting on my bed beside the one guy who has tormented me for too long.

"Fine," I say, annoyed with him for looking so damn good while I try to regain my sanity. "If you must know, it's because you're still a playground bully."

Vaguely I'm aware that those words sounded so much better in my head—where they should have stayed.

His eyes go wide in surprise before turning amused, and he stares at me, making me feel mocked before he even opens his mouth. When his lips twitch, all I want to do is take my stupid words back.

"So what are you saying, Tria? That I'm a kid in a man's body? That if I pull your pigtails that means I like you?"

My cheeks heat because that's not what I meant. At all. Just to make it more embarrassing, he tugs one of my braids and grins like the cocky asshole he is. I really hate that smile.

"You can't do that stuff," I mumble, pushing at his chest, but finding myself unable to quit touching him once my hand finds the firm lines of his flesh. I was a little too numb to fully appreciate the way he felt the last time my hands were on his body.

Every inch of his body has definition that only the perfect can possess. Those lines at his hips form that mouthwatering V that disappears behind his boxer-briefs. His golden skin has the perfect amount of tan, and his mouth is by far the sexiest mouth on any man.

He pulls up on his elbows, then tugs me down, forcing my head against a pillow before he covers my body with his.

"Can't do what stuff, Tria? I'll tug your pigtails some more if it makes you blush like that again."

His body presses down on mine, and my breaths grow ragged. It's embarrassing when my heartbeat kicks up hard enough for him to feel it against his chest.

"I'm not Rain," I say in a shallow breath, trying to find the will to push him away, but finding nothing but a broken resolve. "I'm not a substitute."

He frowns as he runs his fingers through my hair, his eyes moving to the dark locks.

"Is that why you dyed your hair? Because you didn't want to look like her anymore?"

We really don't look that much alike, which is comforting. At least people can't use me that much.

"It had nothing to do with her. It was for me. Now, please go. Stop using me."

A startled gasp falls out of my lips when he surprises me with a bruising kiss, and he starts running his hands over my body, grazing the undersides of my breasts with his thumbs. When he pulls back just barely to look into my eyes, I'm breathless.

"There's only one way I want to use you, Tria, and it hasn't got a damn thing to do with Rain. Now, shut the hell up and use me, too."

If I was a girl who didn't know Kode Sterling at all, I'd probably slap him for that. Unfortunately, I do know him, and despite his crude way with words, I've always been fascinated with his blunt honesty. Even when that honesty was brutal and hurtful toward me. If he says he's not using me to get to Rain, then it has to be true. Right?

"And then what, Kode? Go another few days without speaking or acting like we know each other? Are you going to show up in my room every time you see another guy pay me attention?"

A frown mars his beautiful face, and I take the loss for words as a reprieve. But it's only a short reprieve.

"Tria, I don't know what's going to happen when I walk out of this room—*tomorrow*. You want a commitment or something?"

I can't help but laugh at how confused he looks. He's either really unrehearsed with repeat encounters, or he's used to getting his way without resistance. I'm guessing it's the latter of the two.

"No, Kode. I really don't want that. But I also don't want to have sex with you and have to feel like an idiot tomorrow. No more pushing me into pools."

When his lips brush mine teasingly, my hips arch up involuntarily, pushing against the part of his body I want the most.

"No more pools," he agrees.

"And can you not be a dick to me in public?" I ask hopefully.

"I'm a dick to everyone," he admits, and for some bizarre reason, that makes me laugh.

His grin comes up fully as he stares into my eyes, and I gaze back into the pools of grayish-blue that are almost silver.

"Don't be an extra big dick to me just because you don't want to want to fuck me."

He laughs lightly before messing with the bottom hem of my short shorts, slowly moving his hand up my thigh.

"That's a mouthful, but I won't be an extra big dig just because I don't want to want to fuck you. Right now, I'm perfectly fine with wanting to fuck you."

I'll probably strangle him at some point, but this could work out to my benefit. If Kode isn't making my life a living hell, then the others might be nicer to me. I'm not naïve enough to think he'll ever be nice, but as long as he's not being an over-the-top jackass, it could be better.

"So until we work this out of our systems, you're going to be pleasant?"

He nods, his grin growing as he starts working my shorts down my body, only shifting away from me enough to get them down.

"I'll be as pleasant as I can be. Very few people can tolerate me even then, though. I'm not Dane."

I snort derisively, because he makes it sound as though that's what I'm looking for. Obviously that was meant for my sister, more so than me.

"And I'm not Rain. So if you're using me to get to her, it's not going to—"

He kisses me. Hard. And for a brief moment, I forget he's the enemy while I spread my legs wider and dig my heels into his ass. When he withdraws from the kiss, I bite back the urge to demand he resume kissing me.

"I'm not using you to get to Rain, Tria," he says against my lips, his hands doing a slow exploration of my body. "I'm a dick, but I know what it's like to feel used so that someone can get to your sibling. Not my style."

"Someone used you to get to Dane?" I ask, surprised.

His eyes don't look so cold when he's being so genuine.

"A lot of people have used me for a lot of reasons. And a lot more have tried. Can you shut up and let me remind you what all I can do to make this night a little more fun? I really don't want to talk about my brother or your sister while I'm trying to get you worked up."

His cocky smirk returns, and his eyes shift from genuine to mischievous. Grinning, I pull him down to me and kiss him, deciding to be the one to initiate things for a change.

"But this stays quiet," I add, breaking the kiss quickly.

"I agree," he says while letting his lips trail down to my neck, slowly working his way down my body in a way that has my breaths coming out short and quick.

"People will think we're crazy if they find out, and it'll distract Rain and Dane from their wedding plans."

"I won't say anything, Tria," he assures me absently while pushing my shirt up and latching on to a nipple.

Whimpering, my body starts to squirm beneath his long frame, but it only gives him the incentive to work me over harder. His finger dips inside my panties, pushing in to find my heat, and I moan while he growls.

From there, everything changes. It goes from a slow seduction to a primal claiming. My panties are unceremoniously stripped from my body and cast aside like an offensive article. Roughly, he pushes my legs apart farther, and my head pounds the pillow while my back arches off the bed when his tongue—his amazing, talented, devilishly divine tongue—connects with that bundle of nerves at my center.

"Easy, Tria," he says, grinning against me. "I'm going to make sure you don't forget it this time. That way I never have to work so hard for a *yes* again."

A litany of curses fly from my lips in a dirty praise that would have roughnecks blushing when Kode makes good on his word, sucking, biting, and flicking his tongue in a pattern that has me almost seeing stars in a matter of moments.

I sure as hell don't know how this part of our first night together got lost amongst my fuzzy memories, because I'm fairly positive I might have begged him in front of everyone to give this to me again.

My fingers shamelessly tangle in his hair and pull him to be impossibly closer. The heat of his breath mixed with the ungodly things he's doing with his blessedly relentless mouth becomes too much, and his name comes out with a worshipful breath that will have me hating myself later.

I shudder as he kisses the inside of my thighs, my body overly sensitive to the point I'm ticklish. He grins as he trails his lips up my stomach, kissing and nipping at me all the way up to my breasts where he stops to devote more attention.

He leans up when I start pushing his underwear down, and his erection springs free to pop me across my stomach, eliciting a flinch and tiny whimper from me. His throaty chuckle is too sexy as he slowly moves closer once again.

He reaches under the pillow to pull out a condom package he apparently stashed there, but we both freeze when his bare tip pushes against my wet center. Swallowing hard, he pushes just the head in, and I groan in protest when he quickly pulls it back out and starts fumbling with the foil packet.

"I swear you're making me crazy," he says as he rises up and slowly encases himself in the latex sheathe.

If I'm making him crazy, then he's driving me mad.

With one hard thrust, he pushes himself inside me, and we both moan as though it's the best thing we've ever felt in our lives. My whole body relaxes against him, feeling far too familiar with his touch, considering there has only ever been one other night.

His lips come down on mine as he rocks in and out of me, driving me closer to the edge with every toe-curling stroke. It's hard, rough, and... Kode. And I love the way it all feels.

Our attempt to kiss is futile, because our wildly thrashing bodies make it impossible. Breathing becomes harder as the pace quickens, and he pushes his thumb down on a spot that elicits a spasm in my muscles while my body tries to buck off the bed. The double stimulation of him inside me, claiming me without any inhibitions, and his thumb spinning circles that can only be described as divine is too much.

His name comes out in a cursed praise, and he thrusts in harder until his bottom lip slides between his teeth and his face... Well, it's a mix of predatory excitement and euphoria when he shudders inside me.

His forehead drops down to mine, and we both pant for air, unable to move. Finally, after somewhat crushing me with his solid frame, he climbs off me and heads to the bathroom. My attempt to stand becomes a mess. My legs tangle on each other, and I'm forced to drop back down to the bed, too exhausted and sated to get my body to cooperate.

Kode's throaty chuckle comes to reach me while I shamelessly lie sprawled across the bed, naked and depleted of any sort of modesty.

"Here," he says, handing me a wet cloth while dropping to my side. "I can do it for you if you don't have the energy."

I laugh while blushing fiercely. That gives me the ability to move, and I manage to stumble toward the bathroom with wobbly legs.

"You should probably go," I manage to say, not willing to give him the chance to say it first.

"Damn. Use me and toss me," he jokes, prompting me to grin like an idiot.

Kode being playful is a good side of him to see.

I manage to walk back into the room after finishing up, and his eyes greedily rake over my body like he's not as thoroughly spent as I am.

He's already wearing his underwear and pants when I start pulling on a fresh pair of shorts and a T-shirt. He looks too good, which reminds me what this is—physical. Nothing else.

"So that's how it is?" he muses, trying and failing not to grin. "Friends with benefits?"

As if it could be anything else. "Don't say that," I groan. "It's too cliché, and I hate clichés. Besides, we're not exactly friends."

He laughs again, a sound I refuse to admit is my favorite thing to hear. "Fine. Not friends with benefits. Enemies with benefits?"

The mocking amusement in his eyes doesn't go unnoticed as I sit down beside him on the bed. He glances down at all the leg my shorts expose, and he draws in a long breath.

"I wouldn't say we're enemies either. Just... casual... whatever."

He grins while lifting his eyes to meet mine, and I get lost in the grayish-blue pits for a moment. It really is too bad that he's one of the most unobtainable men ever.

"Fine. Casual whatever it is. I'll see you when I see you then."

It's blunt and honest. Just like him. We can serve our carnal appetites without getting ourselves in a messy entanglement that would only end badly—oh so badly—for me.

After tossing on his shirt, he moves like he's going to kiss me before stopping just barely. He's so close that my eyes go blurry against the nearness, and his breath coats my lips.

"For the record, I was going to stay the night and make it worth your while. Maybe some other time."

Yeah... breathing... not possible.

I watch with a mixture of awe and confusion as he walks out of the room, letting the door shut behind him. With a few curses, I drop back to lie on the bed, and the ceiling and I have a staring contest as my mind tries to sort through the wreckage and piece together something rational to explain what I've just done. Pathetic.

My phone chirps, and I reach over to grab it. When I see the name on the screen, I tilt my head.

Your Favorite Fuck: This works both ways. Now you've got my number. Use it.

Kode. Only he would program something so crude as that to be a name. Deciding I should respond, I start typing back a message. Then I erase it and start over. Then I erase it again and drop my phone to the bed in frustration.

Never should have left my phone out for him to play with. I'm tempted to tell him I've changed my mind and want him back in here right now. Then my phone chirps again, and I take a deep breath before reading it.

Your Favorite Fuck: Night, Tria.

I guess I missed the opportunity to do something as embarrassing as telling him to come back.

Me: Should I ask what you have me programmed as?

He responds almost instantly, and a grin forms on my face just knowing he has sent me another text.

Your Favorite Fuck: I wouldn't recommend it. ;)

That just makes me smile harder.
I really am stupid.

Chapter 5

Kode

"What the hell happened to you last night?" Maverick asks as I sluggishly drop to the chair next to him. This restaurant has more gold embellishments than I've ever seen before. And the glaring glow of all the reflective surfaces is grating on my already frayed nerves.

"Whiskey happened to me," I grumble.

Tria asked me to leave, which I was actually grateful for, considering I really *did* want to stay. Not sure why the fuck I wanted to stay, but I did.

But like a fucking clingy chick that couldn't wait five minutes, I sent her a text before I even got on the elevator. I regretted it the second I hit send, and when she didn't reply, I reacted by sending another damn text. Christ.

At least she sent something back that time, and I had the chance to keep myself looking somewhat suave.

I got back to my massive suite, and had to literally fight with myself to keep from going back down to her room. In the end, I drank myself into a numb stupor until I passed out.

"That's not what I meant. You disappeared from the party and never came back."

I saw no reason to go back up there.

"You're the best man, Mav. I showed up and did my duty as the brother by playing nice."

59

I'll never forget how shitty I felt when Dane asked Maverick to be his best man. It would have been me, but as usual, I fucked it all up. That's my specialty.

"You call pushing the bride's sister into the pool *playing nice?*"

Well, hell. It's not like I can tell him that I did that out of jealousy. Tria's right about keeping our shit quiet. Dane will flip out right now, because he'll think I'm screwing around with Tria to get at Rain. God forbid something not revolve around the two of them. Considering how sudden my inexplicable attraction to Tria is, I doubt I could convince him otherwise. My relationship with my brother is fragile at best right now. Not that I can blame him.

"That was a fluke. I thought something was—"

"Is this about getting Rain's attention?" he asks in interruption. "I mean, I get it, Kode. Really. I do. But Rain and Dane belong together. And honestly, haven't you fucked with that enough?"

A mistake when I was eighteen will haunt me forever amongst the five of us. God help me if Rain ever finds out that I took the letter she left for Dane. If you ask me, they were both too prideful and stubborn to be together if that's all it took to tear them apart.

"I'm not trying to get Rain's attention. Believe me; I think I got the message loud and clear. She's always looked around me to see Dane. Her rejection wasn't a surprise, Mav. It just pissed me off. A lot of things piss me off, so it's not that big of a deal."

His eyes scream *liar*, but I ignore the silent remark as effectively as I ignore the massive headache that is punishing me for too much liquor last night.

60

A swish of long black hair catches my attention, and like a magnetic draw, I'm forced to look up as Tria walks in. Her smile is forced as she follows a girl to a table to sit... alone. And of course she's wearing a tight dress that fits in too well with Vegas.

Does she ever wear anything else out? Because I'm going to be a raging lunatic if she keeps dressing like that.

Five restaurants. This hotel has five restaurants, and she ends up in the same one as me.

"I feel bad for her," Maverick says, blowing out a breath.

"Why's that?" I ask absently, watching the girl who is unaware of my eyes on her. This corner spot isn't as exposed as her window seat. The place is pretty dead, considering it's a late breakfast and it's the least popular restaurant in the place.

"Ash and Raya didn't come, and Tria doesn't really know anyone besides Rain and Dane. Then you go and push her into the pool. Now she's sitting here and eating alone."

My jaw grinds as I watch her, feeling the urge to go join her. She twirls her finger along the top of her glass of water, her eyes staring out the window at the crowded sidewalk outside.

Corbin walks in, his eyes searching and landing on Tria who looks up and immediately goes still when she sees him. He forces a pleasant smile before scanning the room for us. Dale joins him at his side, and the pair spot us together. The second they move in our direction, Tria's hazel eyes come up to meet mine, going wide in her face.

She says something to herself, while averting my gaze, and she shifts her attention back to the window.

61

"If I invite her to come sit with us, are you going to behave?" Dale asks when he reaches us, always sounding so damn mature.

"I'll behave." The words are clipped, but only because I want to be the one to go save her. She'd probably panic if I went and asked her over.

Just as Dale walks away, the waitress brings a tray of drinks that Maverick must have ordered for us. I've never been so happy to see a glass of orange juice in all my life, and I start guzzling it as my eyes drift over to where Dale is trying to talk Tria into joining us.

"Rain wants us to be friends with her. We're adults now. I realize we didn't like Tria in school, but we're seriously old enough to at least be dignified adults. That includes you, Kode. Try not to do anything crude while she's around," Corbin says.

The word *crude* applies to everything I want to do to her. Images swirl through my mind, memories from both nights. Tria's body underneath mine, the sounds of ecstasy and my name falling off her tongue as her body writhed against me. The sweet taste of her—

I choke and sputter the orange juice when the citrus finds the wrong pipe, invading my lungs like an acidic assassin. Everyone looks at me, and I wave off the attention while coughing louder, trying to get air that isn't infused with the irritating liquid.

Tria walks up, her face a mixture of resentful resign and confusion when her eyes land on me having my strangling fit.

"Wrong... pipe," I say through a rasp strain, earning a few mocking snickers from my asshole cousins.

Tria's lips twitch, but she doesn't say anything or react other than that as Dale takes the seat next to Corbin, leaving the last available seat next to me. Tria takes it without looking my way again, and I refrain from scooting my chair closer.

After a few seconds, and a hefty sip of Maverick's glass of water, I manage to get my air and liquid back into their rightful places, and the conversation gets going. As the guys talk about Maverick's upcoming birthday, my eyes continue to rake over Tria.

Her silky, tan legs are hidden underneath the white tablecloth, but the top part of the dress looks like it was designed to accentuate her phenomenal tits. It's then it dawns on me that she has a meeting later. That's why she's so dressed up.

"We're going to hit a few stores after we leave here, and tonight we're hitting the casinos. You in?" Maverick asks her, trying his damnedest to make her feel welcome.

She fidgets in her seat, her eyes moving to the plate. I never realized how shy she is until recently. It's like she's afraid to talk to people she doesn't know.

"I... don't know."

"We're partying like kings tomorrow and the next night, then Pretty Boy is giving us a ride home in his shiny plane."

I groan at the mention of that hideous nickname. Fucking Pretty Boy.

Tria grins lightly, but hides it behind her hand. Corbin's phone chirps, and he checks it while Maverick lays out all the casinos around.

"Change of plans," Corbin announces. "Rain wants us to meet her and Dane at noon for some random show they scored us tickets to see."

Almost instantly, everyone else's phones chirp, including Tria's. She puts her phone away after reading it, probably getting the same message we all just did.

"You coming?" Corbin asks her, forcing her to squirm uneasily again.

"I suppose so."

Tilting my head, I ask, "Don't you have a lunch meeting about your cosmetic line?"

The words are out of my mouth before I even think about it, and her eyes grow wide in her head as all my cousins turn a questioning look my way. Shit.

"Rain mentioned it," I say quickly, covering my ass.

She breathes out in relief for the fast recovery, and shakes her head. "It... The lady cancelled. It's okay though. She just didn't think my line was a good fit with her store."

The guys instantly start talking to her the second they find common ground—business. Any Sterling can talk business all day when we're not busy partying like rockstars.

Dale is quick to point out the fact she's the niece of a man who owns a chain of the largest fashion stores in the nation, but she shoots him down the same way she did me. Creating your own brand is too hard to do without using contacts. I never thought about her being so prideful.

"Well, I know a few guys in New York that I could put you into contact with," Corbin says, pissing me off when his eyes drop to her cleavage.

No. If he hasn't noticed how sexy she is before, then he doesn't need to start noticing now. I'll kick his ass.

Christ. I'm losing my mind. Or it's already gone. That's a strong possibility.

Tria graciously refuses his offer, promising the table of business enthusiasts that she's going to do this on her own. She's underestimating how hard it is to gain ground in a world that runs based on who you know. If she's not going to trade in on her name and her opportunities, then she's going to fall on her face.

The food comes, and we eat during casual conversations. Tria never says much of anything else, and I keep finding my eyes drifting over to her. The second we're done eating, Tria glances at the time.

"I should get back to my room and change before the show. I got dressed for the meeting. I thought it'd be good to get here early and grab us a good table, but she cancelled just before I got here."

She tries not to show her disappointment, but her crestfallen expression is too hard for her to hide. Everyone tells her *bye* as she leaves, and Corbin lets out a low whistle.

"You know, she's really not so bad," he says, his eyes on her ass as she makes her way out of the restaurant.

If he doesn't stop looking like he's going to run up behind her and mount her, I might throttle him.

"If you're into girls that shy and awkward. Those kinds of chicks are boring in the sack," I lie, trying to dissuade him from doing anything stupid.

"Man, you're a dick," Mav says, rolling his eyes. "The girl is still scared shitless of us. Give her time to warm up. You just pushed her into the damn pool last night, so obviously she's skittish."

Shrugging, I try not to let them see my smug smile. I'm the only one at this table she *is* comfortable with, and I happen to like the hell out of that fact.

Kode

"Didn't know Dane was going to have a bunch of ass-suckers hang out with us at that lame show," I mumble, walking out of the *magic* show three—yes, *three*—hours later.

Maverick laughs under his breath when a dude who seems to be in love with argyle heads our way, his grin too big for his face.

"That douche is totally man-crushing on you," Maverick says just before the guy reaches us.

"It is so awesome to meet the legendary Kode Sterling. I've seen you in so many magazines. I bet the women flock to you on a regular basis," the sweater-vest wearing, annoying-as-hell guy says. "What's it like?"

That's all I can take. This prick took the seat beside me at the show, while Rain took the other side of me. Tria had to sit next to Corbin and Maverick, which pissed me off to no end, and now she's all the way at the end of the sidewalk, turning into the casino with Dale. Everyone is going to steal her away with all their fucking charm.

"It's like hell when I'm being tortured by wanna-be guys like you," I snap.

His lips flatten to a thin, disappointed line. "That's a jerk thing to say," the argyle-wearing fool says, affronted.

"Well, I'm a jerk who doesn't give a shit," I grumble while pushing through the revolving doors.

It doesn't take but a few seconds to find her sweet ass in her tight jeans. The high-heels she's wearing would put her at the perfect height to bend her over. Which I will be doing. Soon.

Maverick is laughing when he catches up with me, telling me something about not being such an ass, but my eyes are zeroed in on someone that is far too close to Tria.

"What the hell is Rye Clanton doing here?" I demand.

He's talking to her with that look in his eyes that *will* get him laid the hell out. Tria knows him because of her cousin, Ethan Noles, and I know damn well Rye has no qualms about fucking his best friend's cousin.

"Rain invited him, but he couldn't make it out here until today," Maverick answers, shrugging as though it's no big deal. "Guess he's meeting everyone here. Lucky bastard. He missed that terrible, horribly long show."

Tria's head falls back as she laughs at something he says. My fists are clenched before I start walking toward them with fury leaking from me, but I'm intercepted by a feisty blonde before I can reach the infuriating brunette.

"Don't you dare embarrass Tria anymore while we're on this trip," Rain says sternly, still assuming she intimidates me.

I usually humor her, just like the rest of the guys, but not right now. Right now, my eyes are on a different Noles girl, and the prick who is inching closer to her to show her something on his phone.

"Are you listening to me?" Rain demands. "Be nice, Kode. She's my sister, and you being a dick to her is the same as being a dick to me."

"I've been very nice to her since the pool debacle," I say as a secretive grin tries to tug at the corners of my mouth. "I was just about to show her how to work the roulette tables."

Rain stares at me like she's unconvinced, then she glances over her shoulder. "No. Not right now," she says, turning back to me with a grin. "Rye is talking to her, and I think she has a thing for him."

The tattoos running down his arms don't bode well for me. Chicks dig ink these days.

"If he wants her, then he can follow her to the roulette table. I'll be drinking soon, Rain. You probably don't want me talking to her after I drink. So I'm going to go talk to her now."

"Don't drink. Problem solved."

I look at her as though she has lost her damn mind. "You made me sit through the worst magic show I've ever seen. Alcohol is a must after that."

She groans while playing with the ends of her hair. "It was supposed to be good. We read the reviews."

"It was three hours long."

"I know, but—"

"Three hours," I repeat, and she starts laughing while rolling her eyes.

"Fine. But wait and see if Rye makes a move before you go interrupt. She could use some attention."

If Rye makes a move, I'll give her some attention when I go caveman and haul her ass out over my shoulder.

Tria's eyes come up to meet mine, and her hazel gaze shifts from me to Rain before she turns her attention back to Rye. She looks tense now. Is she jealous of me talking to Rain?

Rain's phone sings some annoying song, and she holds a finger up to signal for me to stay put as she answers.

"Raya? Hey, whoa… Slow down… Calm down. I can't understand you."

Whatever is going on sounds serious, but I couldn't care less. There's a dark-haired siren calling to me, and I make my way over to her and the tattooed son of a bitch at her side.

Chapter 6

Tria

Kode talking to Rain doesn't bother me. It doesn't. Nope. Not at all. I cannot be jealous of him and her, because they are best friends. And we're a casual whatever. So, no. I'm not jealous.

"We can hit some slots if you want to," Rye says in that deep voice that sounds like silk over gravel.

Damn, he's sexy. But... He's not Kode. No. Kode is temporary. Rye is always a little pissy and not usually approachable, but he's always been nice to me because of Ethan. Which is more than I'm used to.

Just as I open my mouth to answer him, Kode's deep, commanding voice comes from behind me and wraps around me like he's touching me, even though he's not.

"Actually, I promised Tria I'd show her the roulette table."

He what? Is he seriously over here right now because he's jealous of Rye?

I turn toward him, my eyes already brighter than they should be, and I smile despite my best attempt to restrain it. He's sexier when he's jealous.

His smirk curves on his lips, and I start wondering if there's a way we can get out of here without anyone noticing.

"Shit," Rain says, her whole face pale as she joins us. "Where did Dane go? He's not answering his phone, and we have to go. Now."

Kode's body turns away from me when he goes to devote all of his attention to Rain. I'm not sure what's going on, but when she wraps her arms around him, it's more than I can take.

"So… slots?" I ask Rye, turning away from the sight that has me wanting to bite through nails.

I know they're close—best friends. And we're… just… fucking? Ugh, I hate myself right now.

Rye leads me through the casino, walking in a way that has women turning their heads to watch the bad boy. I'm not sure he even means to own such a sexy gait, but the natural prowess he possesses can't go unnoticed.

"Don't think Kode liked me talking to you. Something going on there? I thought you two hated each other," he pries, but he does so with a careless tone that means he's more curious than intrusively nosy.

If he's noticing, then others might notice as well. Crap.

"He pushed me into the pool last night, embarrassed the shit out of me, and now Rain has him apologizing. He just doesn't like you."

Rye isn't much of a laughing person, but he snorts out a small laugh after hearing that. "Dane either. They both thought I had a thing for Rain in high school. She was cute, but she sure as hell wasn't worth the drama. They need to get over it."

So Kode's dislike stems from jealousy over Rain. Now I feel stupid.

"You're the only person that I sort of know here. I thought Ethan and Wren were coming, or I wouldn't have shown up. Where the hell are the lying bastards? I haven't been able to get either one to answer my calls since I got here."

I laugh at his annoyed tone. "Ethan had a last minute business thing and couldn't leave Chicago. Wren came for a few hours, but his lawyer called about needing him to come sign papers. I think divorce papers, or maybe just something leading to divorce papers."

He grimaces. "Damn. Hate that. Wren is too good of a guy to have to deal with Erica's crazy breakdown. She's acting like he's the one who fucked her over. I'm just glad she's gone. She never did like me."

I laugh again, surprised by how sad it sounds. Kode hugging Rain shouldn't be affecting me.

His phone rings, and I pause by the slot machine that looks to be out of order. This place is massive, and it's absolutely chaotic. I don't even see anyone from our party anymore. I didn't even realize we managed to stray so far.

"We're... well, I'd say by the slot machines, but there's like a million. We'll walk back toward the front and meet you there."

He hangs up, his breath coming out in a bit of surprise.

"You sure nothing's going on with you and Kode? That's like the fourth time he's ever called me, but that's certainly the most pissed he's ever been."

Swallowing hard, I follow him as he leads me back toward the front. "I'm sure," I lie. "What'd he say?"

"Sounded pissed and a little... I don't know... scattered? Wanted to know where we were, and then hung up on me when I told him we'd head up front. I guess he was trying to call your phone, but couldn't reach you."

That's because I forgot my phone on the charger after changing for the horrible magic show Rain dragged us to. But he called Rye? I'm going to kill Kode. This is just too—

"Hey!" Maverick says, jogging over to us. "We've been looking everywhere for you. Go pack. We gotta head back."

Kode is suddenly there, right in front of me, and tugging my hand into his.

"Kode, what the hell is going on? Did something happen with Rain?"

Panic sets in. She looked worried, upset even, and I just walked away like a brat when she hugged her friend because of my childish insecurities.

"No. I found Dane, and he took Rain back to their room."

He keeps pulling me, and I'm forced to run a little to keep up with his much longer strides. My panic only grows.

"What's going on?"

"Raya called. We've got to get home."

Now my whole body heats with dread. "Kode, stop! What happened? Is Kade okay? Did something happen to Uncle Paul or Aunt Margaret?"

He finally slows down, his lips tightening as though he doesn't want to be the one to tell me. But realization slams into me almost instantly, and I know what he's going to say before the words leave his mouth.

"It's Thomas Colton. He... passed away a little while ago."

Chapter 7

Kode

There are few things I hate worse than funerals. None come to mind right now. I'm the worst possible person at consoling others. It's never been my strong suit. That's Dane's shining point.

When people cry, I cringe. When people need warm embraces, I'm stiff and unsure of myself. Even Rain. When she hugged me after hearing about Thomas's death, I didn't know how to react.

I tried to comfort her, but I was relieved to see Dane so I could hand her over. Never thought I'd say those words.

Tria... Tria didn't seem to need comforting. Or if she did, she obviously knew I sucked at it and didn't attempt to seek solace in me. Instead, she stayed quiet—utterly silent—the entire plane ride home.

She stared at her hands mostly, never really meeting anyone's gaze. Rain cried a little, but she mostly talked about everything she needed to do to help out her aunt and uncle to prepare for the funeral. Tria said nothing.

I kept looking at her, hoping she'd at least let me know she was okay, but she seemed lost inside her own mind, sorting out her emotions on the death of a man their family loved very deeply, even though he was only their family through marriage.

Yesterday I started to call her, but I had no idea what to say. I assumed she was busy with helping everyone get things ready. Maybe I still should have called her. Ah, hell. I really hate funerals.

Now, sitting here in this massive church while someone gives a eulogy, my eyes are three pews down and across the aisle, trained on the girl with dark hair that can't seem to do anything but stare at her hands again.

She's dressed in a black dress that touches her knees, and though she shouldn't be so beautiful right now, she's the very definition.

I don't know what the hell I'm supposed to do, but I feel like shit for not doing something. And I never feel like shit.

The service draws to an end, and Kade and his family stand together. Raya tries to speak to Kade, but he holds his hands up to stop her, his eyes streaked with tears, and he shakes his head while walking away. He storms through the crowd in an angry blaze, before practically bursting through the church doors.

I'm still uncertain if I should go to the cemetery or not, and right now, Raya looks just as uncertain as I do. As her unshed tears waver on her eyelids, she stares at the doors that close on their own, as though she's willing Kade to come back in.

Paul Colton whispers something in her ear, and she forces a smile while giving him a hug. She knows how to comfort people.

"They're requesting that only the close family and friends go to the cemetery," Maverick says, coming to stand beside me as I watch Tria go to hug her aunt and uncle.

"That's wise. The cemetery won't have enough room for all these people."

Maverick smiles as he looks around at the two-story church that is almost filled to maximum capacity. One thing is for sure; the Colton family is loved.

Tria moves behind the family, and I make my way toward her after offering a few awkward embraces to a couple of people who surprise me. I really suck at this.

Hazel eyes meet mine, and I smile at her, or at least I think it's a smile. She looks around before veering off her path and finding my side on the way out the side entrance and into a massive lobby area. Still moving away from the crowd, we head toward one of the uncrowded exits.

"Do you need a ride to the cemetery?" I ask lamely.

"I'm not going. It's the close family and friends only, and I wasn't really that close with Thomas. I feel like it'd be better to let the ones who loved him the most grieve him with each other."

I almost feel relieved to know she wasn't as close to him as I thought. She's close with Paul and Margaret, so I only assumed she had been close to Thomas, too.

"You were so quiet on the way home. I was worried."

Her sweet smile does something that makes me feel stupid—stupid enough to not see the door until I slam into it. She tightens her lips, refraining from laughing at a time like this, while I grip my aching forehead and mutter a few curses. Motherfucker that hurt.

"Damn door came out of nowhere," I grumble as she heads outside. I follow, eyeing the door one last time, and she walks down the barren sidewalk.

"I was quiet because I didn't really know what to say. I never do at times like these. I'm always worried about saying or doing the wrong thing, and it was a shock. I knew he was sick, but I guess you never see mortality for what it is until someone dies."

And I don't have a clue what to say to that. She's not the only one who lacks the right words for the right moment.

"Where are you parked?" I ask instead.

"I rode with Mom and Rain. Mom is going to the cemetery, and Rain is leaving with Dane. So it looks like you're taking me home, or I'm getting a cab."

I grin down at her as she leans into me, and my arm goes around her shoulders.

"I tried calling my dad to let him know, but he ignored my call. It did a two-ring thing before going straight to voicemail."

"Think he'll come to check on the family he's been a part of for so long?" I ask mildly, trying to find a way to say the right things.

"No. I don't think he will. He only gets more selfish every day."

Again, I have no idea what to say. I hate to sound spoiled, but my parents never had any severe marital problems that stressed me out. So it's impossible to relate to what Tria is going through.

My car is a block away, but she apparently knows which direction I parked in. Right now, I don't care if anyone sees me holding her to me, but no one is within view of the church from this angle. They're all standing around the front, and we're on the side.

"How'd you know where I parked?"

"Lucky guess," she says deadpan.

We make it to the car without her ever moving out from under my arm, and I kiss her head before opening the door for her. As she climbs in, my mind goes to the obvious. What I'm feeling for Tria is a little more than casual, and I'm not yet sure if that's a good thing or a bad thing.

As soon as I get in, she smiles over at me. "Thanks for the ride. I really didn't want to get a cab."

Reaching over, I grab her hand in mine to squeeze it reassuringly, unsure about what else to do. She probably needs rest, so I make a mental note to let her recharge for a few days without me.

When she's ready to see me, then she can always call.

Chapter 8

Tria

Frustrated, and admittedly a little pissed, I wait on Brin Waters—one of my only friends—to show up for lunch. I met her a few months ago, and I swear she was just what I needed.

She walks in, her eyes scanning the room for me. Her dress is much too big for her small body. Her hair is pinned neatly in a bun on her head, and her tiny, black, rectangular frames are perched on her nose. She always seems so collected and put together, even though her wardrobe needs to shrink in size.

She spots me and takes hurried steps to the table to join me, sitting down across from me at the bistro table in the small restaurant. When she takes her glasses off and puts them away, she speaks.

"Sorry I'm late. My jackass neighbor from across the street parked his car right behind mine again, even though he has his own side of the curb. Took me forever to wiggle my car out of the small space he left me with."

"Anyone I know?" I ask idly, my knee bouncing under the table as I impatiently wait for the time to spill it all.

"I don't actually know his name. I've only been living with Maggie for a couple of months."

She sounds as irritated as I feel, but for a completely different reason. I have a major crisis, and Brin is the only one not integrated into our group, so she can give me some insight as to what to do.

"He hasn't called. At all. And now I don't know what to do," I ramble.

Her eyebrows go up in surprise, and then she tilts her head. "O…kay… I feel like I'm missing part of the story. Who hasn't called?"

Groaning, I grip my head. How did I get into this mess? I agreed to casual, but after Thomas's funeral, Kode Sterling seemed to disappear.

"He dropped me off almost two weeks ago after Thomas's funeral, and he hasn't called since. We agreed to a casual thing, but… hell, do I sound crazy? I feel crazy. Yes. I think I'm going crazy."

I curse and drop my head back. Almost two weeks. That's not really a terrible length of time. Then again, it might have just been a Vegas thing. Maybe we're the type of people who only hook up in hotels when real life can't pose a problem.

"Tria, I'm really trying to follow you, but I'm struggling. Who are you talking about?"

My knee bounces harder, and I mentally slap myself for the two—no, three—tall coffees and the one expresso I had. My heart is punishing me by beating painfully in my chest.

"Kode."

"I thought he was dating Raya. And I thought he was your cousin," she says with her nose turning up.

Laughing, I shake my head. "No. That's Kade. Kade Colton. This is *Kode* Sterling."

"That's not confusing at all," she says sardonically, but I'm too on

80

edge to laugh again.

I should have stopped after one large coffee.

"Okay, so Kode Sterling... Wait, is he the one with blonde hair that hangs out with Dane at Silk?"

I nod, swallowing hard.

"Yes. That's Dane's brother."

She lets an appreciative whistle out. "No wonder you're all bent out of shape. He's definitely worth looking at."

"He's... I honestly think he must have done something to me, because I can't seem to get him out of my head."

"So he hasn't called, but nothing bad went down between you two."

It's not a question, so I don't respond. I just wait patiently for her to do the part where she starts giving advice. Soon, hopefully. That's what girlfriends do, right?

"Okay. So where did you hook up? I need some backstory."

Quickly, I run through the sordid details, giving her everything from the first account to the last.

"So he got jealous over the guy at the pool and... Rye? Who the hell is Rye?"

"Rye is not the part for you to focus on here," I remind her, sounding as desperate as I feel.

There's no reason for me to see him for a while, so I'm really hoping she gives me something to work with.

"Sounds like he has it bad, but if he disappeared right after someone in your family died, he might be staying away to show respect."

I snort, and then I think about it, and I snort again. "You obviously haven't heard very much about Kode. So tell me what to do. We agreed to casual, so I know I sound crazy right now. But—"

"But you want him. Got it. How long have you liked this guy?"

I look at her with narrowed eyes, and she points her small finger at me. "Don't give me that look. If you want advice, I need to know details. That's how this works. The more details I have, the better I can advise you."

Shit. Shit. Shit.

"Fine. I've liked him for… a while. Then I hated him. Then I liked him again. But even when I hated him, I sort of liked him."

She groans while gripping her head. I'm stressing her out? Does she realize the caffeine overdose I've had? It does *not* make me a patient person, and my mind is running a thousand miles a minute.

"Timeframe, Tria. How long ago was it when you developed this crush?"

Admitting this will just make me look all the more pathetic. But I cave and acquiesce, "Thirteen years ago." I was just a kid with a crush for two years, but he never noticed me. Then Rain came along, and Kode hated me.

Her eyes swell up to be softballs. Then she coughs and takes a sip of her drink.

"And you're just now doing something about it?"

Here's where it all starts getting complicated. "He sort of, well, he was too busy being in love with Rain."

"Oh," she mouths. "So it's definitely important to you that this thing works out. Then you've got to pull out all the stops."

"And those stops would be?" I ask her, wringing my hands in my lap as the caffeine buzz maddens me with jitters.

"It's apparent that he wants you, but since he's not making any moves, that means it's up to you. So, send him a picture."

As much as I adore her, right now I'd like to strangle her for not making any sense.

"I don't think sending him a picture is going to do anything but make me look like an idiot."

"Naked," she adds, winking at me.

My mouth forms an "O" while I sit back and think that over. I guess it can't hurt to try. It's not like he hasn't seen my body before. Might as well remind him what made him want me to begin with.

Kode

"The back nine and you are not getting along today," Dale says as we drive along the cart-path of the eleventh hole.

My ball is in the second cut of the rough grass… on the fairway of the fifth hole that is way off to the side. My mind is on one thing, and for the hundredth time since almost two weeks ago, I check my phone, making sure I haven't missed a call or a message.

Nothing. Fucking nothing.

"The front nine didn't like me too much either," I mumble, hopping out of the cart when we stop.

After grabbing a club, I walk over to my poor golf ball that has been treated like shit all day. Golf is supposed to be relaxing, but I'm tense from head to toe. Should I just call her? I should at least text and see how she's doing. No. That would seem less casual than what we agreed on.

"For Christ's sake, are you going to hit the ball or not?" Corbin yells from the putting green—on the correct hole.

Bastard has a pro game going today. Why did I agree to come golfing?

After flipping him off, I hit the ball, and watch it… land in the first cut of the rough grass. At least I'm back in the right fairway now.

"Dude, at this rate, we're going to have to let people play around us," Maverick says as Dale chuckles, sinking his ball in the hole effortlessly.

Jackasses.

It takes me a few more swings, but I finally get the resistant ball into the fucking hole, and we head on to the twelfth hole. Corbin steps out, preparing his masterful shot, but I become distracted when my phone buzzes in my pocket.

I juggle it out, hoping it's her as I walk toward them with my driver in my hand. As soon as I swipe the screen, I'm stumbling, falling, and landing in a heap on the ground, with my driver thudding harshly to the ground. But my phone sure as hell doesn't drop, and that's because I have a death-grip on it.

Holy. Fucking. Shit.

Tria… naked… bed… mirror selfie… I have to get the hell out of here.

"Dude! What the hell?" Corbin growls.

I don't acknowledge the fact that I just royally fucked up his shot.

"Gotta go," I call over my shoulder, leaving behind the fallen club while jogging over to one of the carts.

They yell at me and curse me a little, but I don't bother looking back as I drive away and head toward the clubhouse. It takes me less than two minutes to run to my car after parking the golf cart, and even less time to ditch my clubs in the trunk and get on the road.

It's about damn time.

Tria

I'm so stupid. Why oh why did I listen to Brin? How will I ever look at him again?

He could have said *anything*. But he ignored my message. I sent it over twenty minutes ago. There's no way he hasn't read it, because he *always* has his phone on him.

Stupid, stupid, stupid, stupid. Great. Now I'll have to miss my own sister's wedding, because I'm a coward like that. I'll never be able to face Kode Sterling again.

A pounding on my door has me jumping and squealing, but I race toward it, tightening my robe as I reach it and swing it open.

In a blur of motion, lips are suddenly bruising mine with a hungry kiss, and I barely gauge who it is before my legs are wrapping around his waist. When did he pick me up?

The door shuts behind him, which means he most likely kicked it, but I'm too wrapped up in kissing the hell out of him to notice anything else going on. His hands are just as greedy as his lips, squeezing me tightly to him as he makes up for lost time.

The kiss only breaks off when Kode stops it, looking around the inside of my new home for the first time. I moved to escape Pete Mercer after I found out he was out of prison and looking for me.

Fortunately, it's been a while, and he doesn't seem at all interested in stalking me down anymore.

My thoughts of Pete are vanquished when Kode pushes me against the wall, jerking my robe open.

"Fuck the bedroom," he says randomly.

Ah. He couldn't find my bedroom.

I start to tell him where it is, when the sound of a foil wrapper crinkling catches my ears, and I realize he's about to screw me against the wall. The wall. Yes. Definitely the wall. It sounds so much better than the bed right now.

"I missed you, too," I say just before his lips reattach themselves to mine.

He pulls back, his eyes narrowing on me. "Then you should have called sooner."

A small fluttering happens in my chest, and I suck in a coarse breath. He wasn't avoiding me. He was waiting on me to call.

I really am stupid.

Before that thought can fully take root, he's pushing into me, letting my robe hang open and baring my body to him fully. My breath catches in my throat as my back continuously thuds against the wall.

Kode out of control because he wants me this much... well, it's hot as hell. And it just makes me kiss him that much harder, that much wilder, and with that much more excitement.

Our bodies thrash like it's been years instead of almost two weeks. The build inside me comes swiftly, almost painfully, and I'm falling over the edge before I can help myself. I go limp in his arms, putting the burden of my weight on him, but he holds me up without a problem, his hips still rocking with a vicious pace. He bites on my lower lip as he grunts and goes still, and then he seals his mouth over mine for a kiss that has me almost begging for more.

"You're not kicking me out," he says as he comes to rest his head close to my cheek.

I grin while running my fingers through his soft blonde hair, still impaled and suspended between the wall and him.

"Nope. I plan on using you more tonight, so I need you to stick around."

He laughs while sliding out of me and dropping me to my feet. As I start tying the robe around me again, he swats my ass, and I squeal in surprise.

"Point me in the direction of a bathroom," he says, moving his hand down to start removing the condom.

That really shouldn't be sexy, but somehow, Kode manages to make every action impossibly hot. Right now, I've almost got whiplash from how fast that all happened, and all I can think about is slowing it down the next time.

"My room is just down the hall. There's a bathroom in it."

He starts to walk away, and then he pulls me to him to kiss me again, grinning against my lips. "By the way," he says as he tugs his slacks back up, "love that picture."

I grin at his retreating figure. "Clearly," I say with a small smile.

He laughs while disappearing into my room, and I sag to the couch. That was so not what I was expecting to happen. He looks a little preppy, which is not typical Kode, so I can't help but wonder what I interrupted.

"Just so you know, the guys are blowing up my phone because I walked out during the middle of a golf game," he says as he comes back into the room. His white polo shirt is untucked, but other than that, you can't tell he just took me against the wall.

He drops down to the couch, and then he pulls me over onto him as he kicks his shoes off.

"I'm fucking starving, too," he says, and I bite back a grin.

"Gripe much?" I ask playfully, rewarded by his throaty chuckle.

"Care if I order a pizza?"

"As long as you get enough for me, I don't care what you do."

He smiles against my head, and I lean into him while flipping on the gigantic flat screen my cousin made me get. Personally, I thought it was too big, but apparently guys like it.

It takes him no time to find a channel and order a pizza. We get far too comfortable on the couch, every touch feeling much too familiar and intimate. But I don't bother analyzing it or ruining the moment with the reality that Kode Sterling and I are a match made in hell.

"That picture will pop up every time you call me now," Kode says with a grin as he puts his phone down.

"You had better not let anyone hold your phone then."

He snickers softly before kissing the top of my head again. I'm draped across his body, wearing nothing but my robe.

"I'm the only one who ever touches my phone, so no worries."

I smile against his chest before turning my attention to some weird reality show. His hands are slowly caressing my body, a soothing motion that starts to make my eyes heavy.

"Dane is clearing out Silk tomorrow for Maverick's surprise birthday party," he says idly, now running his fingers through my hair.

My eyes are almost closed, even though it's the middle of the day. I've never felt so comfortable and at ease.

"Oh?" I mumble groggily.

"Can you be there?"

My eyes go wide as I look up to meet his gaze. "I can't just show up to a party I'm not invited to."

"I just invited you. I'll tell Dane I invited you because the guys and I are trying to make you more comfortable around us by including you."

Rain probably didn't ask me to come because she thinks I still hate the Sterling boys. They're not *as* bad as I initially thought. Dale is actually almost as nice as Dane. Corbin and Maverick are surprisingly smart when it comes to business. And Kode... well, Kode has layers I didn't know could exist inside him.

"Okay."

He grins as he runs his hand down my ass, cupping one side with one of his large palms.

"Be warned—I plan to get drunk. And I'll probably be all over you before the night is over. So you'll have to get me out of there if you don't want everyone seeing me pin you up against the wall."

I shouldn't giggle like an idiot, but I do. Just knowing that he's admitting he can't keep his hands off me is nice. Because for once, it's me that someone sees.

Chapter 9

Kode

"You suck," Corbin says, frowning at me.

I glance at the door again, still waiting on Tria to come in. I only left her house an hour ago to run home and change, then get to Silk in time for Maverick's birthday party.

"Why?" I drawl, trying to feign interest in my cousin.

"Because after you left, my damn badass streak came to an end. I had a triple bogey on the thirteenth, and a double on the fourteenth. Then I hit the damn thing into the water on the fifteenth. I think you were my good luck charm."

Laughing, I finally look over at him. "Sorry. Had something important come up."

His eyes narrow suspiciously, and he stares at me for a minute. "You dating someone? Because you've been acting different lately. And you're not sulking over Rain anymore."

Rain is the last thing on my mind these days. It's as though all of my other feelings have been stripped, laid bare, and finally exposed as what they are. She's my friend. For the first time since I was a kid, I see Rain just as she sees me.

Tria wants me. She lets me touch her, hold her, do whatever in the hell I want to with her badass body. And she kisses me like I'm the only thing that matters every time I'm with her. There's no hesitancy in her touch. And she's not waiting on someone else to take my place.

It feels damn good to be wanted by the person you want. It's also a feeling I'm not accustomed to, but quickly getting addicted to. I feel high every time I'm with her.

"Hello," Corbin says in an exasperated tone. "I asked if you're dating someone."

Shrugging, I turn my attention back to the door. "Not yet." It's not a lie, per se, but it's also not the truth. Maybe after the wedding happens, Tria and I can discuss something more serious. I don't want a real relationship until I don't have to hide it, and until we sort through what's going on between us, we need to keep it quiet.

"Rain is running late," Dane says with a pout as he joins us.

I used to feel the jealous rage course through me when he relayed any message from Rain, but now... nothing. It's actually amazing to feel... free.

"Why?" Corbin asks.

"Raya showed up at her house. Kade... Man, Kade's in a bad place right now. He's taking his grandfather's death hard. Rain called Tria, so she's on her way over to help out. She might stay with Raya so that Rain can come and be here for Mav's party."

Shit. Why didn't she—

My phone buzzes in my pocket, and I quickly pull it out to see I have two unread messages. Well, hell. I guess she did try to tell me.

The first one is from twenty minutes ago, essentially relaying everything Dane just said. The second is from right now, and it's her saying she'll try to come see me if Raya gets to feeling better.

"Should we go talk to Kade?" Corbin asks.

Dane shakes his head, blowing out a harsh breath. "Nah. Wren, Rye, and Tag have this. They're not coming tonight because they're up at the vineyard, doing what they can to piece Kade back together. He keeps lashing out at everyone. I think Raya just needed a break. She's a hell of a lot stronger than most people."

"No," I say, sighing. "She just loves him a hell of a lot more than people realize."

I've seen the way they both look at each other, so I'm surprised Kade is pushing her away right now when he needs her the most.

The talk of death goes away the second Maverick walks through the door, and we all yell *surprise* in unison.

Tria

Raya is fast asleep on my bed. She finally cried herself to sleep. After Rain left to go meet the guys at the surprise party, I brought Raya to my house.

I'm not as good with consoling as Rain is, but I've done everything I knew to do, including calling Brin and Ash over to help me.

"She's asleep," I say with a sigh as I head into the living room.

Ash smiles softly while taking a sip of water. Brin and I both grab the wine bottle we've almost finished off.

"No wine?" I ask Ash.

"I wish. But no. Tag rode with Wren and Rye out to the vineyard, so if Melanie calls with an emergency for Trip, I need to be stone-cold sober."

"Are you worried there will be an emergency?" I ask, concerned.

93

"Always. It sort of goes with the territory of being a mother."

I grin at her before getting comfortable on the couch next to Brin.

"You can head to the party," Brin says, nudging me with her shoulder. Ash doesn't know about Kode, so Brin doesn't elaborate.

"Nah. I'll stay in case she wakes up."

Ash starts to speak, but someone knocks at my door, prompting me to run over and answer. Brin says something that has Ash laughing hysterically, and I smile like I'm infected on the way to greet whoever.

Since it could be Kode, I stop in front of the mirror to make sure my hair isn't wild all over my head. Then I swing open the door, only to gasp in shock and try to slam it shut immediately.

My heart fires out rapid beats, thumping and pounding against my chest as panic sets in. A heavy black boot lands in front of the door, halting it from closing, and Pete Mercer shoulders his way in.

"Thanks," he says sardonically. "I'd love to come in."

I stumble backwards, looking at his freshly shaven head, his twisted grin, and his dark eyes that didn't used to scare me so much. Blood hums through my veins, leaving me with a fearful fever. There's not an inch of him that isn't covered in menace.

Man, maybe I do have daddy issues if I slept with this psycho.

"You're breaking the restraining order," I say, pissed that my voice breaks three times.

He laughs while shaking his head. "Prove it."

His long body is clad in jeans and a red T-shirt—blood red. His arms are corded with bulging muscles he didn't have when we were together. If he were to hit me now, he'd probably break me with very little effort.

"Why can't you just leave me alone?" I ask cautiously, stalling for time.

"Why? Fuck, Tria, it's your fault I went to prison. You have no fucking clue what happens in a place like that. But I'll show you. I'll make sure you understand the hell I endured." He grins the scariest smile I've ever seen in my life, and he cracks his fingers. "We'll have long lessons that explain exactly what I went through."

Swallowing hard, I look up to see the determination in his eyes. It's sharing space with his hatred that is seeping through every visible feature on his body. Even his muscles are straining with rage.

He keeps stepping closer and closer, but suddenly he's backing away, eyes wide in confusion. "Who the fuck are you?" he spits.

"The bitch who just snapped a picture of you with her phone after you broke a restraining order," Brin says flippantly, making my stomach lurch.

She's being way too brave. With a guy like Pete, you play submissive even if it's just an act. He's not a bully; he's a psychopath. Standing up to him is the same as goading him to do his worst.

"I wouldn't do that if I were you," Ash says, joining us, my metal bat in her hands. "Cops are already on the way."

Pete looks like he's about to take on all three of us—and he probably could—but after a beat, he curses and turns to stalk away, leaving my door wide open and an ominous chill in his wake.

My sanctuary is gone. This place was supposed to keep me hidden from him. Sterling Shore is a place packed full of homes and condos, so how did he find me?

Ash blows out a breath while putting the bat down, her hands trembling. I can't believe that was enough to intimidate him.

"Who the hell was that?" Raya asks from behind us, startling the hell out of me. I turn to see her lowering her Taser gun. When the hell did she pull that thing out? How long has she been in here?

"Pete Mercer. I guess he was a little surprised. You have a Taser gun?" I ask, noticing her poker face in place of her teary-eyed one.

"Yeah, my dad's FBI partner gave it to me as a birthday gift. Pepper spray, too."

"Man, I thought he was scared of me and the bat," Ash says, laughing humorlessly while leaning back against the wall.

Raya runs a hand through her already disheveled hair, and then she looks back toward the door.

"Good thing you weren't here alone. You need to go stay with someone," Raya says, her own troubles forgotten as she focuses on my crazy drama.

"You can stay with us," Ash immediately offers.

"Or you can stay with me and Maggie. You won't have a parking spot unless you use the space across the road that my jackass neighbor doesn't use," Brin adds, forcing humor into the situation, something she always does to make people more at ease.

"I'll let you know," I say with a harsh breath. Shit. I don't want to stay with anyone. I hate feeling like I have to hide.

"I need to get back to check on how the guys are doing with Kade," Raya says while putting away her Taser gun, tucking it back into her purse.

"You heading to Maverick's party?" Brin asks, running her hand over my arm in a comforting motion. "To see Rain, I mean."

She means Kode, but she can't say that aloud. Oddly enough, I really do want to see Kode right now. More than I did. It feels safe and peaceful in his arms, and right now, I'd give anything to feel that.

"Um… yeah. I think so. I don't want to be here alone; that's for sure."

"We wouldn't leave you alone," Ash says promptly, reminding me how amazing she really is. "I didn't really call the cops. I just ran out here with the first big thing I could find to hit him with. But you need to call them."

The police won't do anything, and I know it. They never have really been of much use to me. I think they believe I'll only go back to him, so they don't see the use in stopping him before he hurts me.

"I'll go talk to them tomorrow. Not tonight."

She frowns, but nods. "You'd better."

I smile and head into the bedroom to change. No matter what, I won't say anything to Kode about this. I'll just suggest we go to his house tonight instead of hanging out at mine the way we planned.

I'll worry about finding somewhere to stay tomorrow.

Chapter 10

Kode

Without Tria here, I'm half drunk with no one to take advantage of me. Maverick is facedown on the table after doing his row of birthday shots. Pansy.

Corbin is surprisingly sober, considering the occasion. And he's relaxing in the booth next to me while the madness rages on.

"Kode Sterling, you drunk enough to play nice yet?" a girl I think I know asks, but I wave her off.

"Not with you."

She says something that sounds reasonably insulting, and I shrug while Corbin laughs.

"Not chasing ass tonight?" I ask him.

"Not tonight. I spent the day helping Ruby set up her new shop."

My eyebrows shoot up in surprise. "Ruby was in town?"

"Yeah. She's going to be moving here soon. Her new shop is opening soon to the public. So I spent the day helping her look for a place to live. I also set up the finishing touches on her shop, and now I'm completely exhausted."

"She already gone?"

"Yeah. She left about two hours before I had to leave to come here."

Before anything else can be said, a body is sliding into the booth beside me. "Not interested," I say without looking. "Go find a guy who is."

"Okay," Tria—oh shit, Tria—says, sliding back out.

"Hey, sorry," I say quickly, grabbing her hand and tugging her back toward me. A groan passes through my lips when I take in her strapless white dress that hugs her perfectly. "Didn't know it was you."

She seems to relax as though she's relieved.

"Hey, Tria," Corbin says, his eyes going back and forth between us when I pull her flush against my side.

Damn, she smells so good.

"Hey," she says shyly, leaning against my side when I tug her even closer.

"Kode, dude. You're getting a little too touchy," Corbin warns, but I flip him off while leaning over to Tria's ear.

"You look too sexy not to touch," I tell her, kissing the side of her neck and smiling when she shivers.

"Kode!" Corbin warns, growling at me like I'm an errant child that has to be chastened.

"I can handle it," Tria says while rubbing my knee under the table.

I continue kissing a trail down her neck, ignoring my cousin's exasperated groans. She tastes as good as she smells.

"Tria, you don't have to handle it. He gets a little too hands-on when he's been drinking liquor. But he hasn't been doing this shit tonight. Sorry. Just go find Rain, and I'll deal with him."

I flip him off again before pressing harder against her. I've wanted to feel her pulled up against me since I left her house earlier.

"Really, Corbin. It's fine. I swear to you I'm a big girl and can handle him."

"You know exactly how to handle me," I say against her ear, and her hand slides up higher on my thigh, pushing closer to the hard part of my body that has been dying to get back inside her.

"If Dane sees him all over you, he'll kick his ass—or try to—and that won't be good. Then Rain will also try to kick his ass."

"Corbin, please. Don't worry. I've got this. Promise."

Corbin sighs, but he slides out of the booth. "Well, I'm going to go make sure Dane and Rain stay away from the booth. Let me know when he passes out or if you need any help."

She laughs lightly, and I'm pretty sure she nods, but I'm too busy kissing my way down her neck to care.

"You're a little drunk, aren't you?" she muses as Corbin leaves.

Maverick snores loudly at that moment, eliciting a laugh from her. "I'm not as bad off as he is," I tell her, glancing up to meet those endless hazel eyes. "Damn, you're gorgeous."

She grins while leaning over and brushing her lips against mine. In this tall corner booth, it's hard for anyone to see us. "Still want me to stay with you tonight?" I ask her, hoping she says yes.

"Actually, I was hoping we could go to your place. You've invaded my space, so I think it's only fair that I invade yours."

I grin while pulling her closer for a much better kiss, and she melts in my arms while kissing me back, not complaining about the fact I'm a little drunk, or the fact that I'm practically mauling her in the booth. She feels so right like this.

"I'm good with that," I say when our lips break apart.

"I should go say hey to Rain before she comes looking for me. Can you behave in front of them?" she asks me, leaning over to kiss my neck.

I groan while trying to get her in my lap. I'd fuck her here in the booth if I knew no one would see us. But someone would see, and I'd rather they not get that image in their head of my girl. I'd hate to have to go to prison after killing someone.

"I can behave, but not for long. We can get out of here whenever you're ready."

Her lips twitch in amusement before brushing mine again. "Just let me say hey to my sister. I'd wish Maverick a happy birthday, but it looks like it might have been too *happy* for him."

Her eyes land on Sleeping Beauty, and I snicker while nodding.

She climbs out of the booth first, and I squeeze her ass once, earning a quick hand slap. But she grins over her shoulder at me, letting me know she's just as into me as I am her. It's a reassurance I wasn't aware I needed. Apparently chasing a girl who was chasing my brother for all those years has done a number on my ego.

But Tria isn't chasing anyone but me. She came here tonight and didn't hesitate to climb into the booth beside me. I'm the first person she came in to find, and her mind was focused on only me. It makes me want to kiss the hell out of her in front of everyone, but I know that would cause all sorts of problems. Especially if she found out the truth about that fucking letter.

Damn. I really wish that terrible thought hadn't just crossed my mind. Why the hell did I ever try to split Rain and Dane apart? I should have left it alone. Then I might have noticed Tria a little sooner instead of uselessly pining for a girl who was completely unobtainable.

It's not until we reach the others that I see her smile slip, but she quickly puts it back in place. The alcohol has dulled my senses, so I didn't notice how forced that pretty grin was. But now I see it clearly.

"I'm too tired to keep standing," I say to the group, but it's intended for Tria to step in.

"Someone has to drive you home," Rain says quickly. "You've had way too much to drink."

"I'll drop him off. I'm still tired from having the girls over," Tria says, stepping in like the angel she is.

Corbin groans, apparently sensing something is up, and he narrows his eyes on me. I just shrug, acting bored with the whole scene, when really all I want to do is get the hell out of here and find out what's wrong with Tria.

"Tria, you don't have to do that. We can call a cab and one of us can go," Dane says, looking around for someone other than himself to take me.

"It's fine. Really. I'll see you guys tomorrow."

As she hugs the group, Corbin grabs me at my elbow to drag me toward the door, stopping when we're a safe distance away.

"I seriously hope you're not fucking around with Tria to get at Rain. I can't believe I didn't catch on sooner. Dude, you're going to destroy your relationship with your brother if you're trying this shit."

I knock his hand away, and then I take a very menacing step toward him. I'm so sick of this shit.

"I get it. I fucked up. Dane deserves to be pissed, but what I'm doing or not doing with Tria hasn't got a fucking thing to do with Rain."

He tilts his head, looking more curious than intimidated. All this alcohol must be making me lose my edge.

"You like her," he says simply. "That's why you—even though you've got too much liquor in your system—never touched a girl tonight. Well, I'll be damned."

His taunting grin takes over his scowl, and I curse myself for revealing anything to the dick. Rolling my eyes, I take a step back. Before I can respond, Tria is at my side, and my arm drops to land on her shoulders.

"Take care of him," Corbin says with his wry grin. He winks at Tria before pushing off from the bar and heading back toward the others.

Tria doesn't acknowledge him as she helps me out the door. Well, I let her think she's helping me. I'm plenty sober enough to walk, but she might not have let me keep my arm around her in front of everyone if I wasn't faking a stagger.

As soon as we're outside, I straighten up, and her eyes narrow on me as I pull her closer.

"Faker," she says under her breath, eliciting a laugh from me.

"I've been drinking, but I'm plenty sober. How's Raya?"

Her sigh says it all. "She's really worried about Kade right now. She's lost because she has no clue what to do or how to help. She feels useless. She basically just needed some friends to vent to more than anything. She went back to the vineyard earlier."

I motion toward my car as she fills me in on the night. She says it was rather dull before she came to see me. I suppose her forced smile is because of her worry over Raya and Kade.

She digs her hand into my pocket suddenly, and I grab her ass in response.

"Down, boy. Just getting your keys."

She grins up at me, but it's weighted, only partially sincere. She looks around as if she's wary as we approach my car. I open the driver's side door for her, and she pulls me down to kiss me. Hard. Surprising me.

The door hangs open and forgotten as I move her to the solid back and push against her, kissing her back just as passionately. Her explorative tongue sweeps into my mouth, searching and seeking, and I grip her ass with both hands as I devour her.

As quickly as it started, it's over. She pushes me back, looking around again, and then she meets my eyes.

"Sorry. I just really needed that."

My wolfish grin slips into place and I waggle my eyebrows at her. "At your service, Tria. You've got me all to yourself tonight."

"Then let's go."

Chapter 11

Kode

Godforsaken hangovers. Hate them. And I hate me. Christ, my head is killing me. I hate my head.

A loud screaming song roars to life, reminding me what woke me up to begin with. That's the third time I've heard that obnoxious motherfucker this morning. Tria groans while trying to untangle herself from me and answer it. Apparently someone really wants to talk to her.

I hate Tria's phone.

Her bare body is next to mine, the sheet barely covering her as she swats blindly for the phone, not opening her eyes. It's too early for phone calls. Shit, it's seven in the morning, and we didn't even get in until after three.

As Tria answers—her *hello* mumbled—I grin and slide in behind her, wrapping my arms around her waist and kissing the back of her neck. Her dark hair is all draped to one side, giving me an angle on every side of her neck except for the side facing the bed.

"Oh. Hey, Rain," Tria says slowly, warning me to keep quiet, her voice suddenly very alert.

I keep kissing her, but I also keep my mouth shut. I've reached the point where I don't care if they know. But I know Tria is like everyone else—unsure if I'm really over Rain.

I honestly think I got over Rain the minute I saw Tria in a completely different light.

"I'm at... Brin's house. Why are you at my house?" she asks, and my phone buzzes loudly on the nightstand, forcing me to let her go and grab it.

I walk out of the room to answer so that Rain doesn't overhear my voice. Dane is calling? Both of them calling this early? Is it possible that Corbin ratted me out?

"Why the hell are you calling me so early?" I ask, clearing my throat from the early morning rasp.

"Sorry. But it's sort of important. Raya called Rain this morning to find out if Tria stayed with us. Apparently that douche you fucked up a few months ago showed up over at her house last night."

My entire body goes stiff, and my jaw grinds. I'll fucking kill him—after I throttle Tria for not telling me. That's why she acted so upset last night, and she didn't bother including me. The only thing keeping me from storming in there right now is the fact that she stayed with me. She came to me.

"I had no idea," I say in a deceptively calm tone, my eyes moving toward the bedroom door that I shut on my way out.

As I move out to the deck that overlooks the ocean, Dane continues. "Yeah. Raya had a Taser gun, and Brin—Tria's friend—snapped a picture. They're at the police station now because they were worried Tria wouldn't act soon enough. But they need Tria down there now."

"Because it doesn't matter where I'm really at." Tria's voice carries through the open sliding-glass door when she emerges in an angry storm from the bedroom.

I shut it quickly, blocking Dane from hearing her, and shake my head. Apparently Rain called her out on the lie about being at Brin's house, since Brin is at the police station.

"I'll take care of Pete Mercer again. Maybe the message will stick this time." His name tastes like acid on my tongue. I hate that son of a bitch more than anyone right now.

"Don't. Rain is worried Pete wants that. She thinks he's working an angle this time, and I think she's right. Why else would he emerge so soon after the last beating? We don't need to play into his hand."

I run a frustrated hand through my hair, and ignore the neighbors who are staring at me for wearing nothing but my boxer-briefs.

"Then what do we do?" I ask, trying not to lose my cool right now.

"We take care of her. She's going to stay here. Rain is trying to convince her to stay right now, but she's arguing with her about it. We don't want her staying with one of the other girls unless it's Ash. Brin lives with a girl roommate. Pete would consider that a fun challenge— the sick fuck. And Raya already has her hands full with Kade."

"I've got several houses. Tria doesn't seem like the type to want to live with someone, so I doubt you'll convince her. It's probably why she hasn't already told Rain yes. She can stay in one of my condos. He'd never look for her there. He'd be searching all your properties for her, though."

I wait patiently for him to take the bait.

"You wouldn't mind doing that?"

I lean back against the railing as Tria paces through the living room, my shirt covering her up.

"I don't mind at all. In fact, mention it to her right now."

I hear Dane talking to an exasperated Rain, and I listen as the message is relayed. Tria looks through the glass at me, her eyes wide.

That's right, baby. I know everything.

Her lips tighten before her shoulders slump in defeat. Her lips move, most likely giving in, since she knows she's not going to get to argue with me.

"Thanks," Dane says in a slow breath. "You're right. He'd never think to look for her in one of your places, since the two of you hate each other."

I smirk, carrying the secretive gaze that reflects back at me from against the pane of glass.

"Sure. No problem. I'll get it set up."

I hang up at the same time Tria does, and I head back inside to go to war.

"So you didn't think to mention that a psychopath showed up at your house last night?" I ask, doing all I can to mask my anger.

Tria

Ah, hell.

I hate it when he's pissed, and though his face is not exactly contorted in anger, I can feel the fury rolling off him in waves.

"Sorry. But it was Maverick's night, and everyone was in such a good mood… I just didn't want to be the one to ruin it."

He just watches me. Silence envelops the room, making it

108

awkward and uncomfortable. I haven't cried. I don't want to cry. Pete Mercer scares the ever living hell out of me, but I refuse to shed another tear because of his psychotic vendetta against me.

He's already beaten the hell out of me once—though that's not a fact I've shared with anyone. It's embarrassing enough to know I dated the lunatic. They don't need to know I stuck it out until he finally struck me. I'd rather he never got close enough to do it again. But I refuse to give him the power right now by crying about it.

"You're staying with me," is Kode's response after an eternity of silence.

"You mean one of your empty homes," I correct, following him as he moves through the massive house to the kitchen.

"No. I mean you're staying with me. Wherever I go, you go. Speaking of which, I'm going to New York next weekend. So think about what you want to pack."

I stumble over my own feet, trying to slowly sort out what he just said.

"Kode, I can't start living with you. Whatever is going on between us… It's way too soon for me to just move in. And I can't go to New York with you. You've got work to do, and I'll be in the way."

He doesn't respond for a few minutes as he grabs orange juice from the fridge—his favorite thing to drink in the mornings, I've noticed. After he pours a glass, he looks up at me.

"Tria, even if I have to chain you to my side, you'll stay with me. That's not negotiable. I'm not stupid enough to think this isn't way too soon for us to start having that sort of intimacy as far as living arrangements, but I'll be damned if I leave you out there for him to torment without any line of defense. So, get used to it. You're moving in."

Groaning, I lean over the chair, propping my elbows on the top while staring at him. He's really beautiful when he's protective. I didn't know he had it in him.

"Kode, as much as I appreciate your concern—and I do appreciate it—I can't stay. Not live with you. I happen to like this thing we've got going on, and I don't want Pete Mercer to screw it up. He's messed up enough things in my life."

I never thought I'd see the day when Kode Sterling's eyes softened to be so compassionate, but right now, he looks like all he wants to do is save me. I've never had anyone look at me like that. Ever.

"Tria, you're staying here. It's not going to mess anything up."

He moves around the side of the bar, and without any warning, his lips press gently against mine as he pulls me close to him. His hand grabs a fistful of the shirt I'm wearing, gathering it at the back as I move to my tiptoes to deepen the kiss.

He pulls back, nuzzling his nose against mine. "Right now, you need to get dressed. You have to go deliver a statement to the police station."

I groan again while leaning against him, and he holds me to him. I'm starting to wonder if I've spent all these years judging him wrong, or if he's changing toward me.

"My car is at my house," I remind him. "I took a cab to the club last night so that I could drive your car here."

"Your car will have to stay at whatever condo I tell Rain and Dane I'm putting you in. We'll take one of my cars to the police station."

"You can't come in," I say through a sigh.

"Fine. I'll wait in the car and do some business via phone while you go press charges."

This isn't how I pictured this morning going.

Chapter 12

Tria

"Tell me we're on the road to success," Leo, my business partner—the brain behind the formula of Beauty Graffiti—says over the phone.

I feel like a constant failure. His part is done, but I keep falling short on my end.

"Another *no*. Sorry, Leo. Regret taking this leap with me yet?"

He sighs over the phone, but he doesn't say anything negative. Never does. "It takes time, Tria. We're new and trying to compete with brands that have been out there for forever. You fronted all the cash, so that means you're taking the majority of the risk. You gave me a chance to do this when no one else would even review my proposal, so no. I sure as hell don't regret going into business with you. I have faith you'll get it out there. Internet sales are doing decent for a new launch at least."

Only because Ash knows all the tricks to get our line to show up in search engines. But the sales aren't enough to keep the business afloat. Very few people internet shop for new makeup. Leo just assumes those numbers are big, when in reality, they're actually very small.

"I've got more lined up. I'll drive them all crazy before I give up," I assure him.

He laughs before saying, "I'm sure you will. Hey, is something up?

Darla said she was forwarding all your mail to another address when I asked her to send you some fresh samples."

Damn. One more person who has to know. "I'll be fine. Just staying with a friend until some drama gets sorted out."

"Guy or girl?" he asks, prying. I can almost hear his smile.

"Guy, and no, it's not anyone you know."

He snickers before speaking again. "Fine. Fine. Well, let me know if you need anything else for the meetings."

"Thanks, Leo. I swear I'll eventually get us a break."

"I know you will. And let me know if you ever need a place to stay. Jake wouldn't mind you staying with us."

"Thanks, Leo."

Hanging up, I continue going over my short notes from the meeting. I barely got to tell her my opening line before she started taking calls and ignoring me. How do I keep someone's attention?

It's hard to focus on work when your personal life is all twisted up.

I hate drama. I really do. There should be a screening process and background check done on men before they're allowed to date someone. All that information should go to the woman considering a relationship. That would be a great way to avoid lunatics like Pete.

"How'd your meeting go?" Kode asks as he walks in, loosening his tie while dropping off his briefcase by the bedroom door.

He apparently has to work late some nights.

"It... went." That's all I can stomach divulging. It's hard to distribute a line of cosmetics when no one will even look over your proposal. Five minutes into the meeting, the woman was standing,

113

making up a lame excuse as to why she was cutting our visit short. Then I was shown out of the office by a very smug secretary who seemed to revel in my misery.

He comes to drop beside me on the bed, and I snuggle over to him. It has been three days since Pete Mercer showed up and rocked my world, but Kode has been amazing. It'd be really easy to get used to seeing him like this.

As his arms slide around me, he tugs me to him. "You want to show me your proposal? I can look it over and see if I can point out anything you might need to adjust for maximum potential."

It's like he actually cares, which is making me grin like a fool. "No. I need you to tell me how to keep people interested long enough to make it to the proposal portion of the meeting."

He frowns as he looks down at me.

"I can do that, Tria. Whenever you want."

Wearing only one of his T-shirts and my panties, I roll over to straddle his waist, staring down at him as I prepare to recite my presentation. "Beauty Graffiti has been developed by some of the—"

"I'll buy in," he says, grinning down at the lacy red panties his fingers are strumming over.

Rolling my eyes, I continue, "Has been developed by one of the industries newest and brightest minds. It's a mineral compound that guarantees anything from light acne coverage to fine line coverage that is only found in products that cost twice as much to manufacture—"

"You need to move that to the front of your entry," he says more seriously, running his hands up and down my legs. "If they know they have a good product for half the price, they're immediately intrigued. Lead with that, and have valid proof ready to show them. Maybe a binder with that as the first, non-introductory page. That's what would sell me. Don't mention the one who manufactured it unless you have a name worth dropping. That's essentially saying you have someone no one has heard of yet."

That's actually helpful, and I lean over to grab my phone and make a note of it. He grins up at me as I finish typing it into my notepad app, and then I put my phone back down.

"Keep going," he says.

His fingers start tracing lines on my legs as I continue, trying to remember the rest of my key points.

"The urban style packaging will appeal to anyone from ages thirteen to forty—"

"Age gap is too much. Slim it down, since it sounds unrealistic. Even if you have studies to prove it, it still seems too farfetched, and it will make them apprehensive about trusting any of your other information."

Again I make a note, because that makes perfect sense. "Thirteen to thirty?" I ask.

"Better. You can always add styles to represent other ages, then add that to your explanation as to why the age gap is so vast."

I grin down at him and brush my lips over his in a silent show of appreciation.

"Keep going," he prompts, and I do. I finish the entire speech, only pausing for him to insert his notes. It's amazing how much better my opening sounds by the time he has it tweaked. What I wouldn't do to constantly have him around to bounce ideas off of.

He has built numerous businesses, so I trust he knows exactly what he's doing. And he's explanatory, giving details as to why certain things should be omitted or should be expanded upon. He shifts the order of some things around, and by the time we're finished, it's a masterfully prepared presentation.

What I thought was going to be a playful bed conversation, turns into a two hour event, and I'm excited instead of nervous about my business for once. We've broken out a bottle of wine, spread out a makeshift workspace on the bedroom floor, and turned this into a fun tweaking session.

He helps me rearrange my binders, sitting with me and talking about the graffiti styled casing, brushes, and bags that go with it. He's actually wowed with the visual appeal, because he believes it's definitely going to catch eyes.

Graffiti is safe, because it's something that has always been cool in a *bad* sort of way. It's also classy when used right, and I rode the thin line of hip and refined.

"This is really impressive," he says, grinning over at me as we finish the last of the binders. "I see this taking off for you, as long as you find the right people to present it to."

For the first time since I started this line, I feel completely and totally vindicated. The sting of all those rejections slowly fades away, because Kode Sterling doesn't bullshit to spare your feelings. When he says it's good, then it's good.

"That's what I'm working on," I say with a sigh.

"You're aiming mostly at smaller department store chains, right?" he asks, taking a sip of his wine as he leans back.

"Yeah. They're the only ones willing to even pretend to take meetings with me."

Great. I sound like I'm pouting.

He studies me for a moment, looking intense. "Can I suggest changing your strategy?"

I shrug, willing to take any guidance he has.

"Department stores expect merchandise at their demand, so that's the main reason they're dismissing you. You won't be able to outsource the manufacturing if this takes off. It's fine to outsource for samples and such, but it's not a long term plan."

That's something I've already figured out. "I know, but it's not like I can set up my own manufacturing company right now. I'm a Noles, but not even I have that sort of cash to toss out for workers, buildings, equipment—"

"I wasn't suggesting that," he interrupts, smiling over at me. "I was suggesting taking a meeting with some of the big, already established cosmetic lines. It's the best way to get your foot in the door. Get yourself an umbrella company spot that allows you to use their resources and contacts. You'd still be in charge and doing most of the work as far as getting your line in stores, but you'd have their support and access to their facilities. You'd of course have to share a chunk of the profits, but eventually your name and line would be big enough to branch out and form your own independent company."

"I actually tried that," I say with a grin, enjoying the fact he looks surprised. I guess he thought I was going all out without considering other options that made more sense.

"But?" he asks, shifting to face me better.

It sucks to keep sounding like such a failure in front of someone so successful. "As you said, I had no name to trade in on. So the ones I tried to get meetings with wouldn't even see me. It sucks, but it is what it is. Now I'm going this route."

He frowns while opening one of the binders to the page of the before and after pictures. "They won't see you," he says to himself, not looking incredibly happy about that. The frown that puckers at his brow is adorable, because he's a little upset about someone not taking a chance on me.

It shouldn't feel that good to know he cares, but it does.

"Thank you for helping me," I say, trying to rid him of his train of thought.

He slides toward me and kisses me gently. "No one else is helping you out?"

It's a question that I don't really know how to answer. "I have an assistant, Darla, but she's only supposed to help with certain things. My business partner is brilliant, and he came up with the compound and the actual makeup. I'm supposed to be the bankroll and the one getting us into stores. I've paid for the manufacturing of a first launch, buying enough to fill initial orders if anyone wants to buy in. And—"

"That's not what I'm talking about, Tria. I'm talking about anyone—someone else you can run a practice speech with. Someone who can help you repackage and arrange binders. Someone who can point you in the direction of graphic designers. That sort of thing."

"Well, Brin listens, but she doesn't really know how to help. My partner is solely the brains—not the marketing type. Rain is crazy busy with the wedding and her movie deal. Ash designed my website and helped design the graffiti graphics, since that's what she does."

"But no one like me?" he asks, his smile almost precious.

"No one like you," I confirm, and his grin only grows.

Kode

I love waking up with her tangled around me. It's amazing how something can change completely.

Before Tria, I couldn't sit around and talk to anyone but Rain—well, no girl. Rain always seemed like the exception. And in a way she was, but not in the same way Tria is.

Rain could sleep beside me in the same bed without wanting to touch me. Tria can't sleep beside me without wrapping herself around me as tightly as she can get. There's nothing better than that early morning feeling of peace. It's a tranquil high that seems to surpass any drug I've ever encountered.

Tria looks at me with hunger, awe, and gratitude. And she has different tones. She has a tone for her close friends and family, a tone for business conversations, a tone for people she's formally acquainted with, and a tone for people she just meets.

But my favorite tone is the one reserved just for me. No one else hears her speak to them the way she speaks to me. It's a touch lower than her family octave, but it's a feminine sort of husky that has me desperate to get her underneath me any chance I get.

She's not even aware that she does it, which is what makes it even better. I'm special to her, and she doesn't have a problem with letting me know that with all her small actions—things most people would take for granted.

They wouldn't take it for granted if they had lived in the friend-hell I was stuck in for eleven years.

"You have a meeting," she says in her sleepy rasp, prompting me to smile as she snuggles against me.

"Not for another two hours. Has your dad called you back?" I ask her, thinking back to the way she called him three times before we went to bed last night.

"Nope. I just wanted him to call Aunt Margaret and Uncle Paul and send his condolences. I give up."

My fingers start running through her hair, and she snuggles her head into a different spot on my chest.

"Can I ask something and you not get mad?" she asks softly, her voice thick with hesitation.

"Sure," I say, figuring it's probably something about Rain.

"Why aren't you the best man in the wedding? And why do things seem so tense between you and Dane?"

Well, it's inadvertently about Rain.

I start to tell her the whole damn story, but I can't. I know I can't. As much as I want to do it, it would destroy my relationship with Rain. But what scares me the worst is the fact that it could shred what I have with Tria, too.

"Do you really want the answer to that?"

I can't blatantly lie to her, because I don't want to.

She gets quiet for a moment, and her body gets a little more rigid in my arms. But she has to lead this conversation. I can't.

"Because of Rain," she says simply. I maintain my silence—guilty by omission—and she blows out a breath that has me worried. "Did you... I mean... Do you love her?"

I thought I did. In fact, I was convinced Rain Noles was the only girl in the world for me. It was as simple as that. She was the only person I tried to be different with. And I tried real damn hard to be just as fucking nice, sweet, understanding, and patient as Dane.

Then I met Tria. I don't know what's going on with us, but I don't feel like I have to try to be someone else with her. In fact, she doesn't make me try at all. She doesn't expect me to be like Dane because she prefers the way I am. It's... damn, it's nice.

"I'll be honest, Tria. I used to think I was in love with her, but I wasn't. I couldn't have been. I know I love her, but it's not the kind of love I once thought it was."

I'm starting to realize you can't love someone that doesn't love you the way you are. I was just Rain's go-to best friend—the one she trusted but never loved in that way.

Tria relaxes against me, and I bask in the way she curls her arms around me, holding me as though she's afraid this moment might vanish if she looks away. I've never had anyone be this way about me.

"Good," she tells me, and I grin.

121

"You must like me a little if you're starting to ask those kinds of questions."

She smiles against my chest before placing a delicate kiss on my sternum.

"I guess I do like you a little, but I…" Her voice trails off as she sits up, her eyes meeting mine with a great deal of seriousness. I keep my arm around her waist, not willing to give up touching her.

"Kode, I've spent most of my life feeling ostracized because of everyone's awe for Rain. My mom never treated us differently, but I could still tell that she was extra careful with Rain. As a child, you don't understand that, and it causes you to be bitter. Then at school… things were bad for me. And the Sterlings and Rain were a massive part of that."

A wave of nausea rolls over my stomach, and I immediately feel guilt for the first time about how shitty we all treated her in school. We were stupid kids, though. Well, I was just an uncaring ass, but the others were just kids.

"I can't go back and undo the way we treated you, Tria."

She nods slowly, her eyes falling down to my bare upper half to where the sheet meets my flesh at my hips.

"I know. But that's not the point I was making. I've spent a lifetime feeling like the world chose Rain over me—that she was so much better than I was. I worked twice as hard in school, college, and in life as she did. She makes it seem effortless to do exactly what she wants to with her life and obtain undying loyalty and love from amazing people. I have to work for those things, and yet it seems like I can't ever achieve the things that come so easily to her."

She pauses, and my lips tighten. I never realized how much we have in common.

"I'm not bitter—not anymore. I was for a really long time. When I found out Eleanor wasn't really my mother, I was crushed, and no one was there for me besides the woman who had played my mother all these years. My dad—the only person who ever chose me over Rain—cut me out of his life for finding out the truth. He was too cowardly to face the disappointment in my eyes, and too stubborn to realize that I would love him anyway. I thought after people found out that they would possibly look at me the way they looked at Rain, maybe realize I wasn't the spoiled girl with the perfect life, and then they could see me. But no one did."

Dane had mentioned this, but at the time, I was too busy pining for the other Noles sister to fully listen or even care. Now, it's like my world has reversed its rotation. Rain Noles is no longer the center of my universe.

Tria takes a deep breath, and I lie there unmoving. After a spell of silence, I finally decide I should say something.

"I'm sorry, Tria. I know it's not worth a damn thing, but I rarely apologize. I mean it sincerely. I'm sorry."

Her eyes glisten as they look up to meet mine again, and she gives me a sad smile before looking back down.

"I'm not trying to make you feel bad, nor am I trying to make you apologize. I'm trying to make you understand that this thing between us has to stop if you have any feelings for Rain that extend beyond friendship."

I start to speak, to ensure her that those feelings were slain by her hands, but she holds her hand up and speaks again.

"Rain and I are the same age, separated by only a few months. We have one thing tying us to blood, and that's the cowardly father we share. We have a woman who loves us both like her true daughters, and that's kept us afloat. I'm finally building a relationship with my sister, Kode. It's important that I have this. It's important that Mom has this. So I can't play second place again. This thing between us is meaning more to me than I should admit. If you still want Rain as more than a friend—even a little bit—then end it now, because it'll hurt, and I'll get bitter again. I'm finally moving past it, so don't make me feel as though she once again has everything I want."

The words keep playing over in my head, sounding so much like the way I've felt for years, only for different reasons. But she just admitted that I mean something to her, which is shocking. She hated me not too long ago.

I sit up, push her to her back, and put my body over hers to stare down into her eyes. She swallows hard, probably worried about what I'm going to say, so I end the suspense.

"Nothing—that's what I feel for Rain. Well, as I said, I still love her, but purely in the platonic sense of the word. Pretty sure I like you a little bit, too, and I'd prefer it if this—you and me—could keep moving forward the way we are."

Her hand moves to my bare side, slowly sliding down my body in a way that has me trying not to be a jerk and just start something with her right now before we're done talking.

"We're moving forward?" she asks with a sweet smile.

I lean down to kiss her, groaning when my erect cock brushes against her soft skin. When her legs spread wider in invitation, I barely refrain from doing something stupid.

"Yeah. Forward." Gazing into her hopeful hazel eyes, I brush my thumb over her very enticing lips. "I've spent my life getting overlooked for Dane. I wouldn't do that to you—not now. Rain loved him. She couldn't ever see me. Believe me when I say those ties have been burned.

"Dane has always been the wonder for the world to see—the boy who came from the streets but managed to morph into the perfect specimen. It's hard to compete with. And you know how Dane is—too damn perfect. So I get it, Tria. What I felt for Rain is gone. Completely."

It's a freeing confession that has me breathing easily. I feel like I've been tied to Rain for way too long. I did it to myself. She never once led me to believe we were ever going to be more, but I clung to her for all the wrong reasons. Now I'm staring down at the girl I really missed out on.

"As long as you're sure, Kode. I mean completely positive."

"No doubt whatsoever," I murmur softly, brushing her lips again with mine. "I'm not looking at Rain, Tria. I see you. Sorry it took me so long to do that, but I see you now."

She kisses me hard, and briefly I consider fucking her now without breaking contact, but my condoms are in the drawer. I return the kiss with as much fervor and hunger, trembling when it becomes painful not to be inside her.

Forced to break away to grab protection, I quickly scramble to grab a foil pack, stretching across the bed and fumbling blindly so that I don't have to move completely. Just as I get one out and start rolling it on, Tria speaks words so softly that I don't think I was meant to hear them.

"I've always seen you."

For a second, I wonder if I heard her wrong, because I'm pretty sure she has always hated me. But I don't question it. Even if it's not true, it feels good to hear, and I move back to her lips to pay gratitude while thrusting into her soaking wet sheathe.

Chapter 13

Kode

It's odd. I haven't lived with anyone since I moved out of my parents' house at eighteen. But strangely enough, seeing all of Tria's things comingling with mine for the past two weeks hasn't freaked me out. It's actually a little nice to see her stuff lounging comfortably within my house.

I've gotten used to the bathroom counter being covered in girly stuff. And I've grown used to seeing bras in very odd places—such as a doorknob or on the towel rack. We've developed a system quickly. And damn she can cook. Well, she can cook some things.

The only thing that is pissing me off is not being able to go out in public. I'll be glad when the damn wedding is over and Tria and I can come out and announce we're together. But next weekend we'll be in New York, and I can finally take her out on an actual date. It sucks that I had to push the trip back, but I needed to handle a few deals here this weekend.

"Kode, you in here?" Corbin's voice booms through the house, and I make a mental note to kick his ass for using his emergency key. If Tria had been in here naked, I would already be kicking his ass.

"What's up?" I ask, closing the door to the bedroom behind me as I head toward the living room.

"Tria here?" He walks in holding a coffee cup, and he takes a sip before cursing it for being too hot.

"Why would Tria be here?" I ask, shrugging as though he hasn't figured it out already.

He picks up a bra that is hanging over the back of a chair. Damn. She really does find bizarre places to leave those things. Or maybe I tossed that one there. It's hard to keep up.

"Really?" he drawls, dropping the bra to the chair again. Depositing his cup to the small end table, he gives me a pointed look before continuing. "You gonna keep trying to play the dumb card with me?"

"That bra could belong to any girl," I say flippantly.

He rolls his eyes while coming to drop down on the sofa. "Any word on Pete Mercer?"

My jaw ticks at the mention of his name. "Cops aren't looking for him. Apparently all they do is issue an arrest warrant for breaking a restraining order. I'm looking into hiring a bounty hunter. Considering they usually work for bondsmen, that's proving to be a little difficult."

He nods while leaning back, and I take a seat next to him.

"Rain went to the condo where Tria is supposedly staying. Her car was there but she wasn't, so she freaked out. I covered for you and told her that Tria was with me because she was blocked in. Since I conveniently live just down the road, she bought it."

Rain is becoming a pain in the ass with her worry. I want to tell her to stop freaking out because I'm taking care of Tria.

"Where's she at right now?" Corbin asks.

"Out. Her friend Brin came and picked her up. Tria wanted something new to wear to New York next weekend, but I wouldn't let

128

her leave alone. Not until Pete is found."

His eyebrows go up in surprise. "You're taking her to New York? Damn. I guess you really do care about her."

"You thought I was lying?"

"Well, you never really said one way or the other, and you've been avoiding me like I'm the devil since Maverick's party. Thought I'd come over and squash the awkwardness."

Looking toward the door, I take a deep breath. Finally, I meet Corbin's eyes again. Now that he's here, everything I've wanted to get off my chest to someone is trying to bubble out. There's only one thing driving me absolutely crazy in a bad way right now.

"I wish Dane had told the truth about the letter."

He strangles on air as his eyes widen. "Seriously? Rain would hate you right now."

"I know. But it would be out in the open, and Rain would eventually forgive me. Maybe. Dane and I could try to move on from it. And it wouldn't be hanging over my head like a lit stick of dynamite right now. I'm seriously considering telling Tria after the wedding is over. I wouldn't risk Rain finding out and it messing up her wedding."

Corbin blows out a breath, and he leans forward to put his elbows on his knees. "You must really have it bad for Tria. I think it's best to just let this one die with time. Dane knew she'd forgive him, but she wouldn't forgive you, man. Not for that. And Tria... You could lose her, too. Rain and her are tight now."

"I was eighteen when I stole the damn thing. It's not like any of us thought rationally at that age. I was lovesick. And I swear I thought

Dane was fucking anything that walked."

He shakes his head slowly, probably wondering how things got so messed up so badly. Leave it to me to turn a stumble into a train wreck.

"You were eighteen when you stole it, but the fact that you kept it a secret for six years... A lot happened to both of them in those six years. You want Rain putting that shit on your shoulders?"

My stomach roils. It's not like I haven't already thought of that.

"This deep conversation isn't what I came here to have," Corbin continues. "Rain wants us all to go out tonight for Maverick's do-over birthday. He's pissed because he passed out too early to really enjoy his party. So we're all meeting at Silk, partying there for a while, and then letting Maverick call the shots. And she's calling to invite Tria."

Grinning, I think of all the secret places inside Silk where I can have my way with her.

"Fine. But we can't get too wasted. Tria has a breakfast meeting tomorrow via conference call about her makeup line."

"No problem, old man. Two weeks and the girl has domesticated you."

I flip him off, not bothering to tell him this thing between us really started over a month ago. He still hasn't figured out that Tria was the girl from the bar that I dumped them for that night.

The front door opens and shuts, and Tria's voice fills the house immediately.

"Well, I definitely have the underwear portion of the trip covered. I hope you like lacy—"

Her words halt immediately, and the sexiest piece of lingerie I've ever seen is quickly shoved back into a bag as her cheeks turn twelve shades of red in an instant. Her mouth opens and closes several times in an attempt to dig herself out of that hole.

Corbin restrains his laughter, but his body shakes from the silent riot going on inside him. I'm openly grinning at her, taunting her without any shame.

"By the way," I drawl, "Corbin is here."

She squeaks when she tries to speak, and then quickly clears her throat. "I'm... um... I didn't... um... no car."

Corbin's laughter sneaks out, but he coughs quickly to cover it up, and then smothers the dueling sounds with his hand. After a beat, he finally manages to explain.

"I walked here from the coffee shop down the street. My car was blocked in, and this was where I was coming anyway. Seemed to just make sense to walk it, as opposed to waiting for the jackass to come out and move his illegally parked car."

Her face is still scarlet, and I stand to walk over to her. That bag is definitely getting packed. I want a better look at whatever lingerie she was just swinging around.

"Stop freaking out. Corbin has seen more lacy underwear than a Victoria's Secret model."

Corbin bursts out laughing, but Tria's face only blushes deeper as she scolds me with her eyes. After I take the bag from her, I peek inside. Yep. It's going to be a hell of a weekend.

"Corbin figured it out the night of Maverick's party," I say distractedly. Is that a corset? Shit. She's going to make it hard to leave the hotel room, and I really want to take her out on a date.

"Oh," she says on a long breath. "I guess it was obvious, since he was in the booth with us."

I put the bag down before I start getting hard. Corbin doesn't need to be here if that happens.

When I turn around, Corbin has a daring little grin on his smug face.

Tria stands beside me, her body stiff enough to break. So I take her hand and tug her over to the oversized leather chair. When I sit down, I drag her onto my lap. To my surprise, she relaxes against me almost immediately.

"We're giving Maverick a redo party. Rain call you?" Corbin asks her, trying not to dwell on the awkwardness.

"Yeah. Um… She called me a few minutes ago."

"Then I guess I'll see you two later."

Corbin grabs his coffee before he stands and leaves us, as Tria groans and buries her head in the crook of my neck. "That wasn't embarrassing at all."

"Maybe we should just come clean," I say thoughtfully, even though it sounds incredibly random.

"After the wedding," she says, snuggling into me. "People will have plenty of speculations to make, and it will distract from Rain's wedding."

As much as I hate to wait another month, I agree with her, begrudgingly. I'm sick of hiding her, and I want the fucking world to know that no one else can touch her.

My phone buzzes, and I check it to see it's Dane who has sent a message. A groan escapes me when I see the updated location of our redo party for Maverick. Dane and Rain's house. Fuck. Now I'll barely be able to touch Tria.

"There's no way to change your mind about that? Because I'm not looking forward to spending all night without being able to touch you."

I show her the message that states the change of location, and she sighs softly.

"It's just one night, Kode. You spent eleven years hating me. You can pretend as though we're nothing to each other for one night."

I don't know why, but it pisses me off that she can say that so easily.

Chapter 14

Tria

My strapless dress is a shimmery silver, my cleavage is pumped to the nth degree, and the dress has a fitted feel that Kode seems to love. But… it seems to be completely ineffective tonight.

Kode is talking with some of the guys. I'm with Ash. And the distance between us feels like it's suffocating me. He's done well pretending I mean nothing to him. Very frigging well. He hasn't even glanced in my direction all night.

I hate this—hate hiding *us*.

"Damn. The Sterling boys are looking mighty fine these days. I think they only get better the older they get," Courtney Hughes says while joining us.

I hate her. I don't even know why she's here, other than to try and weasel in on Kade. Fortunately, Kade and Raya aren't here for her to try and destroy. Unfortunately, her eyes keep raking over Kode every time he walks by.

"Yep," Ash says, trying to be nice, but I can see her inwardly gagging every time Courtney speaks.

After grabbing another glass of champagne from a passing tray, I start chugging it. If I don't bitch slap Courtney, I might crunch Kode's balls. Neither would make me look very sane, so I need to drink so I can be nice.

"Brin couldn't come?" Ash asks, trying to shift the subject off the

Sterlings when Courtney talks about Corbin's ass.

"No. She works at a museum, and tonight they've got some fundraising party there."

I would really love to have Brin here right now.

"Damn. If Kode is smiling at Leisa Mosely, then he must be drunk."

At Courtney's words, I look up. Sure enough, Leisa is wrapping her pink manicured nails around Kode's arm, and he's smiling down at her. My stomach twists with a gnawing knot of jealousy that seems to be relentlessly clawing at me.

"Grip that glass any tighter, and it might break," Ash says, eyeing me with curiosity.

I slowly loosen my hold on the champagne flute. This is torture.

"Well, if he's paying her some attention, then I know I have a chance. Especially since we have history that I know he wouldn't mind repeating." Courtney's smug declaration has my head spinning and my teeth crunching.

I shouldn't be this jealous. We've barely been dating for any real amount of time. Hell, we can't even go on an actual date. Yet I feel as though I could grind nails into dust with my teeth right now.

"Hey," Ash says, nudging me. "Rye's here. You know, I was thinking… If you don't find a date for the wedding between now and then, you might consider asking him. He's really a great guy."

Other than the fact he never really smiles. Kode's smile is my favorite part of the day.

Crap. Now I'm waxing poetic nonsense. I hate myself.

135

"Um… Yeah… We'll see."

My eyes are forced to peel themselves away from Kode and move to the duo walking into the large living room that is filled with guests. Ethan is beside Rye, both of them looking relaxed in their jeans and T-shirts with all their tattoos slithering down their skin. They should have been brothers.

Wren quickly joins them just as Rye's eyes meet mine. He gives me a forced smile that doesn't come close to looking real, and then he turns his attention back to the guys.

"He's gorgeous," Ash adds, as if I'm blind.

My eyes fall over to Kode who is now smiling and talking to Courtney *and* Leisa. He's never this nice to anyone. Well, no one but his cousins, Rain, and me. But right now… Is he trying to hurt me? Because it's working.

"Damn. Kode and Corbin look some kind of good right now," Julie Crane says, causing me to groan. "Oh, and wow. Just saw Maverick and Dale. And damn, Wren, Ethan, and Rye are here, too. It's like a Sterling Shore edible single men buffet."

Ash laughs while turning her attention toward the socialite woman who doesn't mean any harm. "Courtney is competing with Leisa for Kode," Ash chuckles, unaware of the knife jabbing into my heart.

"Ah, well, that should end up in a cat fight. Then again, Kode enjoys watching drama. He's a bit of an ass like that. I wouldn't be surprised if he was intentionally pitting them against each other right now just for the fun of a showdown," Julie says, further provoking the anger within me.

It's on the tip of my tongue to defend him, but I rein in the urge. My champagne flute is suddenly empty, just like my tolerance-level for Kode's antics.

"I think he's gay," I brazenly and randomly state.

Both women swivel their heads toward me, eyes wide in their faces. But Julie, the gossip she is, quickly pounces.

"Why?"

Shrugging, I prepare to wage a little war between myself and the sex god who is flaunting himself like a steak in front of two starving lionesses. He doesn't date women from Sterling Shore very often. He's barely had any real affairs here. I assume that had a lot to do with the fact he was into Rain for so long and didn't want her thinking he was as bad as Corbin or Maverick.

But his lifestyle sets the stage for this little rumor that I'm about to spread.

"You said it yourself; he thrives on drama. What heterosexual male would prefer to pit two women against each other in hopes of a fight, as opposed to trying to appease them and get one—if not both—into bed? And when do you ever see him with a date? Never. He's in the closet, obviously, and doing what he can to keep up pretenses, but if he were straight, wouldn't he have already made a move on someone by now?"

Ha. Julie's expression is priceless, and I watch as the light bulb goes on in her mind, her wheels slowly turning. It's easy to manipulate someone who is eager for something as juicy as this detail.

Ash starts to speak, but then doesn't. Instead, she suppresses a

137

grin as Julie excuses herself for some ridiculous reason. She runs a whole two steps before whispering in the ears of two women. When their heads snap to the right to look at Kode, I bite back a grin.

"You're so going to have to pay for that. What the hell are you thinking?" Ash asks, but the humor in her voice is evident.

"Couldn't help myself," I say without shame, swapping my empty glass with a full one on another passing tray.

A few gasps ring out, letting me know the rumor has more than likely been spiced up and morphed into something jarring by now. Crap. There's no telling what it'll be by the time it reaches him.

No. I refuse to regret it. He's being an ass right now, so he deserves this. Maybe all the women will leave him alone if they hear he's yet another delicious bit of eye candy that is batting for the other team.

Rye waves me over, and I smirk in Kode's direction. Of course he doesn't notice me. If he wants to be this big of a dick, then let the games begin.

Kode

Tria isn't in my peripheral anymore, and it's irking me because if I turn and try to find her, it'll be obvious to her that I'm seeking her out.

I'm ready to rip Courtney's head off and spit down her throat. One time. I got drunk enough to stupidly end up in bed with her *one* time. Now she acts as though it was supposed to be a night to remember. Hell, she would much rather be with Kade, and right now, I'm wishing he was here to deal with her drama instead of me.

Leisa... I swear she has some serious self-image issues. I actually feel bad for her, which is unusual, but not bad enough to keep letting her grate on my nerves.

Why me?

"Corbin is close to launching his newest website. You really should talk to him about it," I say, throwing him under the bus in an effort to save myself.

Neither girl stops talking to me. My head is going to explode.

Don't look at Tria. Don't look at Tria. That's been tonight's mantra for me.

She said for me to treat her like I used to, and I've decided to be maliciously obedient—do *exactly* as she said. If she wants me to be a cold and dismissive dick toward her in front of everyone, then she's going to get the full effect. Maybe next time she won't be so eager to toss that out there like it's not a big fucking deal.

Dane is holding onto Rain, his arms draped casually around her shoulders and holding her back to his front. That sight used to sicken me, but now I feel... not a damn thing. It's like I've had chains unlocked, and it feels so damn good.

The growing number of older socialites is annoying me. I get sick of going to my parents' functions and having to deal with the elite crowd who want to speak to a Sterling. This was supposed to be a reprieve.

Deciding to note that to Corbin, I move to his side, also hoping to leave behind the women vying for my attention. I'm seconds away from exploding on them. It was fun to play when Tria was watching.

Now that she's not, all I can think about is pointing out all their flaws and giving them complexes to last a lifetime just to get them the hell away from me.

"Why the hell are there so many of our parents' friends here? I thought it was just going to be us tonight," I say to Corbin.

I try to disentangle myself from the two sets of hands that seem to have followed me to Corbin's side. Stupid fucking party.

Corbin snickers while Dane groans, his eyes burning down at Rain who bats her lashes with faux innocence.

"Rain invited our neighbors because she didn't want to be rude. And from there, well, apparently no one had anything to do tonight."

Corbin continues laughing when Rain gets cornered by one of her stepmother's friends. Man, I can go to these elite functions anytime. This was supposed to just be our close friends for Maverick's birthday. He's going to demand another—

"You guys owe me another birthday night," Maverick says while walking up, scowling at Rain who is engaged in some asinine conversation about petunias versus roses for a garden.

Leisa weighs in on the flower conversation, while Courtney tugs on my arm, asking me about my next trip to New York. I wisely don't mention when I'm going.

"I love Tria's dress. I want one like it," Ash says, sidling up next to Tag just as he joins us.

Shit. I love Tria's dress, too. In fact, if it were any sexier, I'd probably have already hauled her out of here.

"Get one," Tag says, sliding his hand around Ash's waist before kissing her cheek.

It must be nice to not have to hide a relationship. Never thought I'd envy Tag Masters for any reason.

I keep waiting on Tria to get pissed enough to end the charade and claim me in front of everyone. She was staring at me forever, and now I have no idea where she has gone.

Discreetly, I turn and move to the bar that is set up, letting my eyes lazily roam over the crowd. I order a crown and coke, and tap my fingers restlessly while letting my eyes peruse the crowd once more.

Then I see her. She's right beside Rye Fucking Clanton. Shit. I didn't consider the fact that if I pushed her, that she might push me back. My teeth grind, but I take a deep breath instead of losing my mind.

Sylvia Pratt walks up to me, smiling as though she has a secret. Since she's one of my mother's friends, I muster up the courtesy to acknowledge her. That proves to be a mistake when she takes it as an invitation for conversation.

"Well, Kode, at least I finally understand why you never would ask Ilene out."

Ilene? Oh, yeah. Her daughter that she'd love to marry off to a Sterling.

"Mrs. Pratt, sorry. I must have forgotten. My schedule stays rather busy."

She pats my arm, but it almost seems patronizing for some reason. "It's okay, Kode. Really. This is the twenty-first century. And this is a great area that doesn't judge for such things."

What? I have no idea what rocks are loose inside her head.

"Um… I'm missing something," I say unsurely.

"You poor thing. You shouldn't be ashamed. I tell you what I'll do. My sister has a son, and he's very nice, charming, and a very good catch. I'll introduce you."

It takes me a second to wrap my mind around her words, but when I do, I'm positive I heard her wrong. Had to.

"Say what now?" I ask in an unusual octave that has me immediately clearing my throat.

"His name is Martin. He's a lovely man. He's in law school right now, but he's not far from taking the bar exam."

What… the… hell?

"Um… Mrs. Pratt, I think you've… There's a mistake here. I'm not gay."

A few snickers emerge from women nearby, their eyes moving over to me. The collar on my shirt seems to start choking me when all the eyes say the same thing. What the hell is going on?

"Kode, sweetie, it's time to be honest with yourself and everyone else. I've always thought you were a little too angry for a man with such a wonderful family. I understand it now. You sad, sweet boy. If someone can't be themselves, it makes them a bottle of fury."

Oh, I'm a bottle of fury alright. Especially when Tria finds my eyes and gives me a conspiratorial wink. I glare at her, but she merely smiles and raises her glass of champagne in a toasting motion, as if to say she just screwed me over and loves it.

Cracking my neck to the side, I rein in all that anger that I apparently don't deserve to have—according to Sylvia Pratt.

"Well, Mrs. Pratt, I'm sorry to disappoint you, but I'm angry without a cause. I happen to love women, especially when my dick is buried to the hilt inside them."

She chokes and sputters on her drink as I walk away, leaving her to gasp in horror at my crude words. Courtney is disputing the rumor when I pass her, telling a group of girls just how amazing I am in bed. Never thought I'd appreciate that so much.

"You know, I always did wonder about you," Maverick drawls as he follows me out onto the patio. I need air before I strangle Tria. "Always thought you were just a little too pretty."

I flip him off, but he just laughs at my back. Tria apparently wants to play, so let the games begin. Our old war was always a little one-sided, since she was too scared to ever retaliate. I guess she has found a set of brass balls. Well, I'm about to break them.

Tria

The mixture of terror and excitement collide as I shake with conflicting spurts of adrenaline. My smile hurts. Rye looks down at me, clearly amused as Wren and Ethan talk about boring work stuff.

"So *you* started that rumor?" he asks, clearly smarter than I ever gave him credit for being.

I shrug noncommittally, and he actually laughs, which still surprises me. Rye always seems angrier than Kode.

There's nothing wrong with a good-natured feud amongst lovers. Right? He'll have to forgive me and forgo any sort of retribution if he

143

wants to get me back in bed. So I'm playing with the upper hand right now.

Why do I not feel totally confident with that thought? Oh. Yeah. Because it's Kode Sterling I'm talking about.

The party seems to be gravitating outside, where I know Kode is. Whispers of what he said to Sylvia Pratt find me, and I burst out laughing. Rye is also grinning—a look that works for him—while shaking his head.

"Man, you're in so much trouble," Ethan says from beside me.

"I don't know what you're talking about," I say with as much innocence as I can muster, following the crowd out to the patio with Rye at my side and Ethan and Wren walking close behind.

"Puh-lease. It's not like he didn't have it coming, considering the hell he used to put you through, but you're playing with fire."

I'm not playing with fire; I'm playing with an atomic bomb.

At least Ethan hasn't figured out that Kode and I are together. Apparently Wren hasn't either, because he looks truly terrified for me.

We make it outside, and Rye tries to walk away. Hell no. I need someone with a lot of muscle nearby just in case I've pushed Kode too far. There's a pool out here, after all.

"Uh-uh," Rye says as I scurry up beside him, putting my side against his for protection.

"Uh-uh what?" I ask idly, my eyes scanning the crowd for the man who is surely plotting something vicious.

"I'm not going to be your jealousy date or your buffer. Too much drama for me," he says while cutting toward a girl with a chest that doesn't look safe. She could tilt over with those things.

"Please," I whisper pleadingly.

He stands closer to the girl while raising a brow at me. Just as the girl starts to speak, he shakes his head at me.

"Nope. Not my style. Drama-free zone right here." He motions up and down his body to punctuate his point.

I scowl at him, and he gives me a wink before turning to offer his attention to the girl who is talking to him about his garage. Apparently she knows him.

Damn. I just lost my one line of defense. Ethan is the kind of guy to help Kode toss me into the pool. And Wren will just step aside with a shit-eating grin if Kode comes for me.

Rain walks out, her face drawn up in agonizing boredom, and I rush over to her without actually running. Kode won't hurt me with her around. She's too small to inflict any damage on the wall of steel, but she has a hold on all the Sterlings that makes them behave.

"Hey," she says, groaning as she loops an arm through mine. "Remind to never again be neighborly."

I have no idea what that means, but I latch on to the arm she has given me like it's a lifeline.

"Sure. No problem," I say distractedly, still looking around for the man who is missing.

"Have you seen any of the boys?" she asks. "Including Dane? He abandoned me when the conversations turned to appropriate dinner parties and how to plan them. Kill me now."

I just laugh, but then Dane Sterling swoops in to acquire the scowling blonde.

"You totally left me hanging," she scolds.

"Baby, you invited the neighborhood. Not me. It's every man or woman for themselves at this point."

He smiles that lopsided grin that has her wobbling beside me. Lost in his thrall, she forgets she's even mad and pulls him down for a very socially unacceptable show of affection. I start feeling weird standing next to them when the heated kiss leads to sounds of wanting more.

Cursing her silently, I walk away with no armor to shield me from the stormy wrath of Kode. Corbin. Hell yes. Corbin knows what's going on, and he's keeping it quiet. Plus, he has very handy muscles.

Never thought I'd see the day where I was intentionally going to see a Sterling for help. Then again, I never thought I'd be spending hours upon hours in Kode Sterling's bed.

Corbin grins widely the second he sees me coming to him. He apparently knows what's going on.

"You think I can protect you?" he asks, his eyes glistening with flakes of humor.

"I was kind of hoping."

He laughs while shaking his head. "I'll do what I can, but no promises. Kode has more determination than me."

Crap.

"How mad is he?" I ask quietly, still unable to find the blonde hair of the devil himself.

"I don't know. I haven't talked to him since the rumor mill went wild inside the party. But he has had some fairly attractive offers. I know that much. Jamie gave him his number."

Laughter escapes me before I can help it. Jamie Burton is one of the most gorgeous men in Sterling Shore, but he's also very much dedicated to men.

"Tria," Olivia Preston says, an odd look in her eyes that seems like concern, or disappointment, maybe. Does she know, too?

"Mrs. Preston," I say with my ingrained greeting manners.

Why are so many older socialites here?

"I'm not usually so forward, and I know it's not any of my business, but after all your poor mother went through with Edward, I expected so much better from you."

The blood drains from my face. What has he told them?

"I feel as though I should apologize, but I have no idea as to why, Mrs. Preston. Could you explain exactly what I've done to encourage you to be so forward?"

Forced eloquence is my specialty. Years of training have me resisting the urge to shake her and make her spit it out when she takes much too long to answer. Finally, she sighs and spikes my blood with ice.

"Rygan Clanton is a good man. He has horrible choices in women, but I would have assumed you'd treat him better than the others."

Corbin chokes on a laugh, but quickly clears his throat to recover. His eyes look anywhere but at me, as though he has caught on. But I'm lost.

Rygan is Rye's father—a hermit who rarely leaves his home since his wife's death years and years ago. Somehow he manages to snag very young women—usually younger than his son—but they always cheat on him, and they often do it without discretion. Most of them openly chase after Rye, but he *never* messes with them. That would be so gross.

But what the hell does it have to do with me?

"Um… I'm sorry, Mrs. Preston, but what's going on?"

She tsks me as though she's disappointed in my denial. "Sweetie, Rygan has had numerous women go after the younger version of himself. Most of them are gold-diggers, but you… Why on earth would you be so cruel to such a gentle man?"

It's then the dots connect, and my anger slowly begins to boil. That bastard!

I've been following Rye around the party, playing directly into Kode's hand, underestimating the evil genius he is. Now I look like all the opportunists who go after the senior Clanton and then try to take on the sexier junior Clanton.

In my moment of silent outrage, I'm left open to another attack from her. "Rye never sleeps with the women who chase him and bed his father. He has too much self-respect and class for that. I realize he looks like a rough brute, but he's a very attractive man with plenty of untainted offers."

Sickness roils in my stomach. This is crossing a line.

Corbin is doing all he can not to burst out in a fit of laughter, while steam figuratively rolls out of my ears.

"Mrs. Preston, I've never dated Rygan Clanton. In fact, I've never dated a man my father's age or older. Ever. Not that I'm opposed to age gaps in relationships, but only if they are truly in that said relationship for the right reasons—unlike you. I don't need to climb the social ladder by marrying a man twice my age just because of his wallet size. And I don't screw the gardener behind his back, either, like you and every cliché there is," I bite out, earning a shocked and indignant gasp from her.

She rattles something off while I stalk away, ignoring Corbin's eruption of laughter that he can no longer contain. Then I see the devil.

Most people envision a pitchfork, pointy ears, black eyes, and a wicked tail. No. The devil wears a designer suit, sexy blonde hair that always looks purposely bedroom-messy, eyes that are almost silver, and a grin that could slay multitudes.

He stares at me from across the pool, that grin only growing as I glare at him. He winks at me and raises his glass in a silent toast, mocking my victorious actions from earlier.

He's fighting dirty. Well, that's just fine. He'll tell everyone the truth or he'll never get me again.

Charging through the crowd and ignoring the judgmental eyes on my back, I make it to the bar that has been set up outside. I don't let the bartender ask for my order. Instead, I grab the bottle of chilled vodka and pour it directly into a glass.

He doesn't stop me, but merely watches with amusement as I turn the glass up and chug the contents without any regard for my churning stomach. It almost comes back up, but I manage to keep it down by sheer willpower alone.

"You look pissed," Rain says while coming up beside me.

After pouring another glass, I nod. "I'm furious."

She exhales loudly, her eyes looking around. "What'd he do?"

It's sad that she already suspects him. But she has no idea what's going on here.

"Nothing I won't punish him for."

Her eyes go wide in fear. "Tria, you can't play this game with Kode. He doesn't fold. Ever."

We'll see about that.

His back is turned now, his attention on Courtney Hughes as she runs her finger up his chest. Rain calls my name as I walk away, my heels whining as I pound them into the hard surface on my way to the man I hate in this moment.

Rye says something to me, but I deliberately ignore him, knowing damn well that will only fuel the chatter around me. He never sees me coming, so he doesn't know to brace for impact. With one hard, unexpected shove from my small hands, Kode stumbles, losing his balance, and yelps before crashing into the pool.

I glare at him under the surface as the water splashes up to hit innocent bystanders in their expensive apparel. Stunned silence descends upon the crowd while Kode pushes up to the top, surfacing with murderous eyes that immediately find me.

"Mistake, Tria. Big mistake," he threatens.

I dust my hands, proving I'm not scared of him, and I salute him with my middle finger on my way back into the house. Dane's driver is out front, and he quickly runs around to the passenger side door to open it for me when I ask him to take me home. I'll grab a cab from there.

I climb in, ignoring the laughter that is now booming from the backside of the house. This is going to be a dirty war, and there's only one way to win. It's not like I can go head-to-head in a battle of cruel attacks with him. I'm no match.

But there's one game I can win.

Kode

She's asleep. In my bed. Naked. Does she really think it's going to be that easy to get out of this?

I flip on the light before I begin stripping out of the dry clothes I borrowed from Dane. Tria stirs just barely, but she doesn't open her eyes.

"Feel better now that you've thoroughly pissed me off?" I ask the girl who I know isn't really asleep.

"Much," she says in a clipped tone.

I don't know whether to fuck her or grab her up and toss her into the ocean right now. Ignoring my cock's input, I move to her side of the bed to glare down at her.

"I think we need to talk about what the hell happened tonight."

She smiles up at me sweetly, her eyes fluttering open, and she shifts up onto her elbows so that the sheet slides down and reveals her perfect tits. How dare she look like every fucking wet dream I've ever had when I'm trying to be pissed.

"You mean you're ready to apologize to me?"

My mouth falls open in shocked disbelief.

"Me? Apologize to you? Tria, you started this. I just reacted. You owe me the apology."

She yawns as though I'm boring her and lies back down while pulling the sheet back over her bare chest. I almost demand for her to remove the sheet again while we discuss this, but it's probably better that she doesn't distract me.

"You started it, Kode. I was the one who reacted. You spent most of the night flirting with one girl who has fucked you, and another who clearly wants to. When you want to apologize, just let me know."

She closes her eyes again, acting as though her conscience is clear enough to sleep.

"Tria, you're the one who refused to tell anyone we're together, and you told me to treat you like I used to in front of everyone."

Her eyes open again, and they narrow at me. "I didn't tell you to let to girls paw all over you."

Okay, so she has me there. "I was trying to make you jealous," I admit.

"You succeeded. It also means you're admitting that you started this."

Her eyes close again, and she shifts so that she's on her stomach, letting the sheet travel down her bare back. It's times like these that I hate the fact she loves to sleep in the nude.

Deciding it's not worth the effort to keep arguing with her, I move to climb in on the other side of the bed. I'd rather be fucking her than arguing anyway.

Wearing nothing but my boxer-briefs, I slide in behind her and wrap my arms around her waist before assaulting her neck with a rough trail of kisses.

"Uh… what are you doing?" she asks, but she only angles her head to give me better access.

"Do you really need me to spell it out for you?" I ask while running my hand down her hip, slowly working my way toward her—

"Ow!" I yelp, drawing back the hand she just pinched the fuck out of. "What the hell was that for?"

She sighs as though she's annoyed. She's annoyed? She's not the one with a wounded hand and a rapidly swelling whelp.

"You can't have me again until you apologize."

She has to be kidding. The only other alternative explanation is that she has suddenly started living in another universe where unicorns and pixies really do exist.

"I'm not apologizing, Tria."

"You'll apologize, Kode. Every man has a breaking point."

She kicks the sheet off, forcing me to bite back a groan as she uses her body like a weapon against my hungry eyes. Deciding not to show her she has me on the ropes, I move to turn the tables.

Putting my body just inches from hers, I lean down to her ear to whisper, "If anyone caves, Tria, it'll be you. I don't play fair."

Goose bumps visibly rise on her skin, and I smile with a hint of triumph.

"Good thing I don't plan to play fair, either," she says with a daring tone that has me cursing myself for celebrating too soon.

Still feigning confidence, I ask, "Care to place a wager on this? Who caves first?"

One thing I've learned about Tria is that she loves having sex with me. It's what we do better than anything else. She can't hold out for long.

Ah, hell. Why is she grinning? That has me admittedly a little worried.

"Sure. If I win, you have to announce to everyone in Sterling Shore that you're an asshole and that you made up all that shit about Rygan Clanton and me."

My laughter comes out in a harsh breath, but I quickly smother it with my hand in an effort to keep her from getting even more pissed. I needed to keep her away from that fucking tattooed prick that seems to be around more and more. Now I've accomplished that while also getting a little revenge.

I'm so fucking brilliant.

"Fine. If I win, you have to admit to everyone that I'm the greatest lover you've ever had. In public. A few details of my awesomeness wouldn't be discouraged."

She grins, but quickly banishes it.

"Fine," she says in echo to my own answer. "And we have rules."

"What rules are those?" I muse, staying as close as I can without touching her.

"Nothing public, nothing too malicious, and no cheating."

My teeth grind together. "By cheating, I assume you mean other people. If you so much as—"

"By cheating, I mean no self-gratification to take the edge off. It's a given that there won't be anyone else, or this relationship is over."

I breathe out in relief and in pained arousal at once. I can't take things in hand? This is going to be hard.

"Agreed. So this is a battle of seduction. Got it. Personally, I think I'm going to enjoy this little war."

She shivers a little, much to my delight. No. She won't make it at all.

"No more vicious rumors," she says. "This is a sexy game, not an evil contest."

"That goes for you, too," I growl, scowling at her. "My mother already caught wind of this one, and now she feels guilty for not being more supportive of me. Fifteen calls from her, Tria. All of them promising me that she'll love me no matter what my sexual preference."

She snickers quietly while nodding. "No more rumors."

"Then let the games begin," I say, forcing myself to turn over and not curse my painful erection that won't be getting any relief for a while.

Chapter 15

Kode

Cold showers suck. Three days ago, I was getting laid multiple times a day, and now… nothing but icy cold showers to kill the raging hard-ons. And she's still using that fucking sexy, curvy body against me.

After drying off and tossing on a pair of workout pants and a T-shirt, I head into the kitchen, only to stumble to an abrupt halt. Tria is sitting at the bar, her long hair braided in two pigtails, and she feigns interest in a magazine as she licks her popsicle.

I've been imagining her mouth on me like that since we started this relationship, and now we're at a stalemate, making my dreams go awry. Every day she finds a way to look like a motherfucking wet-dream. This isn't war—it's torture.

"Thought you were opposed to clichés," I announce, regaining forced composure while moving to grab the orange juice from the fridge. "Don't you think seducing me by licking something is one of the most cliché things you can do?"

"Just enjoying something cool after a run on the beach," she lies. Even though she is wearing shorts that are much too short, and nothing else but a sports bra, she looks too sexy to have gone running.

Fucking games. How'd I get myself into this mess?

"I had to delay our New York trip. My business associate pushed the meeting back to the next weekend. I suppose that's for the best. It gives you time to fold," I tell her cockily.

She's holding out much better than I am, but I can't let her see that.

She snorts out a laugh before standing and pushing the remaining part of the popsicle into her mouth. She sucks it hard, cleaning the popsicle stick of anything solid before discarding it into the trash.

My knees buckle, and I might whimper internally, but I grab onto the side of the counter to stabilize my weak and pathetic self. She grins over her shoulder before swallowing the chunk of frozen stuff, and she tugs her bra over her head before tossing it at me.

"Kode, you're barely hanging on. I'm not too particularly worried about winning this little bet. Right now, I have to get ready. Brin is coming to pick me up for a shopping trip."

She shakes her ass in shorts that might as well be underwear, walking away with a strut that makes me feel all the weaker. I can't wait to meet up with my trainer. I need to punch something since I can't fuck anything.

Tria

Ow. Ow. Ow! Brainfreeze!

It's so hard not to wince in pain when your head feels like it's stuck in an artic inferno. How can something be so cold and burn so painfully at the same frigging time?

Now I'm standing under the hot water with my mouth wide open under the flow. Stupid popsicle. Even my ears hurt.

The pain finally subsides, and I flip the water on to be cooler—

much cooler. Before Kode, it had been forever since I'd had sex. So obviously thinking I could go a long time without sex again seemed perfectly logical. Only… When you have sex regularly, numerous times a day, with Kode Sterling, and then you stop, but yet you share a home with the man who stars in all your fantasies… It. Is. Painful. Brutally painful. Especially when he spends all his spare time seducing you with every weakness you have.

I swear I don't know who I am anymore, because the old Tria didn't wake up desperate to ravage the man next to her. It'd be easier to sleep in another room, but then he'd know how weak I'm getting.

It's only been three days, yet it feels like months have passed. It's maddening.

The only good thing is that, without sex, we've managed to have very lengthy conversations. Out of all his antics to get me to cave— strutting around naked, brushing his erection against me, talking dirty enough to make me pull my own hair—it's the times when he just talks about nothing in particular that has me wanting to cave.

I didn't judge Kode wrong all these years. He's an asshole. But only to people he doesn't care about. It doesn't make it socially acceptable, but it's the way he is. Unfortunately, I've grown rather attached to the complex enigma he is. Too attached.

By the time I finish getting ready and walk out, Jax Marshall— Kode's friend and personal trainer—is here, and I'm getting a sexy show. The furniture has been pushed against the walls for their session, and mats have been laid down. Usually he goes to Jax's studio for this, but since he's trying to make me swoon, he has moved his workouts to the house.

Both men are shirtless and a sheen of sweat glistens on their sexy bodies. Kode is in the process of taking Jax down, scissoring him between his legs after leaping through the air.

Yeah… It's definitely hot.

Jax struggles to get free, but finally manages, and then he pins Kode to the large black mat with a *thud* that has me wincing. But Kode doesn't flinch before wrangling Jax back down, and pinning him.

He winks at me when he sees me drooling, so I decide to ice his triumph while leisurely strutting through the house, swinging my hips just enough to distract him and earn Jax an opening of escape.

"Great way to prove you're not gay. Invite your sexy male trainer over to have private sessions together."

Jax's eyes grow wide in confusion, and Kode pins him again before shooting me a glare of warning. But of course that doesn't stop me from continuing.

"By the time he leaves, his clothes are rumpled, his hair looks just-fucked, and there's sweat all over his body. Just saying."

Jax strangles on air, coughing out a laugh, and Kode stalks toward me a little too scarily. I stand my ground, trying not to look as intimidated as I feel right now. Probably just crossed a line.

"Keep talking, Tria, and I'll add a public exhibition to my demands for winning the wager."

My cheeks heat in surprise and embarrassment as Jax rises from the mat, his brows high as his eyes glisten with curious amusement. Kode's gaze travels down to the respectable amount of cleavage my shirt is showing.

"Or I can just give you a private demonstration of what I want done in public right now," he dares, his voice full of lust, tempting me more than I want him to know.

Fortunately for me, the doorbell rings, and I send a silent *thank you* to Brin.

With a steeled moment of false bravery, I step into him, forcing contact with our bodies. The magnetic charge between our heady attraction is almost too much to bear, and we both take a deep breath.

"As soon as you fold, you can demonstrate any position you want to." My voice is huskier than intended, but it seems to work, considering how hard he's forced to swallow.

He walks away woodenly to disappear into the bedroom. I start to wonder if he's caving right now, and a thrill shoots through me. Jax starts rolling up the mats while I walk toward the bedroom.

My victorious grin turns into a frown when I hear the water running from the bathroom.

Drat. Cold shower.

"Guess our training session is over," Jax says with his charming grin.

Brin grows impatient and calls out that she's coming in when she realizes the door is unlocked. She walks into the living room, joining us, but she stumbles when her eyes catch sight of the dark-haired MMA fighter.

"Do we have to go shopping?" she asks, her eyes greedily taking in every sexy line of muscle.

"Yep. I need coffee and clothes." And sex, but coffee and clothes will have to do.

Brin pouts playfully, and we laugh as we head out.

"Has he given in yet?" she muses when we reach her small, old Camry. It'll draw less attention than one of Kode's flashy cars. There's no way Pete would be looking for me in this. He assumes I'm a snob that thinks I'm too good for the blue-collar ways. Just like most people, he doesn't know me at all.

My phone rings just as we start down the road, and I frown when I see Rain's name. She probably went by the empty condo again.

"Do me a favor," I tell Brin.

"You need me to talk to you while you're talking to her so that she knows you're really with me. Got it," she says, reading my mind and impressing the hell out of me.

"You really should be doing something more than assisting the director of the museum."

She laughs while nodding. "I agree. Now answer."

As soon as I answer my sister's call, Brin starts speaking as though she was in the middle of talking before promptly apologizing for not realizing I'm on the phone. I mouth *thank you* before moving my attention back to Rain.

"Sorry, we're on our way to do some shopping. What's up?"

"Well, Corbin called to see if we could all get together tonight. I wanted to see if you would go with us. He thought it'd be a good idea, and I totally agree."

Of course Corbin thought it would be a good idea. He's the only one of Kode's friends besides Jax that knows what's going on between us. He wants me to be there for entertainment value.

"Will Kode be there?" I muse, wondering why he didn't bother saying anything to me.

"Probably. Corbin was calling him next. But don't worry; he'll behave. I swear."

Almost immediately, I get a text. I pull the phone away to read it, and groan when I see Kode has changed his name in my phone again.

Master Of Your Universe: We're going out with the guys tonight. Maybe you can fold then, and I can spend the night getting reacquainted with your body.

I stifle a grin while rolling my eyes. "I'll come," I tell Rain.

After she gives me the place and time, I hang up. Another text comes in, and I bite back a grin when I see it's from him.

Master Of Your Universe: If you fold now, I'll cancel on the guys and fuck you like I hate you all night. ☺ Considering the pain I've been in, it wouldn't be too hard to fake it.

"You're grinning," Brin says as I leave Kode hanging.

"Yeah. I think I need a really sexy dress for tonight. Kode is close to breaking."

Chapter 16

Kode

"Any word on finding Mercer?" I ask the private detective I've hired.

"He's hiding good, but I'll find him. He hasn't contacted any of his family or his pre-prison friends in a few months, but he has to be staying with someone. Did something happen to make him take precautions? Because he's definitely been covering his ass since before the warrant for his arrest was issued."

I curse while pulling up at the restaurant. The cab is also rolling up, depositing Tria at the front door, and I watch as she blows me a kiss and gives me a wink before going in. Maybe I should just fold. If she doesn't give in by Saturday, I will. Even though I'm enjoying the spirit of this game.

Who am I kidding? I'm ready for this asinine game to be over with.

"My fist collided with his face a few months ago after he ran Tria off the road. He left her alone for a while, apparently taking time to cover his ass and keep us from finding him again. Keep digging and keep me informed."

"Yes, sir. I'll see if I can't backdate that. If you could send me the exact date, that will help with my search."

I make a note to do so before hanging up, and then I climb out of the car. Tria left a few minutes before me, and the cab driver was hitting on her the second she walked out. She's dressed to kill, but it's only to slay me.

Corbin walks out just as I near the entrance, and he nods for me to follow him. Curious, I do as he silently beckons.

"What's with the cloak-and-dagger exit?" I ask as he leads me around to the side where no one's at.

He sighs while running a hand through his hair.

"Wren's mom called and asked Rain if she would take Edward's boxes to him. Apparently he still had work files in his study at their house. You know Rain's history with her father, so I was hoping you could ask Tria to do it instead."

Immediately, I feel defensive. "Yeah, well, Tria's relationship with him isn't any better than Rain's."

"She was daddy's girl for eighteen years. Rain has never had a relationship—"

"Exactly," I bite out. "She loved him, was close to him, and then he cut her out of his life because he's a coward that can't face someone after he disappoints them."

"You're seriously suggesting that Rain go instead of Tria? You've been dating Tria for a few weeks, but Rain has been like our sister for years."

My anger starts to burn under my skin, radiating off me in waves that has Corbin taking notice.

"Rain has plenty of people defending her and looking out for her. Tria has me. Get me the address. I'll take him his fucking stuff since he can't even find the balls to go get it himself."

Corbin takes a step back, obviously surprised by my anger, which only pisses me off more. Did he really think I'd just put this off on Tria without any concern as to how she'd feel about it?

"Dude, sorry. Didn't realize things were that bad between them. It's no big deal. I'm sure Dane will do it."

"No. I'll do it. Don't mention this to Tria, because it'll just put her in a sad mood. She's got enough shit to deal with since Mercer is being a pain in the ass."

Corbin nods slowly. "I'll tell the others not to mention it."

After running my hand through my hair, I walk away from him and head into the restaurant. Tria's eyes meet mine immediately, and her smile forces me to put on a mask, denying my anger the right to surface. Edward has two great daughters that he can't appreciate because he's too busy wallowing in the miserable bed he made for himself.

"Where'd you two disappear to?" Maverick asks as he sips on his beer, eyeing us like we've got a secret to tell.

"Just had some business to sort out," Corbin says, using a tone that tells Maverick something is up but to drop it.

Maverick heeds the silent warning and flips the subject. Corbin sits next to the empty chair that is next to Tria, and I sit between them, playing it cool for the crowd.

"Kode, you should probably change with Corbin," Dane says, frowning when he sees me next to the girl that is driving me crazy in too many ways.

Tria bites back a grin before using her menu to cover it, trying to act as though she's not secretly enjoying my brother's disapproval. Corbin snickers before taking a sip of his beer, and I ignore Dane while ordering a drink for myself. Before I even think about it, I'm ordering one for Tria, too, which earns a few eyebrow raises.

I shrug it off, pretending as though I didn't just slip up. Tria doesn't acknowledge it. She engages in a conversation with Rain about one of her new books, and we all groan when they start talking about the mushy stuff.

Even though it's not an actual date, it's nice to be sitting beside her in public. The only way it could be better would be if I could just kiss her without causing a few heart attacks. I'm sure there'd also be a few hell-froze-over comments in there, too.

By the time we finish eating—and drinking profusely—the table starts getting louder, and Tria turns to me, keeping her voice low.

"Are you okay? You've been quiet."

She's the only one who has noticed that anything is wrong. Other than Corbin, but only because he knows what's wrong.

"I'm fine. Just bored. You could help out with that if you'd just give in and do to me what you were doing to that popsicle."

She laughs while shaking her head, but Maverick interrupts every conversation as the alcohol takes over.

"Alright, time to do something real. Dane and Rain are getting married. Ruby is coming back, which means Corbin will be spending less and less time with us, and Kode is already missing most of the time these days. It's time we finally get those tattoos."

Corbin glares at Maverick, and the rest of us shake our heads in protest.

"Who's Ruby?" Tria muses, but no one can answer before Maverick continues with his relentless charge.

"We agreed to do this forever ago. Sterling tattoos. Now. Tonight. Before everyone continues to drift apart. Call it a bonding ritual. I rented a limo, and it should be outside by now."

"You can't get tattoos if you've been drinking," Tria points out, sounding soberer than the lot of us.

"You're not *supposed* to. But it's not like we're going to bleed to death getting a Sterling tattoo. Come on," Maverick begs.

"Hell no," I say in objection. "There's no way in hell I'm going to go get something permanently tattooed on my body after I've been drinking."

Tria

"I can't believe you talked us into this," Kode growls while straddling the tattoo chair as the guy buzzes away on his back.

I stifle a laugh when he glares at Maverick who is absolutely beaming while staring down at his arm where "STERLING" is proudly displayed in an Old-English font.

My eyes keep trailing back over to the shirtless man who has done all he can to stay close to me tonight. It actually looks sexy to see his surname being written between his shoulder blades. It's a cliché that actually works.

"I should have gotten it on my ass," Dale says loudly, wincing while they tattoo down his chest to his hipbone on his left side in a vertical line.

"You'd mess up that pretty ass?" Corbin jokes, eliciting heckles from everyone else.

Dale flips them off while rolling his eyes and leaning back. Dane is next to him, getting his own tattoo.

Rain is across from us, wincing as she looks down at her exposed hip. A bald man with a dragon tattooed across his scalp is working quickly to get the name forever inked on her right hip.

"Dane Sterling, you have to marry me now," she says, prompting him to laugh as they buzz away on his chest. Wow. He's built damn well, too.

"Baby, you're stuck with me for life. Now there's proof." He winks at her, which earns him her goofy grin.

"Ah, hell, Rain," Maverick says as he stands up, making room for Corbin to sit down, "you've been a Sterling since you were a kid."

Rain grins over at him, and my heart clenches. I would have killed to have this sort of connection with anyone.

"You can get a Sterling tattoo, too," Kode says, winking at me.

Fortunately, with all the buzzing and chatter going on, no one overhears him. Even though I'm actually starting not to give a damn. Rain and Dane can just get over it. Kode isn't trying to get Rain's attention. I know that without a doubt, because all of his attention stays centered on me. It's the first time I've ever felt so special to anyone.

"Little early to be staking that sort of claim," I playfully quip, enjoying the sound of his rumbled laughter.

"I agree," Corbin chimes in, the only one who is close enough to hear. "But I foresee it happening eventually."

My face heats red, and Kode continues laughing while the tattoo artist remains stoic. Corbin tugs his shirt off when the guy is finally ready to start on his permanent marking, and my head tilts when I see the name etched across his shoulder. He's also got several other tattoos, which I wasn't expecting. But the name of the girl I heard mentioned earlier is proudly displayed in an extravagant font.

"Who is Ruby?" I ask again, hoping to get an answer this time.

Corbin looks up, and he motions around the shop. "She owns this place. It's one of her many shops. It's not open for business yet, but she called in the staff for a trial run on us."

"Are you two dating?"

Kode laughs, apparently finding humor in that question.

"Nah. We're friends."

"But you've got her name tattooed on you?"

Corbin tilts his head, looking down at it as his lips curl into a smile. "It was a triple dare."

That rouses my curiosity even more. "You're serious?"

"Can't deny a triple dare," Corbin says with his bigger grin.

Kode's laughter grows, and the guy tattooing him warns him to be still or have a permanent mistake on his back.

"They have a weird friendship," Kode says as his laughter tapers off.

"She has my name tattooed on her, too, so it levels out."

"Oh, so you're like Rain and Dane. Secretly in love with each other for years but not brave enough to act on it."

Corbin and Kode both tense up for some reason. Corbin is the one to break the uncomfortable silence.

"No, we dated. Three times when we were younger. It never worked out for us, so we just stay friends."

"Why didn't it work out?"

Kode's head pops up, his eyes trained on Corbin like he's just as curious as I am. Corbin looks like he swallowed something sour.

"Long story," he grumbles, his face turning the brightest shade of red I've ever seen.

"What the hell, man?" Kode asks with a mocking grin. "Why are you so red right now?"

"Keep on and I'll ask questions about secrets you two want to keep."

Kode and I immediately shift the subject just as Dale walks over to display his work of art. Unlike the others, he looks more militant than a sexy, laid-back playboy.

"Remind me to kill Maverick for this tomorrow," he announces.

Laughter resumes, and everyone finishes up with their bonding ritual that will be forever branded on their skin and in their minds. I feel like an outsider looking in, but it's fun to watch.

As they all pay for their new ink, I head back out to the limo. Kode is quickly joining me before anyone else, and he leans over to place a kiss on my forehead, refraining from losing his cool and giving in. That's fine. I'm going to give in this weekend if he doesn't cave by then.

"This was actually pretty nice," he says while wrapping an arm around my shoulders.

I lean into him, smiling as I feel his abs through his shirt. "You going to give in so I can claw up your pretty new tattoo?"

He groans while tugging at my head to tilt my face up to meet his, and he kisses me just on the tip of my nose.

"Not yet," he murmurs while grinning that wicked smile of his.

He scoots away just as Corbin climbs in, rolling his eyes at us while taking the seat by Kode.

"You know, whenever you two decide to end this little game of yours, give me a warning."

Kode tilts his head, apparently as confused as I am by that request. "Why?"

"Because it's scorching hot to be around you two with all this pent-up nonsense. I can only imagine how heated it's going to get when you unleash on each other. You're going to burn the whole fucking city down."

Chapter 17

Kode

"I hate Maverick," I tell Dane over the phone as I leave Silk. I had Eleanor meet me with all of Edward's files instead of going to her house where people might see me and ask questions. I don't want Rain or Dane knowing what I'm doing, because then they'd want to know why.

Rain wouldn't mind so much, but Dane would assume I was stepping on his toes and trying to get Rain's attention. Since Dane needed me to meet his alcohol supplier while he was in a meeting, I decided just to have Eleanor meet me here.

"I hate him, too," Dane groans.

Eleanor pulls out of the parking lot as I finish arranging the last of the boxes in the trunk. Just as I shut the lid, the face of the son of the bitch I hate the most is staring at me.

Pete Fucking Mercer.

His smug grin turns up as he leans up against the wall of the club, standing in the alleyway between Silk and a storage building, the same spot where I beat his ass a few months ago.

I don't hesitate to stalk toward him, ready to end this fucking game.

"Dane, call the cops. Pete Mercer is at Silk."

"Shit, Kode. Don't do anything—"

I hang up on him to stay focused on what matters, and slip my phone into my pocket. Pete backs up farther, his smirk etching up. If I wasn't in a blind rage and zeroed in on destroying his face, I might have stopped to pay better attention to the fact that we're now deep into the pit of the alley, almost to the beach gate that connects to the two buildings.

"You're not the Sterling I expected to find, but you're sure as hell the one I'd rather have."

His sinister tone doesn't intimidate me, but the thudding of feet behind me puts me on alert. I turn around to see four guys who look like they love steroids a little too much.

"Oh, look. Turns out you're not the only one with friends."

Ah, hell. I shouldn't have been stupid enough to get this deep. I turn back around just in time to get sucker punched by Pete, but I barely flinch before sending a punch of my own.

Arms try to wrap around me, but I'm swinging and connecting rapidly, my brutal training sessions with Jax finally paying off. One hit connects solidly with a face and breaks a nose, and then I turn and land another one across a jaw that has teeth crunching.

But five on one turns out to be shitty odds, and this time when arms wrap around me, they manage to hold me back as a bloody-mouth Pete steps forward with fury blazing in his eyes.

"Rich, pampered pricks like you shouldn't fuck with guys like me, Sterling."

A hard punch connects with my gut, the blow powerful enough to send my body in a reflexive curl, but the strong bastards holding me just lift me back up. Pete's face isn't as fucked up as I was hoping it would be, but I still manage to laugh.

"This rich, pampered prick kicked your ass all by himself. I didn't need a bunch of gorillas holding you back to do it. I merely had an audience."

Pete scowls and pulls his fist back. I stare, waiting without blinking, ready to take the hit without giving him the satisfaction of seeing me flinch.

"Hands in the air! Hands in the air!" foreign voices yell. I figured they'd react quickly after getting a call from Dane Sterling.

I smile as curses are spewed, and Pete tries to run through the back gate. Unfortunately for him, there are two cops with guns drawn on the other side of that gate, their commanding voices threatening him as he slowly raises his hands in defeat.

"You, too! Hands in the air!" a cop yells at me, and I comply, smiling the whole damn time.

"My name is Kode Sterling. This is my brother's club. I was jumped while trying to leave, and I want to press charges."

"You motherfucker!" Pete roars. "This asshole jumped me months ago! If he's pressing charges, then so am I!"

He can say that all he wants. Pete's face has healed up nicely during these months, and Dane shredded the footage of that night long ago to cover our asses.

I frown when I see my phone has been trampled on the ground. That'll have to go on my never-ending list of things to do—buy a new damn phone. Then I'll have to wait on them to finish swapping all my info—

Cold steel on my wrists snaps me out of my inner reverie. I'm being cuffed like all the others, and the cop behind me leads me to the car to start making calls. He takes my wallet to search for ID, and when he feels satisfied that I'm telling the truth, he moves behind me to remove the cuffs.

"We'll need the video surveillance to corroborate your story."

I grin while nodding. "I'll call my brother so that it's all legit. He'll come—" Dane pulls up, jumping out of the car with Rain and his sister, Britt, on his heels "—right now."

The cop turns as Dane rushes over, and Rain runs to my side to investigate my injuries. Fortunately for me, they're nowhere nearly as bad as they could have been if the police hadn't shown up when they did. Five on one never ends well for the *one*. Not even I'm that badass.

"Any idea who these men are?" a cop asks me.

"Just the bald one that was running his mouth. That's Pete Mercer. You'll find he has a warrant out for his arrest for violating a restraining order held by Tria Noles."

The cop calls in the information I just gave him, while Rain curses me for getting into a fight. I can't wait to tell Tria that Pete is going back to jail. He just got caught jumping a Sterling in Sterling Shore. Big fucking mistake.

Chapter 18

Tria

Rain is driving me nuts. I swear she calls me more everyday. I've already talked to her once today.

"Your sister is seriously freaking out. Maybe she'd feel better if she knew you were safely tucked away with Kode," Brin says.

Sighing, I think that over. "I wish. Rain and Kode have history. I'm still dealing with that. My entire life revolved around everyone seeing Rain, but looking right through me. Kode is a lot like me in that respect. Dane is the shining star in their family. But at the same time, Kode was like everyone else. He never saw me until he stopped seeing Rain."

I sound poetic again. More like a sad poet. Maybe some of Poe's work won't sound so disturbing if I read it now.

"So you think she has feelings for him? Or him for her?"

My laughter comes out before I can stop it, and then I shake my head. "No. Rain is beyond in love with Dane. She never saw Kode as more than a friend. And I don't think Kode has any lingering feelings for her. I know he had the hots for her, but if it was gone that easily, then it couldn't have been a very long crush."

Obviously Kode developed a small crush for a short period of time. He's an intense guy, so it just looked like a bigger deal than it was. Right?

"He's so different with you than anyone I've seen him interact with," she says, grinning. "You know, the guy says five words to me. But he sees you, and he spills all sorts of things. It's really sweet. He's one of those guys girls want to love, but can't get him to love them back. You've landed a white whale, so to speak."

Smiling, I lean back in the seat.

"Have I told you thank you for hanging out with me so much?" I ask her, turning to look as her light brown hair falls out of her ponytail holder.

She curses while pulling it back up, and then she grins over at me while we sit idly in front of Kode's home.

"You don't have to thank me, Tria. Everyone needs someone. If I hadn't had Maggie when I went through my divorce, I don't know what I would have done. You're getting stalked by a psycho, so you need someone. I'm here. Any time you need me."

It's hard to picture Brin getting married so young. She married straight out of high school, which seems so rash for someone as grounded as she is.

Out of the blue, I hug her, surprising her. But she hugs me back affectionately.

Smiling, I release her and head inside, making sure to strategically grab all my bags so that I don't have to make two trips. Kode left earlier and said he probably wouldn't be home until late, so I had Brin take me out to get groceries. My meal tonight will have him caving. No doubt about it.

My phone has been blowing up with calls from Rain and other random numbers, but I've ignored them all. This day is my day. I fully intend to devote all of my attention on Kode and winning this stupid bet.

It takes some finesse, but I manage to get the door open without putting any of the bags down. Moving quickly, I get everything put away. It'll be a while before he gets home, so I decide to go for a run.

Just as I finish pulling on my workout shorts and sports bra, the door opens and closes, and I grin, though I'm surprised. He made it sound like it would be after dark before he got back.

"Just so you know, you'll be on your knees and begging—"

My words catch in my throat when I see the wide eyes staring back into mine. Maverick Sterling has one foot still suspended in the air as I shriek and grab a pillow from the sofa to cover my body.

"What the hell are you doing here?" he asks on a gasp.

"What the hell are you doing here?" I echo, still reeling from his unexpected visit.

"I couldn't get ahold of Kode, so I came over to check on him to make sure Dane wasn't downplaying the damage. Now what the hell are *you* doing here?"

My blood runs cold as I think about all the calls I've ignored.

"What do you mean? What damage? What happe—"

The door opens again, and I drop the pillow to sprint through the house just as Kode rounds the corner. My stomach hits the floor when I see a rough, purplish bruise on his cheek surrounding an angry red gash. He moves like he's sore, and he grins grimly when he sees me.

I'm immediately in front of him, cupping his face so I can examine any further damage, but that's all I see.

"What happened to you?" I ask, my voice hoarse and threaded with dread.

He bends and kisses me softly on the lips before stroking my cheek with his open hand. "Pete Mercer is in jail for good. The police will probably be questioning you soon, so be ready to deal with them."

My stomach lurches, and I barely manage not to vomit. "Pete? This was done by Pete? Kode, I'm so damn sorry. Why did he go after you?"

His grin turns sheepish for some reason. "Probably because I beat his ass after he ran you off the road."

Before I know it, my lips are on his, and I'm kissing him. Hard. The way I should have been kissing him this whole week. Stupid bet. He can win.

His tongue delves into my mouth as his hand curls around my waist, tugging me closer before wincing. I instantly shift back on my heels, and pull at his shirt until I can see the damage on his torso. Shit.

Bruises are slowly forming in large patterns, and tears form heavily in my eyes. This is all my fault.

"Don't look at it like that, babe. You look guilty. This is a reason for celebration. Pete is done for. You don't jump a Sterling and get away with it. He'll be in jail for a while between the assault charges I filed and the broken restraining order with you."

Gingerly, I run my fingers over his stomach, still tracing the lines of the purplish colored parts of his abdomen. Then a throat-clearing emerges, forcing Kode to tense and my whole body to go stiff.

Balls. I forgot about Maverick.

"Something you maybe forgot to mention," Maverick says from the back of the room, gesturing to us, and not looking at all pleased about it.

Kode's jaw tenses as he wraps his arm around my shoulders. "Didn't know you were here," he says, glancing down at me, then back up at his cousin.

Maverick's jaw is set in a hard line, and I'm sure he's restraining something, though I don't know what.

"Clearly," he says acidly, then he shakes his head. "You've tried a lot of shitty things in the past, Kode. I didn't think you could top the last thing. But here you are, proving you're as stupid as ever. Rain is in love with Dane. Get the fuck over it." He turns his eyes toward me, and frowns. "I can't believe he'd do this to you. To Rain. Sorry, Tria."

I roll my eyes, sick of listening to him cut Kode down. "Maverick," Kode says in warning. "Don't. You don't have a clue about what's going on here."

"Don't I, Kode? It's pretty fucking obvious. How long has this been going on? A few days? A week? Convenient timing with the wedding right around the corner. How stupid do you think—"

"One month and two weeks," I say, glaring at Maverick like I'm ready to throttle him.

His eyes widen in surprise, and he glances between us. I continue before he can. "We're keeping it quiet until after the wedding so that no one has a jackass remark like you just had."

His mouth hardens into a thin line, and he leans back on the wall. Kode wraps his fingers around my hip, pulling me to him.

"Go out on the deck or on the beach for a while, Tria. I think I should talk to Maverick."

"No. I'm not letting him try to accuse you of using me to get to Rain. It's like no one thinks I'm worth dating without there being an ulterior motive. It all has to be connected to Rain. It's as though she's the center of the universe, and I'm the shuttle that gets you there. I'm sick of it."

His brows furrow as he looks at me, as though he's trying to think of something to say, but Maverick beats him to it.

"Sorry, Tria. I didn't even think about how insulting that must have sounded to you."

That's a shocking thing to come out of the mouth of Maverick Sterling. I return my gaze to him to see that he really does look truly remorseful.

"Mav, this has nothing at all to do with Rain," Kode adds, running his hand down my back. "This is mine and Tria's relationship. No one else has a say in it."

Maverick pushes off from the wall he's leaning against, and comes to stand nearby, his eyes moving down to where my hand is now on Kode's wounded stomach. When he looks up, his eyes connect with Kode's.

"So when you told Dane you would move Tria into one of your empty condos—"

"I moved her in with me," Kode finishes, as though he's helping Maverick piece together the puzzle.

"What about the pool in Vegas?" he asks, his brows arching.

Kode shrugs, and in true jackass form, says, "She was talking to some douche. Thought I'd break them apart."

This time Maverick's lips twitch.

"And when you went missing after that, you were actually—"

"With Tria," Kode says to finish his sentence again.

"When did this start?"

Kode grins, looking down at me for a second. "That bar. The one where I disappeared on you guys after playing pool with the brunette."

Recognition crosses the eyes of the other Sterling, and he asks, "Tria was the brunette?"

Kode nods.

"That's why you were acting like a fucking weirdo," he says under his breath.

What?

"I didn't realize she had dyed her hair," Kode says, snickering as though there's a secret I'm missing.

"Damn. So all this time that you've been blowing us off has been to spend time—"

"With Tria," Kode says, still grinning.

Maverick takes a deep breath, his head dropping back as all the world stops spinning in the right direction.

"Wow. Head trip. So is it cold in hell now that it has frozen over?"

Kode groans while wrapping his arms around my bare midriff, covering me as though he doesn't want Maverick's eyes seeing any more of me than he already has.

"Think you can keep your mouth shut until after the wedding?"

182

Kode asks him.

"Yeah. I can do that." He sighs like he wants to say more, but he apparently changes his mind. "So this is legit? Like you two are an actual item or whatever?"

This is actually a question I'd like to hear the answer to, so I remain silent and still in Kode's arms.

"Definitely legit. So legit that it's pissing me off that you're seeing her wearing very little. Probably should go."

I grin as Maverick snickers, still seeming to be taken aback by this revelation. Then his eyes narrow on Kode. "That asshole knows, doesn't he? That's why he and you have been talking in code lately—no pun intended."

I have no idea what he's talking about, but Kode laughs while nodding. "He figured it out at the club the night you were passed out and snoring at the table."

Oh. Corbin.

"Son of a bitch. I knew he was keeping something from me. If you'll excuse me, I have an ass to go kick. Since you've already had yours handed to you, I'll give you a free pass."

Kode grins while flipping him off—his favorite gesture by far. Maverick gives me an uneasy smile before heading out, and Kode inhales a fresh breath. When he winces again and clutches his side, I almost cry. This is my fault.

"Maverick took it better than I expected. He and Rain are tight. At least the second worst one is out of the way," he says with a lopsided grin, trying his best to keep my mind off his wounded body.

Not happening.

"Pete did all this?" I ask, lifting his shirt over his head. He's forced to bend in order for me to get it off him, and I gasp when I see the numerous bruises around his shoulders and arms as well.

"Nah. I could have killed Pete with barely any effort. The douche did run from four girls. He had friends today that helped out. No worries. Cops got there in time."

My eyes water again as I trace the outlines of the proof they didn't get there in time. He wouldn't have been touched if they had gotten there in time.

"Stop worrying, Tria. You're killing me with those sad eyes. This is a good thing. Pete can't touch you from inside a cell. Since he violated the terms of his parole, he won't get out on bail either. He's gone."

Like a bomb explodes under me, I launch myself up and crash my lips against his. He quickly picks me up, even though it has to hurt, and settles me on the counter in the kitchen. Stepping in between my legs to draw me closer, he kisses me like he can't get enough.

"I see you're not as bad off as I was expecting," an unwelcome, but friendly voice says, causing us both to jump and me to squeal in surprise.

Dale Sterling is standing there, his buzz-cut looking freshly groomed, and his arms crossed over his chest as he stares at us.

"Fuck," Kode groans, reluctantly turning away from me to glare at his cousin.

"How many people have a key to your place?" I whisper, squirming uncomfortably.

"Too damn many, apparently," he mutters under his breath. Then he addresses Dale in a tone that echoes my own exasperation. "Go ahead. Get going with the bullshit about how I'm doing this to get at Rain and Dane so I can argue and then be with my girl. It's been a shitty day, and I'd like a break—if you don't mind."

His girl. He called me his girl. Yeah... I'm grinning like an idiot over something that stupid.

Dale just grins instead of saying anything right away. He seems more amused than pissed, like Maverick was.

"You know, it's amazing how you and Dane seem to think I'm oblivious. He acted the same way when I confronted him about his feelings for Rain. I've known there was something going on between you two since you couldn't take your eyes off of her at Dane's house before we went to Vegas. By the time we were in Vegas, you were watching her like a possessed man on a mission, and then you flew off the handle because she talked to some guy. You two sit by each other, and you might as well be eye-fucking one another. You're not as clever as you think. The others just don't pay as much attention."

Kode sags against me, while I still sit here thinking about the fact he called me his girl. Nothing Dale is saying really matters because I'm stupidly obsessed with that one piece of the conversation.

"Corbin and Maverick have both figured it out. The only two we don't want knowing are Rain and Dane. Not until after the wedding," he tells Dale, whose eyes widen in surprise.

"Corbin and Maverick figured it out? Damn. I've been carrying this secret around like I was going to explode."

Kode snickers, and I wrap my arms around his waist as he leans his back against me, remaining between my legs. It's a small act of intimacy that proves how comfortable he is with me.

My stupid grin only gets bigger.

"I just came by to make sure you were okay. Dane said your phone got fucked up during the fight. Is this thing with Mercer over?"

His phone got messed up? That's why he didn't call me.

"Yeah. For quite a while. He's about to learn how stupid it is to fuck with me."

Dale's wicked grin doesn't match his usual mature manner. He seems to be happy with the fact that Kode is going to destroy Pete.

"You need me to grab you a phone?" Dale asks.

Kode shakes his head. "Nah. Got one of my tech guys programming one right now."

"Well, I'm about to head out. Unless you need anything."

Kode groans, looking over his shoulder at me like he's torn about something. But I'm still grinning uncontrollably. This thing between us means a lot more to him than I realized, and nothing feels better than knowing that.

Kode

As much as I don't want to leave Tria right now, I've still got an errand to run. I also had some work to do, but I guess that shit will have to wait.

"Actually, I need you to go somewhere with me," I tell Dale. "Just give me a minute with Tria, and I'll meet you outside."

Dale shrugs while heading out, telling Tria *bye*, but she doesn't respond, and I turn in her arms to face her again. She seems a little dazed for some reason, and her beautiful smile infects me, forcing me to smile for no real reason.

"What's that grin for?" I ask her, leaning in to kiss her soft lips gently, trying not to get myself too riled up.

"Nothing," she says shyly while shaking her head, her smile only getting bigger as a light blush creeps up her neck. "How long will you be gone?" she asks.

I'm thankful she isn't asking where I'm going.

"Not long. We can call in some takeout when I get back if you want to."

A night in with Tria sounds great after this hellacious day that is only going to get worse before it can get better.

"I'm cooking for you. Something different," she says with a shrug.

I love it when she cooks for me. There's something sexy about being in the kitchen with her while she strives for perfection. I prefer it when she fucks something up because she's pretty damn cute when she's pouting.

"Don't start cooking without me. I'll help."

Her grin seems to be permanent, and I don't want to say anything at all to take it away.

"I won't. Where are you going?"

Shit. If I tell her, that grin will be lost, and she'll have to deal with a reality she doesn't deserve. But I can't just outright lie.

Fortunately, inspirations strikes.

"Our New York trip is back on for this weekend, so I need to take care of a few things. They called before my phone was obliterated. The meeting was rescheduled at the last minute for Saturday. We'll leave in the morning so we can be in New York tomorrow. Then we'll spend the night tomorrow, Saturday, Sunday, and come home Monday. Unless you've got any meetings or anything else going on here. I can have you back sooner."

She wraps her legs around me, and I try not to get distracted by the fact her tits are barely encased by a tight sports bra and nothing else. Unfortunately, it feels like fucking forever since I was inside her, and right now I'm hating the fact that I need to go.

"I don't have any meetings until next Tuesday," she announces.

She looks so damn happy, and it makes me hate her fucking father that much more for pulling me away.

"Then I'll be back soon. Pack your stuff."

I kiss her while pulling her closer, letting her feel how much I'm affected. She tugs my bottom lip between her teeth, biting down just hard enough to make my erection painful, and I silently curse while forcing myself to release her.

"Hurry," she says while I adjust my cock against the painful zipper of my jeans.

"Believe me; I will."

I wink at her while backing away, but she hops off the counter and grabs my hands, her eyes going down to my battered knuckles. Her eyes soften as her smile fades, and she pulls my hands up to her lips, placing delicate kisses on all the scrapes.

It's an affectionate action that has me breathing in rasp, shallow breaths. Concern and care goes into each kiss, and I watch, fascinated, as she finishes.

"I'll see you when you get back," she says while getting on her tiptoes and pulling me down by my neck to kiss me again.

This kiss is different, carrying with it meaning beyond a simple send off. Waves of conflicting emotions gather inside me, swarming me and confusing the hell out of me. When she finally steps back, I lean forward, almost feeling as though gravity is pushing me closer to her.

"I'll pack your stuff, too. Since you're going to be busy. That way you can just spend the night with me without worrying about it."

I battle with myself, trying not to fucking grin like a damn girl. "Two suits. The rest can be casual."

She turns on her heel, swishing that glorious ass that calls for my attention on her way to the bedroom. I have to literally shake my head to snap out of my daze, and I stagger like I'm drunk on the way out the door, pulling my T-shirt back on as I go. Everything feels off balance, yet exactly right, but I have no idea why.

When I get outside, Dale is propped up on my car that I left in the driveway. His silver Rolls-Royce Phantom is parked beside my black Audi R8 Spyder.

"You can wipe that dopey look off your face if you don't want me gagging in your car," Dale says with an amused grin.

I shake my head again, still trying to get my head around what's wrong with me. All she did was offer to pack my shit. It shouldn't have triggered anything this weird.

He gets in on the passenger side while I climb in on the driver's side, my mind still fuzzy. I go through the motions of cranking the car and pulling out onto the road, driving without focus.

"Dane said you're leaving for New York tomorrow. Taking Tria with you?"

"Yeah," I mumble, still neither here nor there.

He laughs as though something is funny. "I know that look."

"What look?" I ask, though it's merely a reflex. No true coherent thought is forming right now. Did I drink vodka instead of water earlier? No. It was water. Why the fuck do I feel drunk?

"It's called a sucker punch," he says randomly.

"A what?" I hate it when people try to confuse me.

"It's when your life makes perfect sense one day, then suddenly you're knocked on your ass. Everything you thought you knew becomes irrelevant and nothing makes a damn bit of sense anymore because your life is uprooted and shifted on its axis. A sucker punch. Some people call it love."

If this is a sucker punch, I'd hate to know what a knockout feels like. Damn her.

"I wouldn't say love," I grumble, shifting in my seat uncomfortably and earning another mocking snicker from the jerk. "We haven't even been on a real date yet."

"Have to say, Kode, never thought you'd take the time to realize Tria had a thing for you, considering you were too wrapped up in Rain."

That has me swivel my head so fast that I almost run off the road.

"Christ!" Dale gasps, clutching the door and seat like he's scared shitless. I quickly regain control as he relaxes a little.

"What the hell does that mean?" I ask, trying to pay attention to the road. Maybe he should be driving.

"I mean you always looked at Rai—"

"Not the part about Rain," I interrupt, impatient and annoyed. "I meant about realizing Tria had a thing for me. She fucking hated my guts—like most people."

He laughs that condescending laugh he has, and I give him a sideways glare, half watching the road while silently prompting him to elaborate.

"Tria was into you when we were kids. You just got too stuck on Rain to see it. You always griped about everyone looking around you to see Dane, but you never noticed Tria looking around Dane to see you. How else do you think you could have gotten her after all the shit you've done to her in the past? That girl has had a thing for you that probably had her questioning her sanity. I know I always wondered why she was into you."

My stomach clenches as my mind tries to pull forth any memory that would backup his ridiculous theory. But I can't think of anything, because I'm a blind, stupid jackass.

"But I didn't see her because I was too busy looking around her to see Rain," I grumble, losing the euphoric high I had only moments ago.

"It's a bitch, isn't it?"

"What? Irony? The fact that I did to her what I hated to have done to me?'"

Yeah, it's a bitch.

"Well, yeah, but I meant hindsight. Could have saved everyone a lot of trouble if you had just realized which Noles sister was really meant for you instead of chasing the wrong one all these years."

His words are like a knife twisting in my gut. For the first time since everyone found out about what I did to Rain and Dane, I feel a sickening amount of regret. Bile rises in my throat when I see things from a whole new perspective. Dane should have hit me harder. He held back when he came at me. I sure as hell wouldn't have.

"Since you look a little pale, how about telling me where we're going instead of focusing on all the bullshit that still hasn't been fully resolved."

I nod numbly, trying not to let my mind continue traveling in the current direction it's going.

"Edward's house."

His eyes go wide with surprise. "Rain and Tria's father? Why are we going to see that son of a bitch?"

Shifting in my seat, I turn on the next road, the last road until we get there.

"Because he needed shit from his house, but wouldn't go get it. Eleanor didn't want to see him—and her sisters didn't want her to see him—so Melanie asked Rain to deliver it. Corbin didn't want Rain to face him, so—"

"So he asked you to ask Tria, since he knew you two were together. That's a dick move. I suppose he underestimates how much

Edward hurt Tria."

Right now, Dale is my favorite cousin.

"No. His loyalty just lies with Rain, so he didn't even consider Tria's estranged relationship with the bastard."

"But now your loyalty lies with Tria, so here we are. I get it. So is there a lot of heavy stuff? Because your car is rather small, and I don't see anything."

"Files. In the trunk. Just three boxes."

"Then why did you need my help?" he asks, confused.

"I just need you to keep me from killing the asshole if he says anything that pisses me off."

Dale's laughter booms out, and he nods as though he finally understands. It's a relief to have them all know about Tria and me—all but my brother and Rain. I'm still dreading Dane's reaction, but I deserve whatever he says or does. In the end, it has nothing to do with him or his fiancée.

I pull up to the beach house that is just outside the city limits, and Dale joins me at the trunk. It's much smaller than Edward's home with Eleanor, but it's still bigger than most on the street.

Dale grabs a box while I grab the other two, and we make our way to the front door. Since he has a free hand, he's the one to knock. Of course a maid opens the door, even though she's not as sexy as Edward's usual preference.

"Can I help you?" she inquires.

"Mr. Noles asked to have his files brought over from Eleanor's home," Dale says, keeping me from blurting out something less eloquent.

"Names," she says in a no-nonsense way.

"Kode and Dale Sterling," Dale answers.

"Wait here. I'll make sure Mr. Noles wants to take visitors."

The door slams in our faces, and we both exchange a what-the-hell look.

"Well, I'll be damned," Dale says, laughing lightly. "You're no longer the rudest person I know."

Rolling my eyes, I hold onto the heavy boxes of files. It takes forever for her to return, but when she finally does, the files start feeling like they're boulders.

"Mr. Noles will see you now."

"How fucking nice of him," I mutter with a scowl, pissed at the fact it took her over fifteen minutes to get back to us.

She shows us in, and we follow her to a living room where Edward is sitting in an oversized chair, looking a little pale when his eyes land on us.

"Eleanor didn't want to see you, and we didn't want your daughters to have to do this, so here's your shit that you couldn't come get yourself," I growl, dropping the boxes to the ground with a heavy *thud*. Dale drops his as well, looking equally frustrated.

Edward frowns as he stares at them. "I wouldn't have asked my daughters come see me. I was just... I wanted... Never mind. Thank you for delivering them," he says coldly.

Dale bristles beside me as my temper flares.

"Tria has been trying to call you, but you won't answer her. Your ex-wife could have probably used a call from you not too long ago. Yet you can only manage to call when you need something."

I swear that bastard smiles at me, which has me clenching my hands into fists.

"I see. So you finally noticed my other daughter instead of chasing after the one who was taken. I hope you aren't just leading her around."

Of all the arrogant, stupid, brazen things to fucking say.

"As if you have a right to speak," Dale says curtly, surprising me. "Little late to be acting like you care, don't you think?"

Edward nods, his lips thinning. "I just feel better knowing Tria has someone. Rain always had someone from the time she moved in with me. Tria never did. It's... it's a really good thing... to know. Really good."

His breaths get lower, quieter, and he sighs while looking down, seeming lost in thought. Dale and I exchange a confused look, and the maid comes back in, looking over at him with a little worry. He notices her and waves her off, which makes me wonder if he's not screwing her like he did all the others.

"You have two great daughters, no thanks to you," I say, deciding to kick him while he's down because I'm cruel like that.

To my surprise, he smiles again. "I'm perfectly aware of that. Glad *you* finally realized the same thing."

He has no fucking right to sound smug right now. It wasn't too long ago his ex-wife was kicking his ass in front of the entire neighborhood.

Then his eyes connect with mine, and for a minute, I see something raw and conflicted teeming within the depths, though I can't actually name it. When he speaks again, his voice is strained, as though he's fighting real damn hard not to fall apart.

"Tria has a big heart. Most people can't see it because she keeps it hidden from the world like a breakable jewel. She gives everything she has to those she loves without expecting anything in return. Even if you don't deserve it, she'll offer forgiveness. Don't abuse that. She needs someone to care about her the way she cares about others."

He has to be the most confusing fucking person I've ever met in my life. Dale shrugs, acting just as lost as I am. If you didn't know better, you'd believe the selfish asshole cared about his daughter—well, both of them, actually.

I start to speak, but he interjects again. "Rain is strong. So strong. She had to be. She built an extra layer of skin that she needed to endure life, but Tria is so much more fragile. Rain bares her soul, knowing she's safe from the world, but Tria keeps her emotions locked away, too scared of what rejection might come if she risks it all. But she'll risk it all with you. She probably already has."

He's talking in weird riddles that make no sense to me, and he keeps pissing me off by acting as though he cares.

"I think you two should go," the maid says when Edward buries his face in his hands and begins to weep. He's fucking crying?

I honestly don't know if I've ever seen a grown man cry like this right now. His sobs wrack his body, and he doubles over, swaying as though he might pass out.

"Now," the woman demands, shoving me to get me moving.

Shit. She's a mean little thing.

Dale and I both leave the house after being pretty much kicked out, confused bigger than dammit. I'm pissed that I didn't get to lay into him with my prepared rant.

The door slams behind us as the sound of sobbing breaches the home—Edward crying openly and loudly.

"What the hell was that?" Dale asks, his eyes full of horrified fascination.

"Beats the hell out of me. Dude was usually always so unemotional. Hell, I can't even remember him smiling or frowning. He was always just straight-faced. That... that was fucked up."

Dale shakes his head as we make our way back to my car, both of us glancing back at the house.

He follows me, and we climb in, sitting motionless and quiet for a minute as we each try to process and rationalize what just happened.

"Think he finally realizes he lost it all? Divorce can sometimes be an eye-opener," Dale says, sighing gravely.

"Maybe," I say absently, cranking the car and backing out of the driveway.

I don't know what's more disturbing; Edward Noles breaking down and bawling like a baby, or realizing that even he saw his daughter had feelings for me when I was oblivious. I'm starting to think I should have paid more attention.

Chapter 19

Tria

This is probably the most nervous I've ever been. I don't know if it's because this thing with me and Kode is finally real, or if it's because I'm wearing a button-up shirt of his, with nothing else on underneath.

He can win the damn bet. Pete Mercer won't be able to touch me. As sick as it makes me feel that Kode was hurt, seeing those marks on his fists... Well, it may be wrong, immoral, and possibly twisted, but I love knowing that he fought like that because he was protecting me.

Rain's number shows up on my phone, and even though I don't want to answer her right now, I also don't want her calling while Kode and I are ending this stupid drought.

"Hey," I say casually, trying not to let my nerves carry over to my voice.

"Finally!" she barks. "I've been worried to death about you. Pete was—"

"I heard," I interrupt, not wanting her to give me the details.

Corbin came over earlier to check on Kode. Fortunately I had clothes on at that time. He gave me the details, including Rain being there shortly after the fight. I hate that she was there for him and not me.

"Then I guess you heard Kode charged in like an idiot and nearly got himself killed."

I swallow hard against the lump in my throat. Corbin also gave me that gory detail. He also pointed out that Kode might have killed Pete if there hadn't been a herd there to hold him back.

"I did hear that," I say weakly.

"I swear. I don't know what to do about him. It's like he doesn't think. We're not kids anymore, but he can't seem to stop fighting like he's one. I've been talking to the guys, trying to figure out a way to talk to him without pissing him off. I'm the only one of us that he actually listens to, so it's up to me to figure out how to get him to stop losing his cool before he gets himself into major trouble."

I realize she has no idea that she's offending me, but it's still pissing me off. *She* doesn't have to do anything with him.

"Kode is grown man, and he's not the one you're marrying. Don't you think it'd be a little odd to show him so much attention when you're engaged to his brother? Especially given your history together?"

Why did I have to bring that up?

"It's not like that, Tria. Kode had a thing for me, but he's over that. My attention toward him is sisterly, not romantic. You know this. Dane certainly knows. But Kode is, well, he doesn't have anyone besides me and the guys to look out for him. Their parents are great, but they don't interfere in their lives. I'm good at meddling."

I don't know whether to scream at her for wanting to be there for him, or if I want to thank her for being such a good friend to him. This is all becoming a mess. I also want to thank her for acting as though his attraction toward her wasn't as big a deal as I initially thought. That's twice I've had that downplayed, so it makes me feel better.

"Rain, it's not on you to fix Kode. Personally, I think you should trust that he has reasons for everything he does. Kode didn't get this far in life and have the success he has because he's reckless."

I realize I'm essentially giving myself away right now, but I don't care. It doesn't feel right to hear her criticizing him, even though she's only doing it out of love and concern.

"You sound very defensive. Considering what an ass he has been to you lately, I assumed you'd be very onboard with me trying to make him change."

My smile forms without my permission. "People are who they are. They change how they act based on who they're with. Kode might be different than even you know."

Yeah, it's a crappy jab at her, but I'm only human. And Kode is different with me than he is with anyone else. Not because I expect him to be different, but because we're all different based on who we're interacting with. I used to bring out the worst in him, but now I get to see a side of him that no one else does.

Kode's car pulls up as Rain continues talking about his behavior toward me. She just doesn't understand. No one does. Hell, even I don't understand.

I stand at the window, watching him as Rain becomes forgotten. Dale and he are speaking, both of them looking rather confused. They weren't gone a terribly long time, but I managed to get everything packed—since I was incredibly excited.

"Rain, I love you, but I've got to let you go right now."

Kode waves at Dale before he heads toward the house, leaving his car in the driveway instead of pulling it into his spacious garage.

"Fine. Talk to you tomorrow."

I hang up, put my phone on the windowsill, and just watch as Kode nears the door, my eyes inexplicably glued to him. His black T-shirt fits him just right—not too snug, but not too loose. His jeans hang in that way that has me biting my lower lip as he uses his sexy gait without knowledge.

The door opens, and Kode's eyes immediately find me standing in the foyer. His smile slowly spreads, and I don't waste time. Too much time has already been wasted.

I move to him, trying to be sexy, but I'm fairly positive I look too eager to be sexy. Fortunately, he doesn't seem to mind. As soon as I reach him and tug him to me, his lips come down on mine hard.

I want to jump up and wrap my legs around him, but I know he's hurt, so I rein in the urge. Instead, I start kissing him hungrily, letting him know this game is over.

"Missed you, too," he murmurs against my lips, grinning salaciously when he realizes he just won. "And you look damn good in my shirt, baby."

I can't help but grin, and that just makes me kiss him harder. It's a rough kiss, one that turns savage and loses all the romantic taste. We're two sticks of dynamite right now, both of our fuses lit and burning toward an inevitable explosion.

He picks me up by my ass, and I forget about the fact he's hurt—until he winces and grunts. Apparently he forgot, too.

I jump down, which forces the kiss to separate, and he grins sheepishly at me. "Looks like you'll be on top," he says, grinning bigger.

Trying my damnedest to look sexy, I start undoing the button on his jeans, making short work of the zipper next, as he backs me against the wall.

"Or we can fuck on the counter in the kitchen," he says hoarsely as my lips start sliding down his neck.

We're not far from the kitchen, barely out of the foyer.

As soon as his pants drop, I start pushing his black boxer-briefs down, taking only a second to appreciate how good they look hanging just below his hip bones.

"Tria, I can't fuck you against the—*oh shit.*"

His words break off into a rasp whisper when I drop to a crouching position and lick the small droplet of moisture from the tip of his dick, shocking him so much that he has to catch his balance on the wall with both hands.

This is the first time I've done this for him, and with his body all tense and strained, I'm glad that I've held out. It'll make it all the better.

Just barely taking the head into my mouth, I suck and twirl my tongue, forcing him to work harder not to thrust into my mouth.

"Baby, you're fucking killing me right now," he growls.

Kode

She's trying to kill me. That's all there is to it.

Her mouth is heaven and hell, because it's so close to feeling good, but she keeps teasing me. Suddenly, she takes me as deep as she can, forcing me to fist my hands against the wall as my knees try to buckle. Then she wraps her hand around the rest, and with dueling motions, she pumps, sucks, and drives me out of my motherfucking mind with unnatural pleasure.

She sure as fuck knows what the hell she's doing, and I start finding it impossible to hold out much longer. When she does some bizarre, divine, insane combination with her tongue, suction, and the twisting of her fist, my balls tighten, my toes curl until they cramp, and I explode without giving her any warning because words can't form.

But she doesn't stop or even react. She keeps sucking me until she's milked me dry, and my whole body becomes damn near boneless. I can't breathe. No… I can't think, breathe, speak, or even move right now.

"Must have been good," she says while getting up, rising in a slow, sexy way that has me cursing myself for not being able to hold out longer.

I clumsily reach for her, trying to find a way to show appreciation when my body refuses to cooperate. She giggles softly, a sound that warms everything in me, and I finally manage to pull her back to me and kiss her. She grins against my lips, and then she starts pulling me to the bedroom, while I stumble out of my shoes and jeans the rest of the way.

"You need five minutes?" she asks, obviously amused by my damn rubbery legs as I stagger behind her, pulling my shirt over my head.

"Yeah," I scoff, grinning as she starts slowly unbuttoning my shirt that she is wearing.

Still weak, I follow her into the bedroom just as she drops the shirt and stands in front of me completely naked.

Did I just growl?

She crawls onto the bed, smiling over her shoulder at me, and giving me new fantasies to work with. How the hell did I overlook her for so long? She's more perfect for me than Rain ever was.

Like a madman, I pounce, eliciting a giggle from her as I toss her onto her back and push her up onto the bed. I settle between her legs and begin kissing down all the soft flesh of her body, making my way down until my breath brushes the part of her body that I've been dying to get inside.

She moans, making my cock twitch despite my recent release, and my tongue finds the wet heat waiting for me. She bucks and whimpers, but I wrap my arm over her waist to hold her in place, pushing my face closer as I take my time, teasing and arousing her to the point of making her desperate.

Each flick of my tongue has her begging, and I fight the urge to grin. Tria begging is my new favorite thing.

But I continue my leisure pace, giving her the slow build even as my erection becomes painful. Her sweet taste has me deciding this will become a regular thing, especially when her hands tangle in my hair painfully, urging me to end her writhing need.

When she finally goes over the edge, she calls out my name and holds me to her as she shakes and quivers like she never has before. Her entire body goes limp as I work my way back up her, and she gives me a sleepy, satisfied smile that has me feeling like this is exactly what I've been needing.

"Wow," she mumbles, running her fingers through my hair as she continues meeting my gaze.

I start to reach for a condom, but change my mind. We've had these discussions—birth control, tests, all that real shit. I've never had a real relationship because I was too busy staying available for the wrong girl.

This thing with Tria and me is as real as it gets.

My lips come down on hers, and she kisses me like I'm the only thing in the world that matters. If I wasn't already achingly hard, this kiss would have me fully erect and ready to go.

Her tongue dances with mine, making it a kiss unlike any other as we meld together like a unit. Each touch feels so natural, rehearsed, even though it's not.

I deepen the kiss as I slowly guide myself into her, groaning when the heat and wetness invite me in. It's more intense with the unobstructed touch, and I slide in effortlessly, enjoying how she doesn't even question me, even though she knows I'm not wearing a condom.

It's a trust, a bond like I've never had, and it just makes me fall a little fucking harder for this girl who I never saw coming.

When she arches her hips and wraps her legs around my waist, I sink in deeper, until our bases meet, and some primal growl rumbles in my chest. It's tighter, hotter, and so much fucking better than I ever thought possible.

It takes me a minute to start moving because all I want to do is stay like this, connected and joined. When I do move, the friction almost has me cursing, because it's too good.

Our kiss doesn't break, which restricts my movements, but I slowly take her, thrusting in with a gentler motion than I ever have in my life.

Generally, I want it as rough and dirty as possible, but there's something to be said about drawing out the pleasure and slowing things down. Each rock of my hips has her moaning into my mouth, and I swallow her sweet sounds like I don't want anything escaping from her to go anywhere but inside me.

Every movement is mine, and my body absorbs it greedily, staying glued to her. Everything she does right now is for me, and I won't share any piece of this with the world.

The sweat gathers as time passes us by. Nothing else exists. Nothing else matters.

"Kode," she gasps, her mouth breaking away from mine as she pants for air.

I quickly take her mouth again, refusing to separate now that she's so close. I want to feel it, taste her ecstasy, and drink in everything right now. When her walls clamp down on me, I kiss her harder and move my hips just right, letting her ride out the orgasm that has her moaning harder into my mouth.

As if my body has become attuned to hers, my balls tighten, tingling sensations assault me all over my damn body, and I explode inside her almost painfully as my vision becomes blurred by the surreal sensations.

I'm not sure what just happened, but I'm fairly positive Tria Noles just imprinted herself deep inside me.

Chapter 20

Tria

Kode is grinning as he shows me into the hotel room. It's a small, cozy room. Not a suite that would impress a girl, and I laugh while following him in.

"Figured we'd be low-maintenance this weekend," he says while winking, waving his hand around at the small sitting area that shares the room with a king-size bed. The small bathroom off to the side brings back memories of our night in Vegas.

He comes to press a soft kiss to my lips, making me revisit the events of last night when he completely shifted the dynamic between us. Everything that has slowly been building between us exploded in a way that I saw coming, but had been denying.

Kode Sterling has taken me in ways that would have some people running to a confession box. But last night was the first time he has ever made love to me. It wasn't intentional for him to make me admit to myself what I was feeling, but he did it. As much as I wish I could, there's no way I can tell Kode that I've managed to already fall in love with him.

"Get changed. We're going out."

His announcement has me snapping my head up. It's still really early, barely after lunch time.

"Where are we going?" I ask while going to open my suitcase.

"Anywhere. Everywhere. My hands are going to be all over you in front of every-damn-body out there. No reason to keep us a secret here."

I grin stupidly while picking out a pair of jeans and flats to wear. If he wants to make a day out of this, I should be comfortable.

It's amazing how sexy he looks in just his jeans and a white T-shirt with some blue logo on the front. His backwards hat suits him. He doesn't look like an overachieving business guru. He looks like a young, sexy bad boy.

His blonde hair just peeks out under the front rim, and it makes him even more appealing. I know women would kill to be in my spot right now. I'm not about to mess it up with a foolish confession of love.

The swelling on his face has gone down, but the bruise and small cut is still there, reminding me he's hurt. Under his shirt hides the bruises, but he swears he's not hurting.

Even with the bruise and cut on his face, he's still the most gorgeous man I've ever seen. There's nothing that can mar his beauty, which is a little depressing. Maybe I'm even more in love than I realized.

He grins over at me when he catches me checking him out, and those grayish-blue, almost silver eyes sparkle with playful mockery as he arches a light brow.

"Keep looking at me like that, and I won't get us out of here."

I laugh while shaking my head, and I move to the bathroom to change. Getting naked in front of him would lead to being thrown on the bed—or against the wall. As appealing as that sounds, I'm also excited to go out in public and let everyone see this incredible man wrapped around me.

By the time I'm finished, Kode is waiting by the door, his eyes greedily raking over me like I'm wearing a sheet instead of modest clothing.

"We should hurry," he says, shifting as though he's aroused.

I giggle like an idiot while nodding. It's like we're a normal couple here. Nothing is barring us from getting closer, and it feels good—freeing.

His arm immediately goes around my shoulders as we head out, and it doesn't move. When we reach the elevator, he has me pressed against him and kissing me hard, not giving a damn that we're not alone, and I carefully maneuver my body so that it doesn't hurt the bruises hidden beneath his shirt.

Ignoring the disapproving throat-clearings, Kode kisses me like he's flipping the world off, and I kiss him back with the same intentions. This is going to be a good day.

Tria

"I'm too full to eat another bite," I groan.

Kode laughs while taking a small bite of the third piece of chocolate cake he has ordered. He might have a badass personal trainer to keep him from feeling guilty for eating so much, but I don't.

"Just one more bite, Tria, and I swear I'll leave you alone."

He's enjoying feeding me apparently. I'm fairly positive every woman in the restaurant is officially green with envy, because Kode has been against my side since we got here, and he has been feeding me dessert like it's his mission to make me fat.

Opening my mouth, I let him slide the forked bite inside, and I close my lips over it. As he pulls the fork back through my lips, he smiles down at me, looking boyishly adorable and excited. I suppose going into a sugar coma or getting sick from a sugar high is completely worth that look.

He wipes the corner of my lip with his thumb before leaning down and pressing a soft kiss to my lips. Yeah… there's not a woman in here that doesn't hate me right now. And I love it.

"What time is your meeting in the morning?" I ask as he pays the waiter, reluctantly. I think he wants to keep me in the public eye at his side for as long as he can before we have to go back to covert lovers.

"Nine. Let's head back. There's something I sort of need to discuss with you."

The frown that replaces his smile has me worried. It's barely eight at night right now, and I expected us to stay out a little later. Not here, but somewhere.

"You look worried about something."

He'd better not be breaking up with me. That look is filling me with too many insecure thoughts.

"I am, but I hope you'll see things my way. Come on. I'll explain everything at the hotel."

I have no idea what that's supposed to mean, but it fills me with dread. He helps me out of the small, curved booth of the intimate, underappreciated restaurant that definitely surprised me with its food.

211

Deciding not to dwell on the fact he suddenly seems uncomfortable, I try to shift the subject. Maybe I'm overreacting.

"That was a nice place. How'd you find it?" I ask as we reach the sidewalk, leaving the hidden gem behind. The hotel is just a couple of blocks from here, so Kode wraps his arm around me and steers me in the direction.

If he's still holding me like this, then it can't be anything too bad.

"I go there every time I come to New York. I found it by accident. I was starving one day, and staying… close by." He seems hesitant about that last part, but I know why. He always stayed with Rain when he came to New York. He continues, not noting my tension. "I stumbled upon it, and decided it was a better option than waiting forever on a table or eating something from a hotdog stand. Obviously I was shocked at what I found. I would have overlooked it if it hadn't pretty much landed in my lap. It seemed like a fitting place to take you on our first real date."

My tension is replaced by excited butterflies. That last piece had meaning behind it. He would have overlooked me, too, if he hadn't accidentally hit on me in a bar where he never thought he'd run into me.

"My turn to ask you a question," he says when I become too stupidly happy to respond. "Why'd you decide to get into cosmetics? It seems a little random, but I've seen you be passionate about making this work."

He looks down as I snuggle in closer to his side. When he tightens his hold, my worry of what's to come dissipates. He's not leaving me, or he wouldn't be acting like he's scared to let me go.

"I graduated college with no major in anything, no real idea of what to do with my life, and no direction to go. Everyone else seemed to know exactly what they wanted to do. Finally, I started to look into different investments, and stumbled across Leo's work. He needed an investor, and I needed someone to invest in.

"As we've discussed, his name isn't a big name that people know, so he had no one interested in his work. But I was fascinated for some reason. And when I spoke to him, it was impossible not to find his passion contagious. So I funded the rest of his work, and from there, we've been trying to break into the unbreakable."

Kode grins as though he enjoys hearing that, and he pulls me closer, making walking a little difficult, but I'm not complaining.

We remain in comfortable silence the rest of the way to the hotel, and his body remains glued to mine the whole way back.

New York is definitely the place to be for business, and it's definitely my favorite place to be with Kode since we don't have to hide from anyone. But there are still... questions.

"When you were chasing Rain, why didn't you just move to New York? You have business here, and it would have been easier for you to get her while being so close."

He tenses beside me, and I hold my breath. I don't know why I have to ask questions like these, but I do. I need to know that what he felt for her is nothing like what he feels for me.

"Because I didn't... want to?" he says, though it sounds like a question he's thinking over. "I don't know. I guess I never thought of

213

leaving Sterling Shore as an option, and Rain... Well, she wasn't enough incentive for me to leave my home."

That has me grinning and relaxing. If he didn't care enough to move, even though he had other reasons to do so, then he didn't love her. Couldn't have.

As we load the elevator, I notice him still being stiff. Asking about Rain was a stupid thing to do. I should be able to just let it go.

"How can you just pick up and go from place to place while having a life with all the things you own and dabble in?"

He grins, his body relaxing, and I mentally pat myself on the back for ridding the atmosphere of the awkward tension. Just as the elevator lands on our floor, he guides me off while answering.

"Because I don't actually run anything. I'm only in on the business changing conversations. I own a lot, but I have people that run things—good people that enjoy my trust in their abilities. I'm not a workaholic because I want to live life while there's a life to live. It's a Sterling thing in case you haven't noticed. We own a lot, and only work a little."

That's not completely true. They all work a good bit, but they live life in equal parts.

He continues as we reach our room. "I make a lot of money by finding the right people who are workaholics to run things—something I learned from my dad. They put their hearts into their work, and I reap the benefits alongside them. It's a win-win situation. Something I hope you are open to doing as well, because when your business takes off, I don't want to lose you to your corporate love."

My heart speeds up as we head inside, and I look at him, trying to decipher what he's saying. He wants this thing between us to continue, that much is certain.

"Well, I would definitely trust your advice. But I don't see that being a cause for concern any time soon."

His lips thin, and he takes a deep breath before looking truly worried about something.

"Tria, I need you to listen to me about something, and I want you to seriously digest the words I'm saying without freaking out."

I'm already freaking out.

"Kode, you're starting to—"

"The meeting at nine in the morning isn't mine; it's yours."

I'm torn between being confused and surprised, because that's not what I was expecting him to say, and it doesn't make a damn bit of sense.

"What are you talking about?"

Kode

I've been dreading this conversation since we got here, but I know how to sell something. Right now it's time I put on my game face and sell this to her.

Her eyes look confused more than angry, so obviously she's waiting on an explanation and not an excuse as to why I've meddled when she told me not to.

"Five of the leading cosmetic lines in the industry are based here in New York. Tomorrow all five will be in a conference room in one of the businesses I co-own here. You'll be giving your presentation to them. That umbrella company is a possibility, and your line will stand a chance of being seen. I brought your samples, your binders, and your presentation notes."

Silence. Her face is expressionless, and the room in encased in agonizing silence. Am I breathing? I don't think I am.

"Kode," she finally groans, gripping her head. "Have you lost your damn mind?"

At least she's speaking, and she doesn't seem particularly pissed. But before I can speak, she continues.

"I told you that I have to do this on my own. I don't want something I didn't earn, because where is the pride in that?"

Now I know she's getting under my skin, because I respect the hell out of that. Just the promise of bringing Paul Colton's stores into business with a cosmetic line would have sealed her this deal a long time ago, but she didn't want to use her family for professional gain.

"Tria, I didn't get you a deal. I got you a meeting that you can't get on your own. Number one lesson in business is having contacts. You have a contact. Now you have a very important meeting to prepare for. Which I'm going to help you do."

She looks torn between confused and frustrated, but not angry. Thank fuck she's not angry.

"No. I don't have contacts. *You* have contacts, and I can't use you like that. Sorry. But cancel this. I'll find a way to do this on my own, I promise."

Come on, Kode. Get to selling.

"You do have a contact, Tria. *I'm* your contact. I'm not handing you anything at all besides a meeting. You're not using me; I'm investing. Simple. That's what I do, in case you haven't noticed. I don't invest in anything unless I'm positive I'll turn a profit. It's up to you to sell it tomorrow and prove I'm making a wise investment."

Her eyes shift, though I have no idea what they're saying right now.

"You're investing? Why?"

Why? I've been asking myself that same question since I set all this up. Every day is a new answer. Tria is everything to me right now, and though I haven't sorted out exactly what that means, I do know one thing; I can't imagine letting Tria Noles go. I'll do everything I can to make her happy, and she cares about this business.

"Because I see you, Tria. Now I'm giving some others the opportunity to see you, too. Believe me when I say it's them that I'm doing this favor for. Not you. Once they see you, they'll know how much I just helped them out, and they'll owe me some favors in return."

Just like that, the air in the room changes, and she closes the distance between us. I can't tell if she's going to slap me or ravage me. The second she jerks me down to meet her hungry kiss, I moan in relief.

Ravage me it is.

"You're really sweet when you want to be, Kode Sterling," she says against my lips.

"Miss the playground bully?" I tease, already working on getting

217

her out of her jeans.

She pulls back, knocking my hands away, but her grin is enough to make me forget that we're even talking.

"You're still a playground bully, but now I happen to enjoy that side of you. But since you sprung this meeting on me at the last minute, you now have to help me get ready so that I don't waste this chance."

Shit. I should have told her earlier, but I didn't want to take the chance of her being pissed and not getting to enjoy the day with me.

"Then wild sex?" I ask playfully.

She laughs while shaking her head. "Then lots of rest. No sex. I need to be alert tomorrow because I don't want to let you down."

I watch as she goes to sit down and type out a text, probably to her geeky business partner.

"Tria, all you need is for someone to listen. You'll get that tomorrow, and they won't be able to say no."

She looks up at me with eyes full of gratitude that say so much.

"Has anyone ever told you that you're pretty damn incredible?" she asks, forcing my chest to tighten.

No. No they haven't.

"Are you telling me I am?" I ask while grabbing her stuff that I packed in secrecy, and then I take a seat beside her on the floor.

She tugs me to her and kisses me hard, stealing my sanity for just a moment.

"Yes. I am."

Caught off guard, I'm forced to clear my throat when she backs up, just to keep myself from saying something stupid or girl-like.

Turning away, I start spreading out the stuff she needs for tomorrow, ready to rehearse with her as long as she needs to in order to feel confident.

"Kode?" she says, drawing my attention.

I move my eyes back to her, and the smile on her face has me convinced there's nothing better in the world.

"Yeah?"

She stands and pulls her shirt over her head, biting her lip when it hits the floor.

"Maybe a little wild sex before preparation."

My hands and feet are moving before my mind works, and I have her in my arms and kissing her savagely before I finally process what she said. It's then I realize that I'm not just falling for her. Tria Noles fucking owns me.

Chapter 21

Tria

Nervous? No. I'm not nervous. I'm a frigging train wreck.

I've changed clothes three times, and though I can't explain how incredibly grateful I am for this opportunity, I also want to strangle him for not giving me a heads-up. I could have brought more options.

"Tria?" Kode asks in his deep, sleepy voice that I find too sexy as I curse the next dress.

"Sorry," I mumble.

"Babe, it's six in the morning. What the hell are you doing?"

I've been up since four. It's impossible to sleep right now.

"I'm getting ready for this meeting."

He laughs, that deep rumble in his chest doing wild things to my already weakened heart. He really needs to stop being so amazing before I go and tell the big jerk that I love him.

"The place is just a block from here. Come back to bed," he grumbles.

Of course he doesn't understand how nervous I am. He has control and power no matter what room he's in. I'm an absolute mess in front of a small department chain store manager. How in the hell can I handle talking to a room full of representatives for five of the largest cosmetic lines there are?

Kode sighs while getting out of bed, apparently noticing my inner meltdown, and he comes over to where I'm at. Naked. Does the man always have to look like a model?

"I'll get on some clothes, and we'll start working on your presentation again. Just pretend they're me."

It's amazing at how much calmer I can get the second he speaks. With a mixture of fascination and awe, I watch him pull on a pair of track pants, bypassing underwear. That has my mind going in all the wrong directions.

"You don't want me thinking they're you," I mumble, absently licking my lips.

He arches an eyebrow, looking too damn amused. "You're right. Pretend they're all Brin. You talk easily and comfortably with her. Now, let's get to work before the props get here."

"Props?" I ask.

He grins while quickly punching something into his phone. Then he sets it down and ignores my question.

For the next hour, we run through my presentation, and he absorbs it as though it's the first time I've done this with him. He never once seems bored or annoyed, and it's impossible to believe this guy is really Kode Sterling—the playground bully.

Room service has come and gone, delivering breakfast that my stomach refuses to let me eat, so when there's another knock on the door, I'm confused.

Kode goes to answer it, and then he pulls out a key card to hand to a very stunning woman. What the hell?

She thanks him, batting her lashes as she rakes her eyes over his bare chest. He hands her a bag, still not bothering to glance my way. By the time she leaves, my arms are crossed over my chest, and I'm very much glaring at him.

"She's a stylist. She stopped by to get the key to the suite I reserved for her and the two models I hired for your presentation." His cheeky grin tells me he sees the unintentional jealousy I'm wearing like a glowing beacon.

It actually takes a minute to process his words.

"What?" I ask, confused.

"Models, Tria. They'll help you present your stuff with a live example. That was Sarah. She's going to go take care of their makeup and hair. She's only going to do their hair right now. She'll be doing the makeup at the meeting while you're presenting. All you do is introduce them, and make them aware that the models will be getting a makeover while you're presenting. Believe me, a visual will do wonders."

And again he does something that has me wanting to drop down on one knee and propose to him. Is he trying to ruin all other men for me? Because it's working. Which means I need to keep myself in check and not rush things, because I really don't want to ruin this thing between us.

"Thank you," I croak, consumed by so much emotion that I feel foolish.

His grin is rewarding, and he comes over to lightly brush his lips across mine, teasing me with the reverent touch.

"What are their names?" I ask, clearing my throat as he pulls back.

"Emma is the thirteen-year-old model who suffers from a light acne problem. Just as your line is designed for. And Lisa is the forty-year-old model that has fine lines from aging, and a few age spots, just as your line is designed for."

He just keeps getting better. "But I thought you wanted me to slim down the target age."

"For your presentation, yes. But for the visual, it'll show them the reach your line has. You'll get to prove your point, without voicing the numbers aloud in a way that will cause skepticism."

I really do love him. Damn.

"The white dress would look the best, by the way." He grins again when he sees me lost in his thrall, and he walks over to pick it up from the small couch off to the side.

I almost wish I could just take him with me, because it's amazing how much calmer I suddenly am.

Tria

I can't believe it. I really can't.

With shaky hands, I start to type out a quick text, only to see I have three messages.

Leo: Let me know if I'm drinking champagne or tequila as soon as you can.

That has me laughing as the adrenaline rush consumes me. And I send back a quick text while walking toward the hotel.

Me: We're drinking champagne tonight. I'll give you all the

223

incredible details as soon as I can do it without squealing.

Before I can read either of my other texts, my phone chirps with an instant response from Leo's quick messaging abilities.

Leo: Fuck yes! I love you.

Giggling, I respond with a quick *I love you, too,* and then I read the next message.

Rain: Eleanor called. She said Edward wanted to see her for some reason. She's going to see him. Just thought I'd let you know since you're not home. Even though your car is there. Where are you?

No. I'm not letting Dad ruin this day for me, so I refuse to talk to Rain about any home drama. There's enough on my mind. Too much. There's so many things I need to do to prepare for this new launch they want to do. It took several hours of bidding and excitement to get the best deal. It all happened so fast. I was expecting months and months of back-and-forth deals.

If Kode hadn't sent his lawyer, I would have been screwed. I never thought I'd be spending the day negotiating terms. And that lawyer was badass. Nothing this incredibly perfect has ever happened to me so fast.

I'll pick Kode's brain apart when he has time, but I don't want to bombard him tonight. I'm sure he doesn't want to spend the rest of our weekend with me hounding him for his brilliance.

The next text replaces all my thoughts, and I find myself rolling my eyes at the name on the screen.

Your Favorite Playground Bully: I'll be waiting for you at the room.

I really need to break into his phone and find out what he calls me. I've seen *Bitch Boy* pop up on his phone before, and found out it was Corbin. *Douche Brother* is an easy one, considering he only has one brother. *Evil Troll* is his name for his very rude, but incredibly organized personal assistant. And there are numerous *Do Not Answer* phone calls he gets. Apparently he uses that name a lot for people he no longer wishes to speak to.

He never programs anyone as their real name, so obviously I'm curious about my designated title.

I decide not to text him back since I'm already close to walking into the hotel. I'd rather throw my arms around him and surprise him with all my gratitude, starting with a naked *thank you* that will have his knees caving.

I didn't want to ever use anyone to get ahead, but Kode sold it to me. He invested in the company, though I'm not sure how much. I've still got to speak with Darla and Leo about that, since he was crafty enough to go behind my back and have his lawyers contact my normal business lawyer.

The models he hired were icing on the presentation cake. There was no doubt that everyone was impressed with the live demonstration.

As soon as I reach our room, I take a deep breath, and unlock the door with the card, ready to surprise the man who is probably anxious about what news I got. When I push through the door, my jaw drops in disbelief.

Absently I hear the door click shut behind me, but my eyes are taking in the small room that has been lavishly decorated for a king's queen.

Roses are all over the place—dozens and dozens of the reddest roses I've ever seen. There are three silver buckets holding bottles of champagne that are tucked snugly into ice. There's a table that wasn't here this morning—an oversized bistro table with two matching chairs that also weren't here this morning. Several candles are lit, creating ambience that I would usually find cheesy, but right now, it's so surreally perfect.

"Thought we'd celebrate," Kode says as he steps out from the bathroom, smiling as he adjusts the towel around his waist.

His hair is still wet from the shower, and small streams of water are licking trails down his skin, carving out a path for my tongue as my mouth waters.

"How'd you know I got a deal?" I ask in awe, feeling the flutter of various emotions gathering deep within my core.

He grins while pulling me to him and kisses me in a way that is quite possibly illegal in some countries. His tongue mimics the actions of what he did to me with it last night in other places, forcing my entire body to heat. How the hell does he make so many bruises look so sexy?

"Because you're amazing," he says, leaving me breathless when he breaks the kiss and resumes smiling at me, bending down to where his eyes stay on mine. "All they had to do was see that."

Everything inside me turns to mush, and he kisses my nose before heading over to the dresser and dropping his towel.

Yeah… frigging speechless. All I can do is stare and marvel at the man who is slowly pulling on a pair of boxer-briefs.

He grins over his shoulder when he catches my eyes taking in the firm lines of his exquisite ass, but I barely register anything. This is like a dream—a high so unimaginable that it can't be real.

"You can keep staring, or you can grab a glass of champagne," he says while grinning, moving over to the black oak table that seems much too elegant for this room. As he picks up a glass and fills it, he gives me that smirk that tells me he knows exactly what's on my mind. "I'm good with either."

Swallowing hard, I stare at him. *Do not say anything stupid, Tria. Don't you dare.*

"I'll take the champagne while I stare," I say with a flirty grin, proud of myself for doing good.

There's no way he can impress me any more than he already has, so I should be okay for the rest of the night.

"I wanted to take us out tonight, but I also knew what all would be going on in your pretty little head."

I highly doubt that.

"Oh?" I muse, taking a sexy-strutted step toward him and his almost naked body. "What's that?"

He grins that boyish grin that doesn't prove he's seduced, but rather excited.

"First, tell me how the bidding war went."

Tilting my head, I ask, "How'd you know—"

"You've already got a deal, Tria. That means they were thoroughly impressed with you. Enough that they couldn't risk someone else offering you a spot before you left. Considering the rejections you've received, they all most likely worried you'd take the first offer without holding out for a better one. Now, how many were in the bidding war, and how sweet was your deal?"

Grinning like an idiot, I shrug, trying my best not to squeal and jump around like I want to. Unfortunately, I end up squealing and launching myself into his arms, jumping up and wrapping my legs around his waist while I giggle hysterically from the excitement.

He laughs while holding me to him, and I rain kisses all over his face in a sloppy, jerky manner that has him laughing harder.

"Three out of five," I say, though the words are said through my heavy breaths and giggling, so I know they're hard to understand. "And I'll show you the details of the awesome deal I got. Thank you for sending your lawyer there to help me, by the way. You're so unbelievably amazing."

He smiles against my lips while trying to kiss me, and I grip him tighter between my legs. We're both smiling too big to really kiss.

"I like seeing you this happy," he says, drawing his face back just enough to find my eyes.

"Well, you're the one who made me this happy. They wouldn't

have ever met with me if it wasn't for you."

He runs his nose along my jaw, and I lightly kiss his cheek, trying to get my breath back. But now the adrenaline has resurfaced, and I feel like I could dance in the streets without any shame.

"What did you think was on my mind?" I muse, enjoying how he holds me with effortless ease, but then his bruises cross my mind, and I try to wiggle free. I feel like shit for forgetting them.

He doesn't let me go right away, and I seriously become curious about his pain tolerance, because he seemed to really be hurting yesterday, but he acts unaffected today.

"Ah," he says, still grinning as he walks over to the table and slowly puts me on my feet. He reaches down for his briefcase, and he pulls out several thick folders packed full of pages. "These are résumés."

I'm confused, my mind still hazy as I try to stay upright and not pass out from the excitement that is bubbling through me without mercy.

"We're staying in because you'll have a ton of questions, and I'm the best person to answer them. We'll start with assembling your team so that you aren't overwhelmed with things to do. Everyone in these stacks is ready to start work right now; they've passed my screening process—which is very hard to do; and they have negotiable rates that will go with the budget you discussed with me. We'll sort these out and find the perfect fit for you."

Ah, hell.

Tears water up in my eyes, and he looks down at me with

bemusement riddling his expression.

"What'd I do wrong?"

I grin and laugh while the tears slip out. I'm not crying sad tears, but he doesn't understand that. I really don't think I've ever cried happy tears before.

"Nothing." My voice is shaky, and I sniffle while he wipes a tear away from my face.

"You want to start on this or do some celebrating first? This is your night."

I grab his neck to jerk him down, and the kiss I give him is searing. He grips me to him tightly when he feels my desperation to kiss him as hard as I can.

"Take me to bed first. Before I say something stupid," I murmur against his lips.

Tria

Well, after trying to destroy the hotel room like horny teenagers or wild rockstars all night, we manage to get everything sorted out, and I have my first, second, and third picks lined up for every position.

Kode is sleeping peacefully after being thoroughly rewarded for all of his hard work. It's almost noon, but he deserves the rest. Especially since I'll be keeping him up tonight again.

I grin when I see his arm reaching out, searching for me even as he sleeps. My chest swells with emotion when he mutters my name and hugs a pillow to him, substituting it for me.

Grinning, I pull his phone from the counter, curious as to what he calls me while I go to the abandoned room service and finally sit down to finish that piece of celebratory chocolate cake. My ass will need to be in the gym next week to make up for all the food splurges I've had this weekend.

His new phone just got to us in time for our flight the other day. Apparently his tech guy had to swap over all his old information. And his phone is not liking me.

After finally figuring it out somewhat, I check to ensure it is on vibrate, and I send him a text to see what pops up. I hold back a laugh when I see my naked selfie picture, but my heart thumps in my chest when I see my name—*My Sexy Girl.*

It's not as creative as the names he gives himself in my phone, but it's a claiming, warming, and endearing name that has me tearing up again. But then a new message comes through, and that brief moment of triumph is obliterated into ashes as cold heat pumps through my veins.

My Perfect Girl: When are you coming back? I thought we'd get together. Just the two of us. It's been a while, and I miss my best fri...

That's all the preview shows, and I don't want to actually read the whole message. Kode would know I snooped, and this was an accident. A terrible, sickening, jarring accident that I wish had never happened.

If I didn't already know who it was, the picture would tell it all. I've seen his phone numerous times, but I've never seen a text or call from her. Dane usually messages him, even though Rain texts the others a lot. I suppose Dane has the same chip on his shoulder about them as I do.

At least now I know why.

Her picture isn't a scandalous mirror selfie of her lying on a bed, looking desperate to tempt him. She's staring innocently over her shoulder—at him most likely—and grinning as her blond hair bounces under the sun.

Her name and image make her seem wholesome—someone that a man would dedicate his life to. My name and my image sound temporary and scandalous—like I'm the well-kept dirty secret.

Perfect? *His* perfect girl?

I can't do this to myself. He's here with me, and he has gone out of his way to make this weekend extraordinary. If I were temporary, he wouldn't have invested in my company. He wouldn't have pulled out all the stops to make this all work for me.

She might have been his perfect idea of a woman at one time, but I'm the one he's with now. Even if I'm merely a substitute for the girl he can't have.

I wish I had never been curious about the special *pet* name he gave me in his phone. Leave it to me to ruin a dream.

Kode stirs, mumbling my name again, but this time my heart doesn't clench uncontrollably.

"You're up too early," he says, alert but keeping his eyes closed.

Trying to swallow down the painful knot in my throat, I slowly move back toward the bed, my feet feeling weighted to the ground. Without releasing the sigh I want to, I slide in next to him and let him wrap his arms around me until I'm pulled flush against his hard body.

"Much better," he mumbles into my hair, smiling as he kisses my forehead. "What're you doing up?"

Seeing my sister's endearing term on your phone.

"I had some messages to check. It's almost noon."

He groans while throwing a leg over me, cradling me to him tighter in a hold that has some of my tension easing. He wouldn't be holding me like this if he didn't want me. Just me.

Right?

Stupid, immature insecurities. I have to let it go.

"So, do you change the names in your phone as often as you change your name in my phone?" I ask, sounding flirty and playful instead of bitter.

He snickers, unaware of the reasoning behind my seemingly harmless question.

"Nah. Most of the names in my phone have stayed the same since I programmed the numbers back whenever. I only change names to *Do Not Answer* on occasion. Other than that, I don't mess with it."

It's not much relief, but it is some. He might have programmed her that way a long time ago. But then again, that picture of her is less than a year or two old.

Stop, Tria. Don't do this.

Deciding not to sabotage my relationship over useless jealousy, I wrap my arms around him and give in to his strong pull.

"We'll go out tonight. Somewhere nice," he says, sighing into my hair.

Kode Sterling may have wanted Rain Noles, but he's falling for me. That can be enough.

Chapter 22

Kode

"Make sure you contact them. Ms. Noles will be using my personal human resources department until she has formed a staff of her own. Thanks, Sharon," I say, hanging up with my assistant.

She's a bitch, but she's badass at her job.

Scrolling through my messages, I see I have yet another new message from Rain.

My Perfect Girl: Are you avoiding me? We're going to talk, Kode. Text me or call me back.

She has sent three text messages since yesterday, wanting to meet up alone. I'm not stupid. She's pissed about me going after Pete alone, and now she wants to sit me down and scold me like a kid. I should probably change her name in my phone. She's not *my* anything. Never was. And I'm learning that perfect is overrated.

I'm not wasting time with Tria to go get reamed by Rain. No thank you.

My phone buzzes in my hand, and I grin when I see the name on it.

My Sexy Girl: I'm heading home right now to do some work. Leo is coming over, and I'm fairly positive he's going to do a few backflips when I show him everything in writing. The lawyers are still tweaking the fine details, but we should be signing everything soon. I'll see you later tonight. Thanks for this weekend.

Damn. She left when we got home to run some errands, but I thought she'd be coming here when she got done. Something was off yesterday. I'm not sure what, but she wasn't as... free?

Usually she hands herself over to me like there's nothing holding her back. Yesterday she seemed distant, and everything felt a little forced. I'm sure it has a lot to do with her nervousness over her business. It's real for her now, and the adrenaline has worn off, making way for the reality that can be daunting. That's why I've gotten her a team together. They'll help make this launch go seamless.

I decide I'm overdue for a training session with Jax, so I head over to his studio. He's working with a few women when I get there, all of them eyeing him like they want a bite.

Rolling my eyes, I walk his way, and he excuses himself from the admirers who are fanning their faces.

"I swear you get more ass than a rockstar," I say as we head toward the mats.

He laughs while shaking his head, and the women move to the workout equipment, not moving their eyes off us.

"Still with the hottie?" he asks as I start stretching.

"Yeah. Just got back from New York."

"Sounds serious. Long weekend together? Or did she invite herself?"

"It was planned. My idea. Long story, but damn good weekend." Until she started stressing out, it was a damn good weekend. I can help her with anything she needs, so I wish she'd just come over and let me work on it with her.

Christ. I'm the one who sounds clingy.

"Did you ever screw her sister? Or was it one of those friend-zone things?"

I really need to quit talking to him about my shit.

"Never screwed her. Friend-zone hell more like it. But it all seems to be working out for the best."

Tria is so much better for me in so many ways. It's shocking at the things we have in common. And she wants me. No one else even draws her attention in the slightest.

Jax stops talking when we start working out, and he kicks my ass a few times, since my head is a little groggy from the weekend. After a solid two hours, I'm pouring sweat and breathing like an out-of-shape pansy.

Jax mocks me when I drop to the mat to sprawl out, and I flip him off without bothering to lift my head to glare at him. When my phone blares some girly song from my gym bag, I silently curse Tria. When the hell did she do that?

"Dude," Jax says through his laughter, "nice tune."

"Shut the fuck up," I grumble while answering the call from Corbin. "What's up?"

For a minute, there's nothing but a long exhale on the other line.

"Corbin, you called me, man. Why you being all heavy-breathing on the other line?"

Jax continues laughing, but Corbin has me worried.

"You remember when you and Dale went to see Edward? All that weird shit going on?"

I remember, but I never told him. Apparently Dale filled him in. "Yeah," I drawl, not interested in anything dealing with Edward right now.

"Well, that woman that threw you out wasn't his maid. She was his nurse. Apparently Edward has had psoriasis of the liver for a really long while now. It took a turn for the worse recently. I guess he tried to drink his guilt away for years and years."

Ah, shit. "How bad is it? Is there anything they can do?"

Tria doesn't need this shit. She and her father have too many unresolved issues.

"It's pretty bad, and I doubt they can do anything, considering he died just an hour ago."

Just like that, my heart slams into my chest. Shit. Tria. Motherfucker!

"I've got to go. Tria—"

"Rain just went to pick her up and tell her in person. They'll be going over to Eleanor's. If you call—"

"Corbin, I really don't give a fuck if Rain knows right now."

He blows out a breath, and I can almost hear him nodding in agreement. "Alright. Let me know if you need anything."

I hang up without responding, ignoring Jax when he starts sounding worried, and I dial Tria while grabbing my stuff and jogging toward the door. She answers with a voice as dead and dull as I've ever heard.

"Hey."

Taking a deep breath, I search for anything to say. I suck at consoling.

"Hey, where are you? I'll come to you."

She sniffles, and a small whimper escapes her, but she clears her throat as though she doesn't want to be crying.

"I'm with Rain right now. I'm fine. I'll be staying with Mom tonight. They're going to... I can't talk about this right now. I'll call you in a little while."

She hangs up, and I stop in my tracks, trying and failing to come up with what I'm supposed to do. Son of a fucking bitch.

I saw how Kade reacted when he lost his grandfather. Tria just lost her dad. Kade needed space. Hell, he still does. But is that what Tria needs, too? What the hell do I do?

Tria

I stare at the phone, wondering if he'll try calling right back. Fortunately, he doesn't. I'm barely holding myself together right now, and if I fall apart, I want to do it alone. All alone. There shouldn't be any witnesses to see me cry over a man that I should have hated.

"Who is *Sex Master*?" Rain asks, trying to lighten the mood.

She didn't love Dad. How could she have? It's understandable why she's not falling apart, but I don't have it in me to play nice with the perfect girl at the moment.

"I don't want to talk about it right now," I mumble numbly, and I hear her sigh that seems to come from deep within.

"Of course. Sorry, Tria. I was just—"

"I know," I interrupt, still staring out the window as we close in on our childhood home. There are already numerous cars outside. Mom is probably an absolute wreck.

"Why didn't someone call me sooner?" I ask as we near the house.

Rain hated him, yet she found out before I did. It's like I'm always the last on the list, even when my father dies. It's truly impossible for one person to always be so overlooked.

"No one wanted to tell you over the phone, since you actually cared about him."

She sounds sympathetic, and there's pity lacing her tone—pity I don't want or need. Everyone praises her for being strong. She is. She truly and honestly is. I refuse to be the weak one that everyone has to pet while they rave about her being so strong.

Sucking in all my unshed tears and wiping away the few strays, I open the door as soon as we park. Rain has to run to catch up with me, and she laces her fingers with mine as we head toward the door.

"I'm here, Tria. I'm here for you and Eleanor."

Maybe Kode is right. She really is perfect. Can't blame him for taking notice, because right now she's keeping me from falling apart.

"Thanks, Rain. That means a lot."

The tears bang at the backs of my eyelids, but I restrain them. My phone chirps, and I release her hand as we walk in, so I can check the message.

Sex Master: I'm here for you.

Breathing out in relief, I stare at the screen for five long minutes. I'll wait until I'm not on the verge of a sobbing breakdown before calling or responding. Right now, he'd see how weak I really am, and that's something I'd like to keep hidden.

Chapter 23

Kode

"Have you talked to her?" Dale asks while sitting down beside me in the back of the enormous church. It wasn't too long ago we were here for Thomas Colton.

With the amount of people here, the chapels just don't have the necessary seating. But this massive church was built with the town, so it has become the rock for a lot of people in times like this.

"Not much. She's been staying with Eleanor for the past couple of days, and she hasn't really been in a talking mood."

I try not to let anyone see how fucking stressed out I am. Tria is shutting me out, and I don't know whether to let her or stop her. I've always sucked at this sort of thing, and since she's been at her Mom's, I haven't really had the chance to see her. I should be doing something, but I'm clueless as to what.

This is yet another suit I won't be able to wear again. Once they've been tainted by a funeral, they go into the discard pile. I don't want those memories burned into the threads I wear. Especially this one.

Rain and Dane walk in from a door at the front of the church, emerging from a private room where the immediate family has been stashed. He's holding her hand, and she's looking over her shoulder at Eleanor who is clutching the hands of both of her sisters. Her eyes are rimmed red, swollen, and full of tears. I guess she hated him a lot less than she loved him.

But my eyes move away from her when I see the girl with her head bowed, her face clean with no tears. She's staring at her hands as she walks behind everyone, not bothering to make eye contact with a single person.

My eyes never stray, and she sits beside one of her aunts near the front as the minister moves behind the podium to speak. Seeing her look so broken and alone is too much.

"Fuck this," I mumble before getting up.

With long strides, I abandon my cousins and round the back of the church to move toward the girl who has no one holding her hand right now—the girl too afraid to cry on someone's shoulder.

Eyes fall on me from all around as I move into the pew, and Tria's tired gaze meets mine. Her hazel eyes go wide in her face, but then her look softens as I sit beside her and put my arm around her shoulders, pulling her to me before kissing her softly on her head.

It's like something inside her snaps, and she buries her face in my chest as her body starts shaking. Silent sobs wrack her body, and I pull her to be almost in my lap, wrapping her up in both arms as the minister continues to praise the life of the man who destroyed his family.

"I've got you, Tria," I whisper softly.

She fists a handful of my shirt as she weeps against me, and I continue to rub soothing patterns on her back. Eleanor looks over with glassy eyes, noticing her child's pain for what seems to be the first time, and her tears start falling harder before she mouths, "*thank you*," to me.

But when my gaze meets a set of cold green eyes, I realize this day is going to get dramatic. Dane is staring at me with a murderous glare and a clenched jaw, looking every bit ready to punch me in the face.

Rain's eyes are wide in shock, her mouth slightly open in disbelief. I'll deal with them when I have to. This is about Tria right now. Not them.

My eyes go back down as Tria clings to me, and I do all I can to make it easier. For the first time in my life, it's not hard to comfort someone. My movements aren't forced or awkward. I'm not looking for a way to escape. This is exactly where I want to be right now.

By the end of the service, Tria's sobs have gentled, and she's leaning against me as the minister carries on. She threads her fingers through mine with one hand, keeping it in her lap. I use the arm wrapped around her to run my fingers through the soft strands of her hair, trying to relax her any way that I can.

As the service wraps up, I stand with Tria, keeping her hand in mine, and lead her through the church. We stop as people try to offer their condolences, and I wait, never letting go of her hand the entire time.

When we finally reach the outside, my arm slides back around her shoulders, and I tuck her against my body. "I'll drive you to the cemetery."

She looks up with her sad eyes that have me wishing I could do so much more.

"Thank you," she says hoarsely, swallowing back another sob.

After opening the door for her and helping her in, I make my way around to the driver's side. My eyes catch Dane's cold glare, but I don't acknowledge it past that.

Tria's hand finds mine the second I'm in the car. I only let go to shift gears, but I keep taking her hand back in mine in between shifts as we follow the line behind the Hearse to the graveyard.

When we get there, she waits on me to open the door, but Dane is right behind me, calling my name loudly at the wrong time.

"Don't go," Tria says, casting a hard look toward the man everyone adores. "He shouldn't be doing this right now."

Rain is tugging on Dane's arm, probably telling him to cool down. Neither girl knows the extent of our issues, so they don't understand why he's so pissed. Unfortunately, I get it. Now.

"Just let me tell him to shut up," I say softly, kissing her head before making my way toward my fuming brother.

Several others pass by me as I backtrack, and Dane shrugs Rain off as he storms toward me.

"How long have you been scheming this bullshit up?" he growls, drawing a few gasps and head-turns.

"Dane!" Rain hisses, grabbing his arm again and trying to pull him back.

"Later, Dane. Not here. Not now. Your girl might not need you right now, because she didn't love that asshole. But my girl does need me. You can say whatever you want later."

His brow furrows, as if he's confused, and I walk away to rejoin Tria. My arm immediately goes around her shoulders, and I bite back a grin when she flips Dane off. Apparently she doesn't find him so perfect in this moment.

Tria

I don't know what Kode and Dane said to each other, but I can guess. I can't believe Dane would do this right now. Here of all places.

Even though I was trying so hard not to fall apart, I was already on the verge of a breakdown when suddenly Kode was right there, pulling me to him like he knew I needed him. I've never been so grateful for anything in all my life.

I never wanted to lose it in front of him, but I couldn't help it. It was too much, and he held me to him like he couldn't imagine doing anything else. Kode was the only one who knew I was hurting.

Dane saw me in that church. He knows I broke. Yet he wants to accost his brother in the middle of the graveyard for being a damn good person, just because he thinks it has something to do with Rain.

"I've got you," Kode says against my temple as we reach the rest of the crowd. His lips brush my head gently, and I lean into him and wrap my arms around his waist. He doesn't hesitate to return the embrace, and I hold him as my tears slip free.

The gentle patterns he rubs on my back are soothing and comforting as the casket slowly lowers into the ground, burying the two fathers I knew—the one who loved me, and the coward who ran away.

Dane looks our way, but his expression has changed. He doesn't look like he's ready to kill Kode right now. I'm sure I shocked him by giving him the bird in the middle of the graveyard, but he was pissing me off.

Maybe Kode has rubbed off on me more than I realized.

That thought has me smiling ever so slightly for the first time since I heard about my father's death.

Aunt Melanie hands me a rose, and I lean away from Kode as I slowly take it and make my way toward the grave. Rain drops hers in with a sad look, but there are no tears. I've already reached the point of not caring how messy my sobs have gotten. So I don't bother wiping the few tears that fall when I drop in my own rose.

Mom moves toward the grave as I walk back toward Kode. I turn around when I reach him, and he wraps both arms around me and tugs my back flush against his front. I watch with a fractured heart as Mom breaks, her tears bursting free as she shakes with her sobs.

"You son of a bitch!" she yells, dropping to her knees.

Kode moves with me, and my aunts reach her just as I do. Kode helps her back to her feet, and she turns in his arms to sob against his chest. He looks uneasy and uncomfortable while he tries to console her. Just minutes ago he was soothing me with effortless ease.

Dane comes over, and Mom turns to grab him, gripping the lapels of his suit coat while burrowing her face into his chest. Kode looks relieved while coming to my side again.

For two days, Rain and I have slept in Mom's bed like we were little kids that were afraid of the dark. Only we were there to keep her from being afraid of the dark instead of the other way around.

They start covering the hole while Mom continues to unravel on Dane, and he does all he can to ease her pain with his gentle touch. Kode's hand slides back around my waist, tugging me to him and kissing my hair.

"Are you staying with Eleanor tonight?" he asks softly as people start to disperse.

"My aunts are staying with her tonight. I was hoping I could stay with you."

His arms tighten around me, and he nuzzles me gently. "You're welcome to stay as long as you want to, Tria. I didn't want you leaving just because Pete was gone."

For the second time in a long two days, I smile. That's exactly what I needed to hear right now.

"Can we go now?" I ask, looking up at him.

He smiles down at me with those soft eyes no one else ever gets to see. "Anything you want."

Chapter 24

Kode

"Where's Tria?" Dane asks as he steps inside my house.

I've been dreading this conversation since the funeral five days ago. I'm surprised it has taken him this long.

"She had a business meeting with her new team. She'll be back soon."

He looks around as we near the living room, his eyes falling on the several items that prove a girl is living with me. Tria's lip gloss is on the coffee table, her running shoes are setting by the glass doors, and her girly candles are here and there in certain places. If he thinks this is obvious, then he should see the master bathroom.

"I talked to Dale and the guys. They apparently figured it out a while back. Call me stupid or blind." His face is expressionless, and his voice is even, which makes it impossible to read his mood.

"You're about to get married. Your mind is a little preoccupied," I say mildly, trying not to be the one to spark a feud first.

He leans back, propping his ass on the back of my sofa, and stuffs his hands into his jean pockets while studying me.

"Dale seems to think you're in love with her. Why Tria, Kode? You fucking hated her. Why would you go after Tria?"

He's obviously reining in his anger, because he's definitely not happy with the fact I have the other Noles sister. The one actually made for me.

"Well, you kind of can't help who you fall for, Dane. Falls aren't usually planned. If they're planned, they're called jumps."

I expect a grin or something, but I get nothing besides crickets. *Well, this conversation is going great.*

"Dane, I'm not going to apologize for—"

"Do you love her?" he asks, interrupting me.

Though I really don't want to have this conversation with him before I have it with my girl, I guess I sort of owe him an explanation.

With a heavy sigh, I prop up beside him and stare at the wall. There's now a picture hanging there—Tria and me in bed. It's just a face shot with me kissing her cheek while she snaps the picture. But it's probably my favorite thing in the house right now.

"Yeah. I do. And I get it now, Dane. I don't know how you didn't kill me when you found out about what I did."

His eyes widen in surprise, and to my astonishment, he laughs. It's a low, rumble of a laugh that seems to vibrate from his chest.

"Man, you really do love her."

It's almost painful to look back at all the time I wasted thinking I was in love with Rain. It's easy to get confused, but after you've had a taste of the real thing, there's no mistaking it ever again.

"Yeah, well, I haven't told her that yet. Her dad just died five days ago, so I don't think it's the best time."

Dane nods slowly, and then he reaches into his back pocket to extract the envelope that is hanging out. He hands it to me, and I read the messy handwriting on the front that has my girl's name on it.

"What's this?"

"Edward wrote a letter to Tria, Eleanor, and Rain. I told Eleanor I would deliver Tria's. It gave me an excuse to come talk to you about this beehive you stirred. But if you seriously love her, then I'm not going to say anything other than... What the fuck? You *hated* Tria worse than anyone."

His lips curl up in a smile, and for the first time in too long, I feel like my brother is looking at me with something other than hatred. I just laugh, unable to help myself.

"Wish I knew. Dale says I got sucker punched." I rub my jaw to feign a hit I didn't see coming, and Dane laughs hard—harder than I've heard him laugh in so damn long.

As his laughter tapers off, he stares at the picture of Tria and me on the wall. He studies it for a moment, probably noting the stupid smiles on our faces.

"Corbin said he knew you were serious when you mentioned telling Rain about the letter."

The others have spoken about this since Dane and I had this fight, but we've never talked about it. Not since the day he shoved his fist into my face.

"Yeah. I still want to, but I want to wait until after the wedding."

He frowns while continuing to study the picture. "The wedding has been moved back two weeks. It was a pain in the ass to do, but Rain didn't want her father's death messing with our day. She feels that will be sufficient time for people to get over the son of a bitch. Personally, I don't understand grieving him at all."

That has me tightening my lips and trying not to piss him off

251

when we're finally starting to be on good terms again. I thought this thing with Tria would tear us apart, not push us closer.

"That's because he treated Rain like shit from day one. Tria knew him as a father for eighteen years of her life. Eleanor loved him for a really long time, even when he tried to make her hate him. Any idea what's in these letters?"

He shakes his head. "Rain wasn't ready to read hers just yet. She wanted to wait until she had some liquor. Eleanor retreated to her room after giving me Tria's, and Rain hugged her goodbye. I figured I'd give her space to get drunk and read it."

I nod, because there's nothing to really say. Bashing the guy now that he's dead seems pointless.

"I don't think we should tell the truth. Rain will be devastated. I don't want her to lose her best friend. Would you want Tria to lose someone she has thought of as her best friend for six years?"

Looking down shamefully, I stare at my feet, unable to even face the picture of Tria now.

"I was only her best friend because I knocked you out of the picture."

Dane sighs long and loud. "No, Kode. You didn't do that on your own. You provided a speed bump. That's all it should have been. She and I were ridiculous by letting our pride get in the way. But we were eighteen. And sometimes, as you know, you make stupid decisions when you're young based on immature emotions, and then you stick with them because you rationalize the reasons in your mind. It's a hell of a lot harder to swallow your pride and face something after time begins to pass."

That's the fucking truth.

"I wish I had never gone back out to the car that day."

Dane laughs humorlessly. "That makes two of us."

The door opens and closes, silencing us as Tria walks in, her eyes wide. Apparently she has already seen Dane's car in the driveway.

"Tria," Dane says, standing and fidgeting nervously before pocketing his hands again.

"Dane." She stands taller, keeping his gaze. I'm pretty sure she's on the defensive right now, considering she won't let anyone run their mouths about us. She knows how real we are, and she's got my back.

I'll never forget the day she stuck Maverick in his place. He won't ever forget it either.

"I wanted to apologize about what happened at the funeral," Dane continues, looking as shameful as I've ever seen him look before. "It was sure as hell the wrong place and time, and I acted like an idiot kid instead of an adult. I'm sorry."

She crosses her arms over her chest, staring at him like she'll rip him in half if he's says the wrong thing right now. It's so fucking hot.

"Rain is really excited about this," she tells him. "I wish everyone could have that reaction."

Surprisingly, Rain is the biggest fan out there of our relationship. Maybe Dane is right about letting our past bullshit die with the lie.

"I know Rain is happy," Dane says, smiling at her. "So am I. But I'm also a self-centered jerk sometimes. I'm human, after all. Never said I was perfect."

She tenses noticeably, like there's something in there she didn't like to hear. "No one is perfect," she finally says, letting her eyes meet mine briefly, but then she returns her gaze to my brother. "Sorry I flipped you off in the cemetery."

Dane bursts out laughing, and I smother my snickers with my hand while Tria bites back a grin.

"I deserved it," Dane says when at last his laughter fades.

She shrugs, seeming to agree with him, and she reduces the distance between us quickly, moving to my side where I wrap my arms around her and pull her to me. Dane turns to smile at us.

"I'll be taking off. I guess I'll see you two soon."

"Yeah," I say as he walks away.

Tria sighs as the door shuts behind him, and she angles her head to look up at me.

"I didn't know what I'd be walking into when I saw his car."

Obviously I'm just as relieved.

"The guys got to him. They told him how I really feel about you. I actually think we're cool again for the first time in a while."

I'm careful not to bring Rain's name into anything. It's the smartest thing to do.

"Did he tell you the wedding has been pushed back two weeks? It'll be a total of three weeks before we can officially go public," she teases, smiling up at me with her long lashes looking close to her cheeks.

"Ha. I think we're very much public now." Sighing, I hand her the envelope before I change my mind and do something stupid like rip it up—been there, done that, not a good idea. I'd love to save her some pain, but I've learned my lesson about interfering with damn letters.

"What's this?" she asks, looking down at the crisp white envelope.

"It's from your dad. Dane brought it over."

Her breath comes out harsh, and she takes a minute to just stare at it. I wait patiently, ready to do whatever I can to make it better no matter what that damn thing says.

"Here," she says, handing it back to me. "Hold on to it for me. I'm not ready to see what it says."

I take it, though I'm a little confused. "You're sure?"

Her dark hair falls over her shoulder, going down past her breasts and touching her top few ribs.

"Positive. If he's telling me he's sorry and that he loves me, it's going to break my heart. It'll make me feel guilty for all the time we lost because I didn't try harder. If it's something cold and indifferent, then it'll break my heart in a different way. He doesn't get to speak to me from the grave until I'm ready to listen."

I nod, folding the envelope and sliding it into my pocket. "Then I'll keep it until you ask for it."

She smiles, even though it seems forced now.

"Thank you. Now, I got three movies. You can choose which one we watch."

I flip through them and choose the only one that doesn't look like a damn romance. She rolls her eyes at my selection, and then she heads to the kitchen to retrieve a bottle of wine and two glasses.

"How'd the meeting go?" I ask, watching her hips sway in her sexy skirt that hugs her hips and legs all the way down to her knees. Her white shirt is tucked in, and she looks like a dirty dream I want to have.

"Great. You really know how to find some incredible people. It's going to be a well-oiled machine. They already have all the plans worked out, and they essentially just needed me to sign off. I was so impressed that I almost lost my cool and bounced up and down."

Her smile is infectious, and I find myself grinning, too, while tossing the movie in. She heads into the bedroom as I drop to the couch and start pouring our wine. She emerges just as the movie previews start, and I waggle my eyebrows at her new attire—just my shirt.

"There's something to be said about ordering in," I murmur, trying not to be too pushy.

"Definitely," she says in agreement, winking at me.

We've only had sex a couple of times since she heard about her father. I'm trying to give her whatever she needs right now. If it's sex, then it's hers. If it's quiet time, then I shut the hell up. If she needs a bath, I'm turning on the water.

She sits down beside me and slides a leg over my waist while taking her glass. When she cuddles up against me and rests her head on my arm that is draped over the back of the sofa, it feels so right that it's almost suffocating me.

"Tria?" I look at her while she sips the wine, her body slowly tangling around mine like she can't get close enough.

"Mm?"

Instead of saying anything, I just kiss her, a firm kiss that has me wanting more, but not pushing for it. Our glasses go to the table, becoming forgotten as I hold her to me. When she kisses me back and starts pulling me backwards with her, slowly lying down on the sofa while keeping me between her legs, I fight not to rip the buttons off the shirt.

"I'm glad you're here," I finally say against her lips.

"So am I," she says, smiling.

Yeah... I'm pretty fucking in love with Tria Noles.

The damn doorbell rings, announcing the food is here, and Tria laughs as I growl and adjust myself in my jeans. I don't think it's funny. At all.

She sits back up, and I go and pay the douche waiting with our food.

We eat and talk about her meeting, and she fills me in on all the details while we both ignore the movie. She's far more interesting than the screen right now.

When the doorbell rings again, we exchange a confused look. "Kode, Tria, it's Rain. Open up."

Rain's voice is breaking, and Tria scrambles up, stopping by the bedroom to grab shorts while I jog to the front door. Damn glad I didn't give Rain a key.

I open the door, and a wave of blonde hair is all I see before Rain disappears around the corner, more than likely going to find her sister. The strong scent of alcohol wafts toward me, causing me to frown. Did she drive drunk? That's not like her.

"Hello to you, too, Rain," I mumble, sticking my head out the door just in time to see a cab pulling out. Thank fuck she didn't drive. Now I don't have to kick her ass.

When I get back into the living room, Rain is crying, and Tria is hugging her, looking over at me with as much confusion as I feel. What the hell? Dane was just here a few hours ago, and everything was... Oh shit. Her dad's letter.

"Rain, tell me what's going on," Tria soothes, hugging her sister as Rain unravels on her. She never does this.

"The wedding is off."

Cold sweat forms all over my body, and I immediately grab my phone to text Dane while Tria gasps in surprise.

"Why?" Tria asks hoarsely. "What the hell happened?"

Rain sniffles while drawing back, and I tell Dane that she's here via a few key strokes. Something isn't right.

"It's amazing that our asshole father can even ruin my life from the grave. But he did it. That bastard managed to do it. And I hate him even more in death than I did while he was alive."

Edward didn't like Dane?

"Rain, calm down and tell me what's going on." My voice draws the attention of both of them, and Rain dives into my arms like she always has.

Tria moves to sit down on the arm of the chair, now wearing a pair of shorts under my shirt. It's awkward again. Trying to comfort anyone besides Tria just feels weird.

"Edward wrote me a letter, telling me how he has a lot of regrets in life and all that cheap ass shit. Then he has the balls to say that he wishes he could have been a good man. A man good enough to face me and be there for me during everything I went through. He shouldn't get to clean his conscience before his grave. It's wrong. It's cheap. It's so fucking cowardly!"

Her voice is loud and distorted from her tears. I've never seen her so hysterical before.

"What's that got to do with your wedding and Dane?"

She hugs me tighter, and I try to think of what to say. Nothing. I really suck at this.

She finally pulls back while wiping her eyes, and she moves to join Tria on the sofa arm. Tria squeezes her hand, trying to comfort her.

"Life is short. You only have a few glimpses of amazing things. Beauty fades. Life moves at a pace that gives you whiplash. I read that letter, and realized that jerk got to answer questions without actually answering them. So, I did something I told myself I'd never do. I wanted answers. I didn't think it mattered, but it does. I deserve to frigging know."

She's like a rabbit on crack when she gets up and starts pacing, and nothing she's saying is making sense. I've seen her drunk many times, but never this emotional and drunk at the same time.

"What does that have to do with Dane and the wedding?" Tria prompts, echoing my question that wasn't really answered.

"I wanted answers. Like I said, I told myself it didn't matter. But I had to know. So I finally asked him about that damn letter I wrote him six years ago. I wanted to know why he let me go. I deserve to know!"

My body turns into a block of ice as I go stiff from head to toe.

259

The nightmare is playing out into reality, bleeding into the bubble I have with the girl I love. And it's all unfolding in a way that will never turn out good. I should have already fucking told Tria the truth.

"What'd he say?" Tria asks, as the words I need to say start choking me.

"He said he was stupid. That's all he'd say. I told him that was a shitty excuse, and I needed more. He looked so damn torn, Tria. He's hiding something. I don't know what happened, and until I do, I can't marry him. How can I? I refuse to start a marriage with someone who can't be honest with me no matter how much I fucking love him."

Bile rises to my throat, and I lean over to grip the back of a chair.

"Dane didn't do anything wrong, Rain," I say quietly, just as my door slams.

"Rain! Dammit, don't just run out on me!" Dane's booming voice fills the room, and Tria jumps, startled. He must have been close by when I sent that text.

Rain screams at him, cursing him and calling him out as a coward. That's all I can take.

"It was my fault!" I yell. The entire room falls silent other than the few muttered curses from Dane's lips.

Rain blinks at me, her tears still falling. Tria stands and moves to the side of the room, watching me with intense but unreadable eyes.

"How the hell was it your fault?" Rain demands.

This is not what I wanted to do. "Because I took the letter and tore it to pieces. Dane didn't even know it existed until he read your Easton Boys book. I'm sorry, Rain. This is on me. Hate me. Not him."

She shakes her head, and her finger points at me. "You're lying. Why would you do that? You're my best friend. I'm not stupid, Kode. Stop covering for him."

Tria continues watching, her arms crossed under her breasts, and her eyes solely on me.

Fuck. Fuck. Fuck.

"Rain, it really was me. I went to get my sunglasses out of the car and found the letter. I fucked up. Really, really bad. But it was me. Dane didn't tell you the truth because he thought you'd forgive him easier than you'd forgive me, and he loves you so much that he didn't want you to lose your best friend. That's why Maverick's the best man instead of me, Rain. You know I'm telling the truth."

She stares at me, unblinking and silent. Then the rage in her eyes focuses on me, and her fists clench at her sides.

"Why?" she bites out acidly, her tears running harder. "Why the hell would you do that? Did you read it? Do you know what it said?"

My breath hurts. Everything hurts. But I shake my head, revealing more with each passing second.

"I didn't have to read it. I knew what it would say."

She chokes back a sob before covering her mouth. "Then why?"

"Because he loved you," Tria says, her voice quiet and pained.

Her eyes are no longer on me. They've found the floor, and my heart clenches.

"You didn't love me, Kode. Fuck. You didn't love me or you wouldn't have done this. You bastard!"

"Rain, I know that I don't—"

"No," she interrupts. "You don't get to defend yourself. I fell apart, and you just let me. You knew I loved Dane, and you made me think he abandoned me? And you let me continue believing that you didn't know I loved him, so I suffered in silence—agonizing silence from a secret I didn't have to keep. Why? How the hell could you do that to me?"

There aren't words to explain the actions of an eighteen-year-old kid who thought he was in love.

"Because you're his idea of perfection," Tria says, sounding heartbroken as she pinches the bridge of her nose.

In my distraction, I never see Rain approach, but I feel the hard slap that resounds off my face. I wouldn't have stopped her even if I had seen her coming.

"I hate you," she says in a hoarse whisper, her tears falling harder as my eyes come down to meet her teary ones.

"I'm sorry, Rain. I was a stupid kid at the time."

"Sorry? Kode is sorry. Imagine that. Well, Kode, you can't be sorry for this one. I lost six years of my life because of you. I can't have children now. I lost that chance because of you!"

I wish she had just slapped me again. It would have felt better than that.

"Rain!" Tria yells, stepping toward us. "That's not on him. Don't do that."

Rain glares at her, but the knife is already in my heart. Did I really steal something that precious?

"Rain, that's not right," Dane says, shaking his head with tears in his eyes. "We could have gone to each other. You could have had—"

"Shut up," she cries, her eyes so red and raw, and then her attention comes back to me. "Do *not* ever speak to me again."

She storms out of the house, leaving me in pile of rubble as I slump to the chair. Dane walks over and squeezes my shoulder. "That's not on you. She's hurt right now. And she's seriously drunk. She'll calm down. She didn't meant that."

But in the end, the words are there, and I deserve it.

Dane sighs while looking toward Tria, but I can't even bring myself to meet her eyes.

"Sorry, Tria. He… wanted to tell you. I asked him not to."

With that, he starts to leave, but not before Tria says, "Because you didn't want Rain hurt, right?"

Dane's retreat is stalled, and I turn to see his apologetic eyes looking into mine before he answers, "Yeah."

Tria nods solemnly, not giving me any indication as to what she's going to do or say. Dane leaves, and my whole body becomes hot and cold at once. It's hard to do, but I finally look over to meet Tria's eyes.

"Tria, I'm sorry. I was a stupid—"

"How long did you feel like that toward her? Obviously you felt that way before you were eighteen. And you felt that way not long ago. So how long?"

Her voice is even, not rattled anymore. It's almost like she's not surprised, and that hurts almost as badly as what Rain said to me.

"Since I was thirteen. But, Tria, I didn't love her the way I thought I did. I swear to you that I didn't."

Now would be the worst possible time to confess the fact that I know that because I didn't know what love felt like until her. It would sound insincere, and I can't ruin it with this bullshit tainting the words.

"Kode," she sighs, coming to sit beside me on the arm of the chair, and I reflexively wrap my arm around her waist. She doesn't knock it away or recoil from me. So that has to be a good sign.

"I told you once that I wouldn't compete with Rain. Our relationship is still new. We've got bitter ties for different reasons, and we're finally moving past that. I don't want to hate her, but right now, I almost do."

No. Shit. Please don't let her do this.

"Tria, it's you. I swear to you, I never wanted Rain the way I want you."

She laughs humorlessly, and her hand caresses my cheek in a way that almost tells me she's saying goodbye.

She stands, and I stand, too, circling the chair and blocking her path. She looks up at me, and that's when I see the tears glistening in her eyes.

"Give me your phone," she says softly, and I quickly oblige, not giving a damn why she needs it.

She takes it and scrolls through something before handing it to me. "I'm your sexy girl. The one with a nude photo and a good time attached to her name. I realize it turned into a little more, but that was the foundation of us. Relationships like that don't last. You never even had sex with Rain, but yet this is what you have for her."

She takes the phone and scrolls through it again. My heart starts thudding in my ears, and my air becomes heavier. When she hands the phone back to me, I curse myself for my stupid fucking system.

"Your perfect girl. The picture says it all, right alongside her cherished name. She's your dream girl, and I'm the substitute—a poor man's Rain."

She starts to move, but I drop my phone and pull her to me, crushing my lips to hers in a desperate attempt to keep her. She kisses me back, but whimpers against my lips. When she pushes me away, I don't resist.

"Tria, I realize that's how it looks. In the beginning, I was still sprung on Rain. I never changed her name. And yeah, you were initially my sexy girl. But things change. You're everything to me," I promise her.

Her lip trembles, and the first tear falls from her eyes as she reaches up and touches my lips with her fingers.

"Then why did you decide to keep this a secret from me?"

That's the final nail in my coffin. I can tell it.

"Because I didn't want to lose you."

She shakes her head. "No. You wanted to tell me. Dane didn't want Rain hurt. Which means you also didn't want to hurt Rain. I heard what Dane said. Was he lying?"

The hopeful look in her eyes has my heart breaking more. "No," I say in a reluctant whisper. "I didn't want to hurt her, but I also didn't want to lose you."

She smiles, but it's such a sad, resigned, defeated smile that tears find my eyes for the first time since I was a kid. "I wish I knew that was true. But how can I? One thing I always loved about you was your honesty. It might be brutal at times, but it was reliable. Now… I feel like I don't know what to believe, Kode. There's nothing but lies and secrets and lies to keep those secrets."

I start to object, to tell her I'll never lie to her again, but she adds, "And I can't be the girl that keeps getting looked over. I thought… I really thought what we had was too good to be true. Now I know why. For what it's worth, Rain missed out. I would have loved to have been loved by you."

If she ripped my heart out with her bare hands, it would hurt less.

Tria

"Tria, I do—"

"Don't, Kode. Don't finish that sentence. Not now. You don't want to lose me, and that means so much. But it's not enough. I can't compete with my sister, and you've been in love with her for eleven years."

I just want out of here before I drop to the ground and cry myself into dust. If I had realized it would hurt this much to fall in love, I never would have risked it. It's too much.

The knot in my chest makes it hard to breathe. The lump in my throat has me barely able to swallow. And the tears in my eyes are slowly starting to drip out despite my attempts to restrain them.

When Kode admitted that it was him, I realized he was trying to let Rain go. But only because he couldn't ever have her. It's agonizing, but it's understandable. And I saw it coming. I really did, but I fooled myself into believing that I could one day be the only one he saw.

The second choice sister. That's me. And I'm so sick of it.

Now I'm hurting him by forcing him to see this as it is. I know he hasn't been doing this to me on purpose. Not even he is an asshole like that. And if it wasn't for Rain, I'd be enough for him. But I'm not. He just can't see that, and I'm not willing to try outshining eleven years' worth of devotion.

"Kode, if you care about me at all, please let me walk away right now. Don't make me fall apart in front of you."

He takes a step toward me, and my body tenses. I'm terrified he's going to kiss me again, and I love him so much that I'll let him. I'll push him away, but not until our lips have touched and danced to a familiar song that only we seem to hear.

"Fall apart, Tria. Slap me, punch me, kick me, scream at me until you can't breathe... Do whatever you want to, but please don't leave. I swear I'll put you back together if you'll let me."

My sobs break free, and he instantly has me in his arms, drawing me against the body I've sought for so many different reasons. I clutch him for a moment, letting myself be comforted by the same man who has broken me. Then I pull back while shaking my head.

"I need to go. I'm sorry, but I can't do this right now."

"Tria," he groans. "Baby, I'm sorry. I fucked up. I was young and—"

"And still in love with her just a few months ago." Why can't he see this? Why can't he tell he's killing me right now? "Kode, this was doomed from the beginning. You don't love a girl like Rain Noles and get over her with a girl like me. I. Have. To. Go."

I punctuate my words with a hiccupped sob that escapes me just as I barge by him.

"You're wrong, Tria. You're the only girl in the world who could have made me realize that I never could love a girl like Rain Noles."

I keep walking, refusing to let him talk me out of this. I know what I just saw… what I just heard. Believing him now would be the death of me tomorrow.

He doesn't follow, or chase me, or fight for me in any way as I grab my phone from the bar. I walk out, not bothering to put on any shoes. I never got my purse out of my car earlier, so at least I don't have to worry about coming back for that.

I'm so glad Pete is in jail, because I finally have my car and my home back, and I don't plan on getting out from under the covers for a few days.

The second I get into my car, my phone chirps, and I hesitate to read it. Finally, I do.

Your Public Boyfriend: I'm not giving up.

From anyone else, that would make me sick. With Kode, it gives me false hope. There's no way in hell he can ever possibly prove that I won't have to compete with the one who got away.

I know he doesn't realize he's playing with my head, so it's on me to be strong enough for the both of us until he stops giving a damn. That shouldn't take too long.

Chapter 25

Tria

"Tria? Are you in here?"

I shush Rain while chewing on the greasy bag of chips. She walks in, her eyes wide, and gazes over the hell my room has become.

"Leo let me in. I didn't know he was staying with you."

"Yeah. Jack—his brother—got a girlfriend, and it got crowded, so he moved in a few days ago. He's crashing here until he finds something," I mumble absently.

"Have you—"

"Shh!" I interrupt as I move closer to the edge of the bed, waiting for a miracle to happen, but no. No miracle. You have to be kidding me!

My bag of chips go flying across the room, scattering and not inflicting nearly enough damage on the TV.

"Something they said?" she asks dryly, glancing back and forth between the TV and me.

"He dies?!" I yell in disbelief, glaring at the screen, still wondering if something is going to happen to magically bring him back to life.

No. Nothing. He's dead.

"I just spent two hours of my life watching that angst-ridden, gut-clenching, long-as-hell movie to distract me from our miserable existence, and he dies right after they finally get together? How can they classify that as a romance? I'm suing them for false representation!"

Rain comes to sit beside me, sighing as she looks around at the room I've barely left all week.

"She wanted to give it a realistic touch," she says in defense of the heartless person who created this tragedy—not a romance.

"If I want reality, I'll walk outside and breathe in the toxic air, dammit. I'll take a look at my own miserable life. If I read or watch a movie, I'd better get a fucking happily-ever-after."

She frowns as she looks me over. It's not like I'm disgusting. I had a shower yesterday. Or was it the day before?

"Tria, I'm worried about you."

I pick up another bag of chips that I have stashed beside my bed, and I open them while curling up for the next movie on my list. It had so better have a good ending, or I'm buying a plane ticket to Hollywood so I can beat the hell out of someone.

"Why?" I ask casually, even though I'm not stupid enough to not know her reason for concern.

"You haven't answered your phone all week—"

"I have for business related things," I interrupt, letting her know I'm not that far gone. Is it so wrong to need some space from everyone and everything that is connected to the man who unintentionally broke my heart?

"Okay… Are you mad at me?"

I wish I could be. It'd make seeing her less painful. "No," I confess, sighing.

She seems relieved by that, but the worry in her eyes doesn't

271

lighten. If anything it seems to weigh on her even more.

"Tria, you're not leaving your house, and now you're yelling at a movie."

"The wonderful world we live in has so many delivery services. There's no reason for me to leave. And yes. I'm pissed that I ordered a *romance* and got a sick, Shakespearian twist that made it a tragedy."

The new movie starts playing, promising to be a bit comical. Thank God it isn't another tear-jerker.

"Tria, it has been a week."

She underestimates how much I cared about Kode. They all do. I'm sure not even he understands it.

"Rain, if Dane and you split up right now, where would you be?"

Her brow puckers to mimic her frown. "Under the covers," she groans.

"Well, I'm sitting on top of them, so I'm already doing better than you would be. Cut me some slack. I'm not done wallowing."

It takes so much effort not to break down and bawl, but I manage to escape the tears. My trashcan is overflowing with tissues. I'm fairly sure my nose will be forever raw. And my poor stomach is hating me for all the junk I've crammed into it over the past week.

"Has he tried calling?"

Numerous times. And texting. But that's not something I want to share. No one has to know he's still chasing me. It's better if they don't, that way no one gets mad when he finally moves on. If they know he kept trying for me, then they'd think he was merely leading me on.

"Have you talked to him? He was your best friend for a lot longer than he was my boyfriend. I know what he did was shitty, but what you said... Rain, that was way too low."

She looks down, and a tear slips free from her eye. "I know. I felt horrible about it when I woke up the next morning. I was on an emotional high, and I was way too drunk. I had told Dane I didn't want to get married to a liar like my father, and then I called a cab. Dane was taking a minute to get himself together—probably trying not to lose his temper on me—and I left without saying anything."

She takes a deep breath before exhaling it loudly. "Fucking Edward. I never should have read that letter. None of this would have happened. Kode had moved forward, Dane and I are together, and you were happy. I fucked it all up by going crazy."

I pat her leg and offer her the bag of chips. She takes them, and puts the salt-and-vinegar flavored thing in her mouth, cringing when she realizes it wasn't a plain chip. I'd laugh at her face under normal circumstances.

"I always did have a flair for the dramatic," she adds, dusting her hands off. "Guess that's why I started writing."

"It's not your fault that this happened, Rain. It's just one big cluster fuck, and all four of us got weaved into the mess. Shit happens."

I need her to go so I can cry some more. She'll stay if I start crying right now.

"Are you going to forgive him?" I ask, hoping she says yes.

She gives me a weak smile. "If he'll ever talk to me again after what I said, then I probably will. I've been calling, but he won't answer. He told Maverick that he wasn't making up with me until he made up with you. Says he's never letting you think you come second again."

My heart squeezes and aches in a violent, unforgiving rush of painful emotions. But now I feel so guilty for putting this on him.

"Then maybe you should go to him," I say softly, moving my eyes back up to the movie and praying for escape.

"He never loved me, Tria. He never looked at me the way he does you. He has never held anyone so tightly in all his life as he held you at Edward's funeral. Kode would move heaven and hell to be with you."

She just never saw the way he looked at her, because she was too busy looking at Dane.

"He thinks you're perfect," I grumble. So what if I'm sulking. I'm in mourning. I've lost my father and the man I love in a two week span.

"Then he never really paid much attention to me. Dane knows I'm not perfect, which is what makes him love me more. Since Kode hated you for a while, I'm pretty sure he knows you're not perfect, and he loves you anyway."

I groan while leaning back and putting my arm over my eyes. "Rain, I love you for trying, but you don't see things the way I do. Never had to. Please stop pushing this. It's hard enough as it is." I peek out to see her staring at me, and I add, "So you're not mad at him anymore?"

I need her not to be mad at him. And she seemed pretty pissed a week ago. It's hard to believe that fury has died down so soon.

"A lot can happen in a week."

"Go to him. Talk to him. Let him apologize to you. He needs you as his friend. Don't let one thing tear you guys apart."

I see her studying me out of the corner of my eye, but I don't acknowledge it.

"Don't let the same thing tear you apart, Tria. Hollywood doesn't control your happily-ever-after. You do."

I wish it was that easy. I really do.

"Care to tell me what helped you get over everything so fast?"

Her smile forms instantly, and her eyes water as she pulls a picture out of her purse and hands it to me.

"This did."

Kode

"Holy hell," Maverick drawls as he uses the damn emergency key for the wrong reason, just like all my cousins have done this week—my brother, too.

He walks around, looking at the messy house I've let go, as he makes his way toward me. My couch and I have gotten overly friendly this past week. Whiskey has also become a close companion. I haven't started drinking today… yet.

"I leave you alone for a few days, and you go from looking like Pretty Boy to looking like Mountain Man. When's the last time you shaved?" he asks.

I rub the longer hairs on my face and shrug while turning my attention back to the TV.

"Dude, you look about as good as your house right now. You should come out with us tonight or something. This shit isn't healthy."

Well, fucking up the best thing that ever happened to me is unhealthier. I should have come clean from the beginning. I should have made sure she never had a reason to doubt me when I told her the truth. And I should have changed Rain's motherfucking name in my phone. Why did I leave it that way?

Because I'm a procrastinating stupid jackass, that's why.

"Mav, any good reason you're here?" I ask, annoyed and on the verge of punching him just to shut him up.

"Yeah. I just told you. I want you going out with us tonight. We've given you a week."

Rolling my eyes, I shift on the couch, turning over and away from him.

"Not long enough."

He huffs, and I hear a chair shift, clueing me in that he just sat down.

"Have you talked to her at all?" he asks.

I fucking wish. "I've called. And texted. And called. I've sent her flowers. And called. I've emailed her. And called. I've tweeted her. I've even hit her up on Facebook. Nothing. She won't speak to me."

"Well, there's an obvious way to see her. You know where she lives. Just show up."

That fucking crazy dick ruined that option for me.

I turn back over to face him, barely able to hold myself together at this point.

"After everything Pete put her through, I can't do that. I don't want her ever putting me in the same category as that psycho."

Maverick shakes his head, glancing through the sliding glass doors that lead out to my deck.

"Man, you and Pete are not in the same category." His eyes come back to mine. "Tria loves you. She doesn't want to give you up. It's killing Rain, you know. She's blaming herself for this."

"She shouldn't," I grumble. "I fucked this all up on my own."

"Actually," a feminine voice says, causing us both to jump, "there's a lot of people in on this fuck-up."

Rain is moving toward us, her eyes as sad as her slow walk of defeat. I never even heard her come in. Maverick must have left the door unlocked.

Maverick tightens his lips while standing, and he goes to press a kiss to her forehead before waving to me.

"I'll leave you two to talk."

Rain walks closer as Maverick heads out, and she comes to sit down across from me, looking as crestfallen as me.

"Rain," I say hoarsely, instantly choking on all the guilt I didn't feel before Tria.

Sitting up, I meet her sad gaze, and shift uncomfortably.

"Sorry to just show up, but you wouldn't take my calls. Tria and I talked. She wanted me to come."

Hope fills me, and I sit up straighter, leaning forward with eager attention.

"She wanted you to come see me? Can I go to her?"

277

A tear falls from her eye, and she stands to come sit by me, her breath leaving in a sigh.

"I think you should go. She loves you, but she thinks you're in love with me. She's been overlooked for so long, that she refuses to believe someone finally wants her over me."

I swallow the knot in my throat. She knew I saw her before I fucked up.

"That's my fault. I handled everything wrong. Is she okay?"

Rain's eyes drop to the unruly facial hair I've unintentionally grown over the past several days.

"She looks about as great as you—minus the bad beard."

I try to smile, but it doesn't work.

"Do you hate me?" I ask softly.

I don't want to smooth things over with Rain before I fix this shit with Tria. But Tria sent her here.

"No. Kode, I'm sorry for what I said. That was the cruelest, most unfair thing in the world to put on your shoulders. It's not your fault I went six years without confronting Dane. It's sure as hell not your fault that I got uterine cancer and lost the ability to have children. I hate myself for saying that."

I pat her knee, keeping my eyes low.

"But it was true that I'm the reason you two didn't get together soon enough to have children."

Her hand covers mine and squeezes it, a motion that used to mean something to me. Now it feels sisterly—the way it should.

"That's bullshit. You know it. I know. Even Dane knows it. You started the snowball, but we let it turn into an avalanche. Even if we hadn't, there's a very good chance things would have eventually gone wrong back then."

"Doubtful," I scoff, knowing damn well how perfect they are for each other.

"Kode, Dane asked me to marry him after dating me for a very short period of time. And I said yes. If we had gotten together when we were eighteen, we would have gotten married just as fast as we are now. We would have probably gotten divorced just as quickly and destroyed our futures before our lives even really began."

My eyes come up to meet hers, and she smiles sadly at me.

"What do you mean?"

"I mean that Dane and I ignored each other for six years because of one miscommunication. We were just too damn young for what we were feeling. As much as it pains me to admit this, you may have done us a favor."

Guilt spikes my blood, and I shake my head. "Don't do that. Don't justify my actions."

"Oh, I'm not. Believe me, it's not that easy, Kode. I'm still royally pissed at you for what you did and for keeping it a secret. Doesn't mean I had the right to dump the shit on you that I did."

I move my eyes to meet hers, and I smile. I prefer it when people don't sugar coat shit.

"Thanks for that. But I still feel like it's my fault you didn't have any kids."

Another tear falls from her eyes, and she pulls out a picture that she holds with the back facing me. "Kode, if I had been able to have kids, then I might not have ever gotten this chance, because I would have been too busy to consider this."

She hands me a picture of a small girl, and I study it with confusion. Sad blue eyes stare into mine with loneliness and longing. Her lips are turned down in a frown that looks too permanent on her face.

"Who is this?"

Rain sniffles and laughs while wiping her eyes as more tears fall. "This is Carrie. She's five, and she's currently in foster care. Her mother died of a drug overdose; her father died in a drive-by shooting; and she has no other relatives. Despite all that, no one will adopt her because she has a hole in her heart. In her case, it's not a life-threatening thing, as long as she is cared for properly. Dane and your mother are in Louisiana right now, doing all they can to expedite the entire adoption process."

My eyes go wide in shock. Hell, Dane didn't even tell me he was leaving the state.

"Rain, that's incredible."

She hugs me, and I wince when I think of the Noles sister I want to be hugging. As she draws back, she wipes her eyes again.

"I know. Most people don't want a child that has any medical condition. This was a sign, Kode. She was made for us. Elizabeth had a friend call her and tell her about Carrie's situation. She told Dane, and from there, everything went into action quickly. Dane and I fell in love with her after meeting her on Tuesday. We had already decided we were adopting her, but I just had to meet her. I flew back that night, but Dane stayed in Louisiana with Elizabeth."

I look over the picture again, sitting back and staring at my future niece. It's amazing, really.

"Go to Tria, Kode. Don't waste six years making stupid excuses."

Her comment draws my eyes up, and I see her tight expression as I breathe out heavily.

"I'm fighting for her, Rain. I really am. I'm just trying not to push too hard too soon. My biggest fear is losing her forever."

She stands and stares down at me. "The longer you wait, the more convinced she's going to be that you're not in love with her. So go. Before she builds a wall around herself that you won't be able to penetrate a second time. She's in a lot of pain right now. I'm fairly positive she'll never allow herself to go through this again if you wait too long."

Cursing, I close my eyes and search for answers inside my scrambled mind.

"And, Kode?" Rain says, her voice a little sadder again.

I open my eyes, staring expectantly, and Rain continues. "Give her back Edward's letter. She needs the closure whether she realizes it or not. I know I didn't demonstrate it very well, but I'm glad I read it. It's done now. As long as that letter is out there, she won't ever have the closure she needs."

With that, she walks out, and I curse again while heading toward the bathroom. I don't know what the hell I'm going to say. This had so better not backfire on me, because I don't want her thinking I'm just like Pete.

The letter her father left is staring at me when I open the box I hid under the bathroom counter. Rain has never steered me wrong before, but I can't force her to read it. Tria can decide on her own what to do.

After taking a deep breath, steeling myself with the resolve, I grab my razor and prepare to dull a few blades.

It takes me longer than it ever has to get ready, considering I can't go to see her looking my absolute worst. And after getting showered, shaved, and dressed, I finally grab my keys and head over to her house.

My hands are practically shaking by the time I reach her home, and I give myself a minute or two to rehearse what I might say. Her garage is closed, so I can't tell if she's at home or not.

After finally digging up my balls, I make my way to the door. I knock, but hear nothing. So I knock harder. Finally, the door swings open, but it sure as fuck isn't Tria looking back at me.

A fucking beast of a man is standing at the door in nothing but his boxers, looking as though he just woke him up from a nap. It's the middle of the damn day.

His shoulders are broad enough to put him in a linebacker position. And the muscles are rippling all over like he lives in the gym. And he obviously doesn't give a damn who sees him in nothing but his underwear.

"Can I help you?" he asks, seeming bored or tired. Not sure which. And I really don't care. My blood is boiling.

"Who the fuck are you?" I growl.

The dude cocks his eyebrows at me, and he tilts his head, studying me as though he's trying to place my face.

"You're Kode, aren't you?" he finally asks.

I nod slowly, still trying to figure out what this dick is doing in her house, wearing nothing but his damn boxers. And how does he know who I am?

"My name is Leo. I'm Tria's business partner."

Son of a motherfucking bitch. Hell no. This is sure as shit not how I pictured him. He's supposed to be old, short, bald, ugly as fuck, and nerdy as hell. He is *not* supposed to look like *this*.

"You always answer the door in your boxers?" I snarl.

He snickers as though something is funny. There isn't a damn thing funny right now.

"I'm staying with Tria for a while. Come on in. She's in the shower. I need to head to town anyway, and you need to straighten this shit out between the two of you so that she doesn't keep crying herself to sleep."

She's crying herself to sleep?

I visibly relax, and my angry snarl slowly starts to simmer down. He seems a little too amused as he walks down the hall, and I move to drop down on her sofa. My palms are sweating like I'm a kid going out on his first date. Christ. I hope this isn't a bad idea.

Chapter 26

Tria

"Hey," Leo's deep voice says into the bathroom.

I move my head out from under the water, and peek through the crack I make in the doors. "Yeah?"

He steps in, his body clad in his date-night attire instead of his couch-potato or work clothes.

"I'm going to go meet that guy you set me up with. He'd better be as hot as you say."

I smile while nodding. "Jamie is definitely the catch of a lifetime, because he's sexy and nice. Trust me. You look good. Don't worry about coming in late. I sleep hard."

He frowns as he leans a hip against the counter. "You don't sleep at all. It's starting to worry me."

Leo and I have had a mostly professional relationship until he needed a place to stay. Now he has taken on a worried brother role. It's not something I'm used to, and though I appreciate it, it's not something I need right now.

"I'll be fine. Just a bad breakup. Go on your date. Jamie is hot. Women and men all over will be pissed at you."

He grins that full-teeth smile, and he nods. "You sure he wants to do this?"

"Positive," I promise for the fifteenth time. Leo is more insecure than I am.

284

"Alright. Have fun. I'll see you when I see you," he says in that deep rumble of his.

He winks at me, and I return to rinsing my hair under the water, listening as the door clicks shut behind him. It'll probably suck to see Leo wrapped around someone when I'm still pining after Kode, but he needs a good guy. He has dedicated his time to school and work, and now it's time for him to have a life.

When I get out of the shower, I grab my towel and lift my eyebrow. Where did my clothes go? I wore clothes in here, and I hung up new clothes to put on when I was dry. But they're all missing.

Leo. Why the hell would he do that?

Wrapping up in the towel, I head toward the living room, curious as to if he's gone yet or not. But my feet tangle and I almost fall when I see the long body slowly lifting into a standing position from my sofa.

Kode Sterling is here. The man I've avoided all week is in my living room, looking like he just stepped out of a photo shoot for the world's sexiest men, and he's licking his lips as he takes long, slow strides toward me.

"Tria." He says my name in a deep voice that sounds like it's wrapped in velvet, and I shiver. Yes. I'm so damn weak, that just my name from his lips has me ready to drop into a puddle.

"What... When... Um..."

He smiles when I stammer and find myself unable to speak. His sexy blonde hair is in its usual messy style that has me wanting to put my fingers through it before pulling him against me.

"Your roommate let me in," he says softly. "I didn't come to scare you or to make you uneasy." His eyes drop to the towel again, and he shifts as though he's trying to hold himself back. "But I wanted to come talk to you since you won't take my calls."

My body sways to the music of his voice. It's amazing how a week without it has made me even weaker instead of stronger.

"I can't... I'm sorry. I've said all I could," I murmur while dropping my eyes from his silver gaze. It's just too damn hard to look at him.

A warm hand cups my chin, and my breaths stop as he tilts my face up so that our eyes meet again. That smirk on his face looks better than his sad eyes.

"I haven't said all I could. I'm in love with you, Tria. I wish I had said that sooner, but there never seemed to be the perfect time."

My heart breaks, and my tears start falling like he controls my body. I try to back up, but he goes with me, moving me until I'm backed against the wall with nothing but a few inches and my towel barring his hands from my body.

But he doesn't touch me anywhere but on my chin that he's still holding. Instead, he leans down and puts his face close with mine—so close his breath bathes my lips. Like a hungry fool, I soak in the closeness without letting him see it.

"And I'm going to prove it. You'll come back to me, Tria. Or I'll keep chasing you for the rest of my life."

That has my eyes snapping wide, but before I can say anything, he's kissing me. It takes a minute for my mind to decide if I'm dreaming or if it's real, and when I realize this is definitely real, he's pulling away.

"I'll see you soon."

He winks at me before turning and heading for the door, and I sink to the floor as the door shuts behind him. My fingers slide up to my lips, and then my tongue runs along my bottom lip that he had pulled into his mouth.

Thank God I brushed my teeth today. And showered.

Scrambling to get up, I grab my phone, and I send a quick text to Leo, cursing him for not giving me any warning and for stealing my clothes. He sends one back almost immediately.

Leo: You should be fucking him instead of texting me. You sure he's not gay? I can take a go at him to be sure.

I roll my eyes, but a text on my phone draws my attention. It's Rain asking me to come to Maverick's house tonight. A party.

Five minutes ago, I wouldn't have been ready for a party, but now I want to risk running into Kode again.

Yeah. I'm pathetic.

My eyes trail over to the bar, and I see the familiar envelope setting there. With a trembling hand, I pick it up and hold it. Rain went crazy when she read the words our father spoke from the grave.

Why did Kode bring this? I'm not ready to read it yet. Then again, I did break up with him, so maybe he doesn't feel comfortable holding it.

With a sigh, I shove it into the kitchen drawer—one I never use—

and shake my head while staring at nothing. I don't have the strength to be broken again right now, especially at the hands of my dead father.

Tria

"I can't believe you really came," Rain says, beaming as she makes her way toward me.

The bomb she dropped on me earlier shocked me, but I'm so damn happy for her and Dane.

"I'm here. How's Dane doing with Carrie?"

She grins bigger. "He and Elizabeth are a force. We'll have Carrie living with us by next weekend. Elizabeth knows everyone who is anyone, and Dane has the money to get this rushed. He wants to be the savior for Carrie that Elizabeth was for him. It's really so amazing."

"I think so, too," Britt—Dane's sister—says as she joins us.

Her long red locks are a little wild tonight. I smile down at her Wonder Woman shirt and tilt my head.

"You look... different."

She smiles and nods. "I found Comic Con. Dane took me. It's so awesome, and he bought me a ton of comic books that have female superheroes."

The delight in her voice is so new. Normally she's so robotic. Now she's standing here looking like the cutest, happiest girl she can be.

"And he bought her every article of clothing that had her favorite heroines on it," a familiar voice says from close behind me, seconds before a hard body is flush against my back.

I go stiff immediately, and Rain bites back a grin. I came here

288

because of Kode, but now that he's so close, I'm freaking the hell out.

"Hey, Britt, Rain." They both greet him as he leans down to my ear, and in an entirely different, deeper, and sexier tone, he gets against my ear and says, "Tria. You look incredible."

Breathing… How do I breathe? The air goes where?

I don't move—mostly because I can't—and Kode continues talking to Britt who is animatedly recapping the Comic Con experience. His body stays pressed closely to mine until I don't have the strength to endure it anymore.

"I need a drink," I say while quickly walking away.

Rain jogs to catch up with me, and she loops her arm through mine. Her cheeky grin doesn't go with the angry snarl she had a week ago.

"Kode is completely sober and all over you. I love it," she sighs.

I love it and hate it. I suppose that statement is a testament to our entire relationship.

I don't bother commenting, and I fight hard to not look in Kode's direction. The last time we were at a party, he spent the night trying to make me jealous. If he resorts to those tactics, I'll have to leave. I'm not ready to see something like that.

I should have stayed home.

After tossing back a few drinks, my eyes finally do the unthinkable and shift toward the man I love. To my surprise, his eyes are burning against mine, and he winks at me, causing my stupid heart to do painful things.

"Tria," Raya says, drawing my attention.

Rain and I both turn to face her, and I look around to see if Kade is anywhere around.

"No Kade?" Rain asks, frowning.

Raya shrugs, trying not to express anything. "He's still at the vineyard."

"Is he okay?" I ask.

"He's... Well, I hope he will be okay. This has been rough for him. He loved Thomas so much."

She fidgets as though she feels uncomfortable with this topic, so Rain shifts it, telling Raya about Carrie. The way Rain's face lights up when she talks... I've never been so happy for her. Maybe sometimes there's something good at the end of a major fuck-up.

The party has grown, and now there are twice as many women as there are men.

"You can tell this is Maverick's party," Raya remarks dryly, taking in all the sexy, flashy women Sterling Shore has to offer.

The men here seem to be enjoying themselves. Considering the fact I have no control over my urges, I turn to look at Kode. He's talking to Corbin, not paying any attention to the girl who is touching him.

I grimace when I see her press against him, but then he says something to her I can't hear, and she gasps before stomping away angrily. Corbin doubles over in laughter, and a small smile graces my lips.

Ash Masters walks up, forcing me to peel my eyes away from Kode as Tag joins him. But before my eyes fully escape, he catches me looking, and he winks at me before giving me that smile that he only ever gives me.

Swallowing hard, I devote all my attention to Ash with strained focus.

"You seem to be the talk of the night," she drawls, grinning like she has a secret.

I look at Rain and Raya, but they're both looking at me, too.

"Me?" I squeak, quickly clearing my throat from the embarrassing sound.

Ash snickers while nodding. "Apparently Kode is telling every girl in here that he's not on the market because he's in love with you. You don't even want to know what he's telling the few girls that don't take the hint."

My heart leaps into my throat, and I might possibly stagger a little. Raya steadies me, her eyes brighter now that she has something else to focus on other than Kade's dark period.

"Oh," Ash adds, her grin only growing, "and he's telling the guys here that if they like their faces where they're at, then they'd better not even look at you."

Ah, hell. I'm smiling. I'm smiling like a damn fool.

"Well I'll be damned," Raya says while crossing her arms over her chest. "You're in love with him, too."

That destroys my smile, and Rain's eyes lose their momentary excitement.

"What's wrong?" Ash asks, her eyes shifting from me to Rain. "Why do you look like someone just kicked you in the stomach?"

Forcing a smile that I don't feel, I shrug. "Because I love him. Too much. Which is why I'm not willing to put my heart through a grinder again. He only thinks he loves me because he can't have the girl he really wants."

Rain curses while running a hand through her hair, and she begins arguing. She just doesn't get it. She'd understand completely if Dane had been in love with me for eleven years before finally noticing she even existed.

Kode

"So you've talked to her?" Tag asks, still reeling over the fact that I'm confessing my love for Tria to anyone here that will listen.

Yeah, I'm making a bitch out of myself, but I'm determined to prove to Tria that she's the one. The only one.

"Went to her house today," I say, letting my eyes once again trail over to my girl. She's frowning. Why does she look upset? Hell, why does everyone around her look so damn sad?

Resisting the overwhelming urge to go to her, I swallow back the disappointment. I was sure she'd be happier once she started hearing what was circulating tonight.

"And?" Tag prompts.

Reluctantly, I stop trying to read lips and return my attention to talk to Tag.

"And her fucking business partner opened the door in his boxers. She was in the shower, and he went in there. I had to get out of there before I punched a hole through the wall. I wanted to beat the fuck out of him, but I knew that would only piss Tria off, and I'm trying to get her back. So I played it cool, and left her in a way that would only inspire the right thoughts."

Tag smirks. I hate that jackass smirk.

"You forgot to mention that part," Corbin says, his eyebrow raising. "Were they—"

"*Don't* finish that if you want to keep your balls attached," I growl, already on the edge of losing my damn mind. Doesn't he know better than to push me?

Corbin holds his hands up, surrendering, but he's grinning like he just won a prize. Fucker.

Maverick walks up, and he hands me a drink. "You need this, Pretty Boy. That ugly scowl is going to mess up your reconciliation scheme otherwise."

It's hard to plot murder and force a smile for Tria's sake.

Tria glances down at her phone, and I watch as she types in a message. Whoever has just lit up her screen has also lit up her smile. It'd better not be that beast that was at her place.

"Dude, you're still scowling. You're going to freak her out if you look pissed," Maverick says, grinning like the dick he is.

This is torture. I only came here because Rain sent a text saying that Tria was coming. For some stupid reason, I thought spreading the word that I loved her would do the trick. Should have known I'd done more damage than that could fix.

"Tria doesn't freak out when I look pissed," I mumble.

It's one of the many things I love about her.

293

"She used to," Dale says as he joins us, his smile also too fucking big.

"That was before she started trusting me."

And I shredded that trust with one mistake after another.

Deciding I need to loosen up, I chug the drink in my hand, and Tag goes to grab me another. I think they're all trying to keep me in place so that I don't go drop to my knees in front of Tria and beg like a motherfucking baby for her to take me back.

As soon as Tag returns with a new glass full of amber relief, a sight catches my eyes that has me grinding my teeth. That beast is here, and he's scanning the crowd. That's who sent her a text. He probably wanted to know where she was.

"Might want to hold him back," Tag says, laughing. "Before he kills the guy he's eyeing."

I start to move, but Corbin really does start holding me back. Then Jamie Burton walks out onto the patio, joining Leo at his side. A few spurts of mocking laughter come in from behind me as I watch the duo slowly make their way toward my girl.

"Dude, you just went postal over a guy who really isn't looking at Tria in *that* way," Tag jokes.

"Narrow-minded dumbass. They're probably just friends."

I refuse to hope that Leo is on a date with Jamie. It just seems too good to be true, and with the luck I've had lately, I don't see that happening.

Tria hugs Leo in greeting, and Corbin tightens his hold on me when I try moving again. She backs away to shake Jamie's hand, and he laughs as they talk. Then Jamie leans over to Leo to say something in his ear, and I almost do a fucking cartwheel when he bites Leo's earlobe like a lover's nip. When Leo smiles like a fool with a crush, my anger flees to make room for relief.

"Fuck yes," I breathe, sagging back into a relaxed state.

Riotous laughter breaches the air when the guys around me watch in fascination. Yeah. I'm fucking crazy.

Leo tugs at Jamie's arm, and he nods in my direction, apparently noticing the fact I've been burning a hole through them for the twenty minutes they've been here. His mouth tilts up on one side, as if he knew I hated him for a little while. I almost wonder if that's why he showed up. At least I can take him off my people-to-kill list.

Tria looks over at me as Leo walks away, and I give her a real smile because I can't help myself. My feet are moving before I can stop them, and Corbin sidles up to my side as I reduce the distance between myself and Tria.

Her eyes get wide in her head, but it's as though she's trapped and unable to look away. I don't stop walking until I'm right beside her, angling my body so that her side is touching my front.

"Kode Sterling. We thought you had died. Haven't seen you around in a while," Courtney Hughes says.

I hadn't even noticed her over here.

"I've been too busy trying to get my girl to talk to me," I say, watching the blush rise up Tria's neck. It's a good color on her.

Corbin snickers while moving closer to Rain and dropping his arm around her shoulders.

Courtney's voice is like nails on a chalkboard when she continues. "Oh. Really? You two? I had heard the rumors, but I thought that was impossible."

I still haven't looked at her, because my eyes are glued on the brunette who isn't moving away from me. Old habits die hard, and my hand moves to her back, stroking it and almost feeling the static between our touch.

She stiffens at first, but almost as quickly, she relaxes as though she's relishing the feel of my body so close to hers as much as I am. It feels so damn good to be touching her.

"Nope. Not impossible," I finally say to Courtney, still keeping my eyes on Tria who is wearing the sexiest red dress I've ever seen.

It stops just below her ass, and the top part is strapless, giving me a view of the upper swells of her perfect tits.

Fuck. Seven days suddenly feels like ten years.

"You look beautiful," I tell her, not giving a damn when several of the guys make heckling sounds.

Tria smiles up at me, and I brush my thumb across her cheek.

"Thank you. I should probably go."

Shit. I pushed too fast. She was letting me touch her, and I couldn't keep my mouth shut.

"Don't," Rain says, trying to help me out apparently.

Tria turns her attention to her sister, and her body starts to separate from mine. "I need to. I've got an early conference call to make. I'll see you tomorrow."

Tomorrow?

Rain pouts, but sighs, "Fine. Tomorrow. At least you're giving me that."

Making a mental note to grill Rain in a minute, I put my hand back on Tria's waist. "I'll walk you out."

Her breathing hitches, and she looks back up to meet my eyes.

"I don't think that's a good idea," she almost whispers, as though her voice is lost.

"Why?" My voice is low, the way she likes it to be when I seduce her.

I know exactly why she doesn't want me to walk her out. She's weak right now. I've weakened her with my touch, and she's on the verge of giving in.

"I'll walk with you," Courtney says, glaring at us when I scowl at her. "I forgot my phone in my car."

Bitch.

But the phone gives me an idea. I pull up my contacts as Tria bids everyone goodnight, and I hand Tria my phone as she turns back toward me.

"What's this?" she asks, her eyes slowly taking in what I'm showing her. When she sucks in a sharp breath, I can't help but smile.

On the screen, she sees the picture of her with her head resting in my lap, smiling happily as she watches TV. The name I had her under has been changed to *The Girl I Love*. Tears water up in her eyes, and she takes a deep breath.

Reaching over to her hands, I scroll to another contact, and show her a different name. It's Rain, but now it says *Dane's Girl*. And the picture is one of her with Tria.

She looks up to meet my eyes, and gives me a sad smile.

"That's nice, Kode. But doing something after the fact usually implies that it's not very sincere."

She hands me my phone back, and her hand shakes as she does. Cursing internally, I take it back, but not without seizing the opportunity to wrap my other hand around hers, forcing skin-on-skin contact.

I smirk when she sways, acting as though that simple touch is enough to crack her reinforced barrier.

"Just because I'm slow about some things, it doesn't mean they're any less sincere, Tria."

She jerks her hand away from mine like it's on fire, and I frown as she takes another shaky breath.

"Bye, Kode," she says hoarsely, and she starts to walk away, but not before turning around and forcing one last smile for me when she sees me watching.

Groaning, I turn away when she disappears through the gate with Courtney on her heels. Everyone is watching, no one is speaking, and the audience of our friends that was forgotten are now making me feel a little awkward.

Ash sniffles, Rain sighs, and Britt stands there with a dazed expression. All the guys are just wide-eyed as they gawk at me like I'm some exotic creature or an extremely fucked-up science experiment— not sure which.

"What?" I grumble, shrugging as if I don't know what the hell they're all staring at.

"Dude, you're so far gone that it's almost disgusting," Maverick says, his face drawn up as though he has tasted something sour.

"That was heart-wrenching," Ash says on a sigh.

Didn't realize we were putting on a damn show.

"It is what it is," I mumble, kicking at an imaginary stone on the patio while pocketing my hands in my jeans like a surly teen.

"If I was writing this story, I'd have you causing a major, dramatic scene at my wedding where you confessed your love for her on your knees," Rain says thoughtfully, causing me to arch my eyebrow in amusement. "Then she'd run into your arms, you'd kiss, possibly carry her out. It'd be over-the-top romantic."

Deciding I don't have any dignity left, I answer, "Two problems with that. The first is the fact that it wouldn't work. I've already confessed my damn love—"

"To everyone," Maverick points out in exasperation. "Several times."

I continue talking as though he didn't just say something snide. "And interrupting a wedding, begging for her to take me back… All that's a little too cliché for Tria."

Rain nods, seeming lost in thought. "True. Both things."

Courtney returns just as I glance down at my phone, trying to think of anything I can say to Tria.

"Well, now that she's gone, how about I take a look at how you have me programmed in your phone," she purrs, putting her hand on my arm.

I smirk as I quickly pull up my contacts, eager to oblige. She grins as she looks over, but her gasp of outrage makes me smile so damn hard that it hurts. *Do Not Answer* is the name with her number, and a picture of a pointy-nosed goblin is set for her.

"You're an asshole," she spews, furious as she turns away and stalks off in an angry huff.

Corbin looks over and bursts out laughing when he sees what pissed Courtney off, and I put my phone away while grinning triumphantly.

"Where are you taking Tria tomorrow?" I ask Rain, not even bothering to try to be subtle.

She grins as though she has been waiting on me to ask that question. "Silk. We'll be there around eleven. She agreed to go out for my early bachelorette party."

"We crashing a party?" Corbin asks, already smiling like my coconspirator.

Damn straight we're crashing.

As Maverick and Corbin start scheming to help me in my quest, I send a text to Tria. I reprogrammed my name in her phone earlier when I was at her house. She had changed me to *Kode.* That's better than a *Do Not Answer* or *Bastard I Hate.* I wanted to remind her of the good stuff. Now my name is *The Guy Who Loves You.*

Me: I miss you.

Since she hasn't responded all week, I'm surprised when I get a text back.

The Girl I Love: I miss you too.

I clutch the phone in my hand, worried I'm hallucinating. There's no doubt I'll be at Silk tomorrow. And I'll be anywhere else she is as long as she misses me, too.

"Kode," Rain says, smiling secretively.

"Yeah."

"If you're at Silk tomorrow, make sure you're drunk when we get there."

That's an odd request. "I need to be sober. I act like an idiot when I'm drunk, and Tria will completely write me off if I push her too hard."

Hell, she ran out of here after I touched her cheek and told her she was beautiful. If I drink, I'll be all over her.

"Just get drunk. Trust me."

Trust. Well, isn't that word the very crux of this whole damn situation.

Chapter 27

Tria

Tria,

I have a life full of regrets. None of them compare to the regrets I have for the sins against my family. I won't ask you to forgive me. It's not fair. All I want you to do is move on with your life in a way that brings you pride. I didn't tell you about my health, because I knew what you'd do. You would have come. You would have tried to make things better, and I would have hated myself more for putting you in that position. You're so incredible that you would have apologized to me for all my wrongs by somehow justifying them and making them your fault. I may be a bastard, but not even I could have allowed that.

Seeing that you've managed to build a relationship with Rain makes me so happy. If nothing else, the disdain you shared for me gives you common ground. I was thrilled to learn that boy finally wised up. He always did pay his attention to the wrong Noles girl for him. Rain was Dane's from the moment he saw her. But Kode was a fool to overlook you for so long. The day he came over here, I wept with joy and with pain.

Joy for the fact that you would be taken care of the way you deserve. Pain for the fact I'd never get to see your wedding. I'll be surprised if I manage to last until Rain's wedding.

Just so you know, your mother was the love of my life. I was a fool that took her for granted, the greedy man who fell in love with himself and his job and lost sight of the things in life that matter at the end. You won't be like that. I know you won't. Your heart is bigger than I've ever known. I'm just glad others are finally seeing the woman you really are.

This is wrong of me, but I can't help it right now. Consider this the last selfish thing I ever say. I love you, Tria. Always have. Always will.

Dad.

The words of that letter replay over and over in my head. Why I read it just before Rain picked me up in the limo for her bachelorette party, I don't know. Curiosity perhaps? Or maybe my masochistic nature overrode my needs for self-preservation.

Regardless of the reason, the words are etched into my brain forever now—my father's last words to me. Surprisingly, they've given me a sense of calm, whereas they drove Rain to the brink of self-destruction.

The part that is bugging me though, is when did Kode go over there? Did he go to talk to my father? Why did he tell him about us?

I expected my questions about my father to go unanswered—that letter wasn't long enough for him to explain everything he should have. But I didn't expect it to introduce new questions, especially about Kode.

Dusting off the lingering effect of the confusing letter, I follow Rain into the club, trying not to mention anything that might set her off. She doesn't need to know.

Silk is packed tonight, and I already regret the short denim shorts with frayed hems that I'm wearing when a set of creepy eyes drop to my legs. Rain's dress is way more revealing, so I'm hoping that she steals all the attention.

My shirt is a strappy, low-cut white shirt that glows under the black lights, and my wedge-heel sandals put me at least four inches taller than my sister. Should have worn something else.

I didn't feel like dressing up too much, but Rain demanded I change out of my T-shirt. Hell, I was proud I put on makeup and bothered to fix my hair. After seeing Kode yesterday, I spent the night crying in my bed, wishing like hell I could believe everything he was trying to say.

But it'd be the end of me if I had to go through losing him a second time. I'm barely surviving this as it is.

When he sent a text and I realized he had hacked my phone to change his contact name again, I burst into a sobbing fit of tears. In a moment of weak abandon, I sent him back a message. It was stupid. All that did was invite him to continue this game, just like me leaning against him while he was touching me last night.

Why can't I be strong? I couldn't resist reading that letter just as I couldn't resist texting Kode back, although I knew both were a bad idea. Even though the letter actually gave me a sense of peace, ending the suspense I didn't know was there, I still ignored the voice in my head that told me to stay away.

"This is way too many people," Ash says, cursing when a guy bumps into her and spills his drink on her feet.

"Can we go somewhere else?" I ask, yelling over the loud music.

Rain frowns, seeming distracted as she searches the crowd like she's looking for something.

"No," she calls back. "I want to be here. This is my future husband's club. It seems perfect for the occasion."

Perfectly chaotic if you ask me.

People writhe together in places not meant for dancing, blocking the paths for walking, and Rain leads us up to the booth no one else is allowed to sit in besides the Sterlings.

Speaking of Sterlings... Shit.

Kode is sitting at the booth with Maverick and Corbin, and he looks like he's ready to pull me into his lap right now. My heart thuds in my ears as he appraises me with a slow, and steady, heated gaze, scrolling his eyes up and down my legs, and slowly raking his eyes over me like a predator sizing up his prey.

"Looks like we've got party crashers," Rain says with a shrug, and I glare at her.

She did this shit on purpose.

"You can sit by me," Kode says, grinning as he slides over to make room for me. Ash and Rain climb in on the other side, both of them grinning like they plotted this whole damn thing.

The spot beside Kode is the only spot available in the curved booth now. Maverick and Corbin are smiling like cats who ate canaries, and I roll my eyes while dropping in beside Kode.

The second his arm goes around my shoulders, I start fighting the urge to melt against him.

"Love those shorts, baby," he says against my ear. It's then I smell the alcohol on his breath. Too much liquor makes his hands glue themselves to me. Possibly any girl. I guess I'll find out tonight.

"You're drunk," Rain notes, looking pleased for some bizarre reason. Kode's hands have already started pawing at me, but I'm not fighting him.

He won't stop, and everyone will get mad if I fight him and he doesn't stop. I don't want them pissed at him or saying anything negative toward him. It'll only piss me off.

At least that's what I'm telling myself to justify this.

"He's been drunk all week. Last night was the first time he's been sober," Maverick says, sounding somewhat like he's tattling.

"You've been drunk all week?" I ask, turning to meet his smile.

He tugs me to be flush against him, nuzzling my face with his as he leans over.

"I miss you too much when I'm sober," he confesses, making my heart clench.

Drunk people tell the truth all the time, right? Isn't alcohol like a truth serum? Or is that just some myth that I'm trying to convince myself to believe.

Kode's arm slides around my waist, and one hand moves to my ass as he tries to tug me onto his lap. I resist, and he pouts before moving his lips to my neck and starting a trail of searing kisses that have me practically convulsing.

His touch... It's my Achilles heel.

"Tria, if he's too much, just ask for help," Maverick says, though he's grinning.

Rain's smirk says it all. I remember him once being like this with her, but not nearly to this extent. She said the only time he ever kissed her was that time at Dane's party—the night when all hell broke loose. But she said that Kode is like an animal around me when he's been drinking. Right now, he's proving that.

She's right across from him, but even drunk off his ass, he's completely focused on me. It's a small victory, but one that still has me questioning my already fragile resolve.

"I love you," he says against my neck, and another piece of that resolve breaks away.

The table makes conversation, and Corbin pulls Rain out of the booth as Maverick grabs Ash. They abandon us and make their way onto the dance floor as Kode continues his oral assault on my sensitized skin.

"You taste so damn good," he says when he reaches the swells of my breasts. Dale walks toward us, but his grin crawls up when he sees Kode practically devouring me, and he turns and walks away.

"Why'd you go to see my father," I ask, my voice cracking.

He leans back, tilting his head. "How'd you know I did?"

Frowning, I glance around to make sure no one can hear.

"I read the letter."

He brushes his hand across my cheek, and those silver eyes stare softly into mine with more compassion than Kode ever shows anyone else.

"He mentioned that?" I nod to his question, and he continues as his hand slides down to my waist, unable to stop touching me. "He wanted your mom to drop stuff off, but she didn't want to. Melanie asked Rain, but it upset her. Then Corbin asked me to ask you, and it pissed me off. I didn't want you having to deal with that, so I went and took Dale with me so I didn't do something stupid. Did I screw up?"

His question is so sincere, that I almost launch myself into his arms. But instead, I just lean into his touch a little more, which of course has his roaming hands taking full advantage.

"No. You didn't screw up. Why did you tell him about us?" My voice is soft, barely maintaining an audible tone over the music.

"I got defensive when he said something that I took out of context. It took him five seconds to realize I was there to protect you and not Rain. He actually seemed pleased with that."

Oh damn. He's drunk and talking in a way that is almost hard to understand, but there's no doubt that he's telling the truth right now. It's almost enough. Almost.

His mouth returns to trailing kisses down my neck as he says, "I'd do anything to protect you."

In that moment, I completely believe him. His brazen lips make it back down to my shirt, and his tongue darts out to find the line of my cleavage. I'm so glad the music is drowning out the embarrassing sounds I'm making. Kode is the only one hearing them, and it's only fueling him.

I can't breathe, especially when his bold hand grabs my shirt, inching it down to uncover more flesh on my breast for him to attack.

"I have to go to the bar. I'll be back," I hoarsely tell Kode, trying to escape before I end up screwing him in the booth.

He stands when I do, and he grabs my hips, pulling my back to his front, as he moves us toward the bar. "Not without me," he mumbles, stumbling a little. "Too many people."

Again, my heart clenches, swelling with a touch of pride. His eyes are on me. No one else. His hands act as though they'll never let me go.

After ordering my drink, I look over as Rain joins me at my side, ordering her one as well. Kode continues nibbling on my neck until Corbin hauls him off me. I almost beg Corbin to let him go, because it feels so good, but I know I shouldn't.

"Give her just a little room," Corbin says, laughing. "You told me not to let you scare her."

Kode frowns, but he glances over at me for a fleeting second before sighing in defeat. Maverick walks around to hand him another drink, and they talk to each other while Ash squeezes in at the bar with us.

When I turn my attention back to Rain, she's grumbling and knocking some guy's hands away.

"Get the hell away." Her disdain bleeds into her tone, but the creep doesn't take a hint.

"Dude, back the hell up," Maverick growls, glaring at the guy.

The guy just laughs while holding his hands up, staggering to the left a little in a drunken stupor. "Sorry. Didn't know she was yours."

He stumbles in behind me, but the second his hands touch my waist, he's falling and yelping. When he lands on the ground, he starts clutching his nose as it spews blood. Kode's fist drops back to his side as he looks down at the guy he just punched out, and my eyes go wide when I see the murderous glare in his eyes.

He didn't hit the guy while he was all over Rain. This guy barely touched me.

"Kode, don't!" I say, grabbing his arm when he moves toward the guy like he might do more.

"He shouldn't have put his fucking hands on you," he growls, too drunk to know when to stop.

That's my breaking point. All the pieces fall together, and I lose the last ounce of my resolve.

No one is helping me hold Kode back. What the hell?

To keep him from pummeling the guy and going to jail, my hands go to his shoulders as I step in front of him, and I use them as leverage to haul myself up and wrap my legs around his waist. His hands immediately go to my ass, and his eyes lose their angry haze as lust and excitement fills them. His angry scowl turns into a slow, sexy grin that has me tightening my legs around him for an entirely different reason.

"What're you doin', baby?" he asks in a sexy drawl that has me reminding myself to breathe.

"Taking you home with me."

His grin doubles, and he leans in and kisses me hard. My hands go to his hair, and my fingers tangle in the soft blonde strands as I kiss him back with the same need pouring out of me.

I kiss him like I can't ever stop—like I can only breathe his air.

"Take the limo," Rain announces, referring to our girls' night ride she rented.

I wave in the air to acknowledge I heard her because my lips are otherwise engaged. Kode is owning my mouth with his tongue, his teeth, and his growls of pleasure. It's like fire on ice with every twist of his tongue, because I'm fully dissolving right now.

His hands tighten on my ass, and though I don't know how he does it, he makes it outside.

"Home, Ms. Noles?" The limo driver asks, making me realize we've already reached the car.

I start to say yes, even though it's painful to break away from the kiss. Kode puts me down, as Hank—the driver—holds the door, looking very much amused.

"Actually, I have a different address."

Kode tugs me into the car as I laugh and tell Hank Kode's address instead. Leo had another date with Jamie tonight, and I don't want us competing for who can be louder at my house.

Hank grins while closing the door, and Kode pulls me onto his lap, his lips quickly moving back to my neck to resume devouring me. I grin when he thrusts up, mimicking the action he wants to do without clothes as Hank pulls out of Silk.

When his lips reclaim mine, it's so powerful that I moan and grind against him. It takes me a second to realize his hands have moved from my ass and are working against the button on my shorts. My smile grows, and I break the kiss and press my forehead to his.

"Not here. We don't have enough time, and I want more than a limo fuck," I tell him, smiling as he groans.

Then his eyes look up to meet mine, and he tugs me closer, brushing his lips against mine just barely.

"Tell me, Tria," he murmurs against my lips, confusing me.

"What?" I ask, but all coherent thoughts cease when I sink lower onto his lap and feel how hard he is.

Eight days is way too long to go after you've had Kode Sterling.

The question becomes lost as we hungrily kiss each other, desperate sounds of pent-up desire coating the car and possibly scarring Hank's ears. As soon as we reach the house, Kode is lifting me out of the car, keeping my legs strapped against him, as Hank holds the car door for us.

"Have a good evening, Ms. Noles," Hank says, laughing lightly.

I just wave, because talking is impossible while I'm suckling Kode's tongue and swallowing his growls. Kode fumbles to get his door open, but he finally manages, still carrying me.

"Tell me, Tria," he says again, breaking the kiss as we blindly make our way through the dark house.

My body is suddenly being lowered to a familiar bed that smells a lot like my perfume for some reason.

"Tell you what?" I ask around a moan when he pulls my shirt down and puts his mouth around my nipple.

Right now, I'm glad I skipped putting on a bra. But he releases his hold, sliding until his body is hovering over me, and his eyes meet mine, even though his silver pools are hiding in the darkness.

"You know what," he says, that sexy drawl thick and laced with lust.

My whole body heats, and a smile spreads across my face as a lone tear escapes my grasp.

"I love you, Ko—"

His lips crush mine almost painfully, and my clothes become obstacles for him that he's impatient to get rid of. I giggle when he breaks the kiss to curse my stubborn shorts after they don't slide easily over my ass.

He has to move off me, and with one hard tug, he jerks them down my legs, dragging my panties with them. With very jerky movements, he hurries out of his clothes, and I giggle while pulling my shirt over my head.

He stops, looking down at me with hungry eyes that can barely be seen with the sliver of moonlight sneaking through the window. Then my gaze travels down his body, greedily taking in all the hard lines of definition, and of course the hardest part of his body at the moment that has me licking my lips in anticipation.

Very slowly, he lowers himself onto me, running his hands along my sides.

"Say it again," he murmurs as he drops a soft kiss to my chest, eliciting a shiver from me in response.

"I love you," I whisper, sucking in a sharp breath and arching my hips as he continues moving lower with that divine mouth.

He teases me, swiping his tongue across my lower abdomen, and I swear under my breath, making him chuckle against my tingling skin. But his laughter stops when he reaches the spot where I want him, and he flicks his tongue across that bundle of nerves in a way that has me writhing beneath him, ready to explode after only a few seconds.

"Say it again," he whispers against me before flicking his tongue

313

once more, and I cry out, barely able to keep breathing, never mind talking.

"I love you," I whimper, desperate for him to finish.

I start to curse him when he moves, but then suddenly he's on me, in me, thrusting deep with one hard stroke, and I grip his shoulders as we both moan in unison. His lips find mine as he slowly draws back, and I bite his lower lip when he plunges in fiercely once more.

"I love you," I say on my own, earning a growl from him as he sets a furious pace that has me clawing and making feral sounds that don't sound human.

His forehead presses against mine as he grabs both of my knees, angling my body in a way that gives him more depth and more traction for his already hard thrusts.

It's almost too much—too much sensation, too much desire, too much need. I feel like I'm falling and climbing at the same time, holding on while simultaneously letting go, and my body spirals out of control while finding a serene place of control at the same time.

When I cry out his name in unbridled ecstasy, arching off the bed as my body explodes around him, fireworks detonate behind my eyelids. I'm pretty sure I black out, because when I open my eyes again, Kode is stilling inside me.

His eyes open as he gasps for a breath, and he drops to me like he's exhausted. I wrap my legs around his waist, kissing his head as he pants for air. He doesn't seem as drunk, but he's not sober either. I'm really glad he's not one of those guys who suffers performance issues after drinking too much.

"I love you, Tria," he says, grinning against my neck.

I smile like a fool while holding him tighter, and a content sigh flows from my lips. "Need five minutes?" I ask, smiling bigger when he laughs.

It might sound crazy, but I honestly believe Kode Sterling is mine.

Epilogue

Kode

"No," she hisses, glaring at me while I grin triumphantly at her. She's not getting out of this.

"You made a bet, Tria. Obviously I don't want you doing it here, but soon. And somewhere public. You lost. I can recap the night you caved if you'd like."

She puckers her lips in a pout that has my cock twitching happily, and I shift in my seat, making sure the affected area stays hidden under the table.

Rain and Dane are making their rounds as the newlywed couple, and Mom is holding her new grandchild in her lap. This isn't the most appropriate time to tease her about collecting on our little bet, but I love getting Tria riled up. It's not like she'll ever follow through.

"You're an ass," she grumbles, sipping her champagne.

"An ass you happen to love," I say, grinning over at her.

When her lips twitch, she covers her mouth with her hand to hide her growing smile.

"You two make a great couple," Mom says from across the table, unaware of our private conversation. "Will you be getting married next?"

I strangle on my drink while Tria smiles mockingly at me. Marriage? I hadn't even thought of that shit. Then again, there's no way in hell I'm letting Tria go, so it's not like it would be the worst idea.

"That's not on the agenda just yet," I say uncomfortably.

"Really? We discussed it the other night, dear," Tria lies with her overly sweet tone that has me glaring at her.

"Oh?" Mom asks too brightly, clearly excited. Damn. "That's perfect. Then you could start working on some more grandchildren for me."

Tria is the one to strangle on her drink this time when the tables turn, and I grin over at her. Fortunately, Carrie asks to use the bathroom, and Mom stands to oblige and escort her.

"Not in a hurry to have kids?" I muse, teasing her.

She shakes her head, and I laugh. "Me neither. So quit provoking my mother."

She rests her head on my shoulder, and I pull her as close as I can get her. Unfortunately, it's not close enough, so I end up tugging until she's in my lap. The second her sexy ass is pressed against me, and her entire body is resting on mine, I feel better.

"Toasts!" Maverick demands, and then he points to Tria who immediately goes pale. She's been dreading the hell out of this. I've helped her rehearse her speech all week long, but she still doesn't want to stand up in front of everyone and speak.

"We'll start with the Maid of Honor," Maverick adds, smiling tauntingly at her because he knows how much she doesn't want to do this.

The outdoor reception is being held at my parents' enormous home, where Mom insisted to have it. Eleanor is wiping her eyes, still crying happy tears as she watches Tria stand up in front of me shakily.

317

After a few deep breaths, Tria finally starts her speech to the quiet reception as Dane and Rain sit down at their own table.

"Most of you know that the history between myself and my sister is a little rocky. We didn't have the conventional start that most families get to experience. To be honest, I started envying Rain early on. Who couldn't? She was amazing and strong and so damn smart. Then she had the Sterling boys taking care of her, letting the world know she was even more special, and of course that had most of the women in Sterling Shore teeming with envy."

That last part wasn't in the original speech she rehearsed with me.

Everyone chuckles, but it actually hurts me to hear that. Tria had no one, and Rain had an army of support. If I could go back in time… I'll just have to spend my future making it up to her.

"Out of those Sterling boys, she had the attention of the illusive Dane Sterling. It was evident when we were thirteen that they would end up together. They took a long road to get to where they are, but there's no doubt in my mind they took the route designed to make them stronger—to make their relationship stronger.

"It's not easy to find the one person in this world designed specifically for you. But they've found that in each other. It's rock solid, and if you've ever been around them, then you've seen it. You've probably felt it. And more than likely, you've longed for that same thing. So to my sister and my brother-in-law, I want to say I love you both, and I'm so unbelievably happy that you two managed to find each other."

Everyone starts clapping, and Rain smiles while dabbing the tears from her eyes. Dane leans over to kiss Rain, and a few catcalls sound out.

I keep waiting on Tria to sit back down in my lap, but she doesn't. Instead, the second the cheers start dying down, she continues speaking.

"While I have your attention, there's something else I need to say." She turns to me, and I tilt my head, curious as to what she's up to. She grins, and then faces the crowd again. "Most of you know Kode Sterling, and not too long ago, I started a small rumor about the fact he might not be all that into women."

Oh shit. She's really doing this? Here?

Everyone snickers, and Tria shrugs innocently before adding, "The truth is, well, I guess you know we're together. But what you don't know is that he's probably the most phenomenal lover in the world. He's the only man who has ever made my toes curl, and I swear I can't get enough. So please don't doubt that Kode Sterling is a woman's dream."

Yeah... I'm fairly positive this is one of the few times I've ever blushed in my life, and the sounds of people choking, gasping, or laughing has me turning even redder. I'm kicking her ass.

Tria drops back down to my lap, covering her laughter with her hand, and I glare at the back of her head as everyone hoots and mocks me.

"That backfired, didn't it?" she whispers, apparently finding amusement in this bullshit.

"I told you I *didn't* want you to do it here," I growl, but she only

319

laughs harder.

"Did you? I must have misunderstood," she says, feigning innocence.

If I didn't love her so damn much, I'd probably drop her ass to the ground. At this moment, I really wish I didn't love her.

Maverick is still roaring with laughter when he goes to make his toast as the best man, and Tria turns in my arms, grinning that teasing smile as she presses a soft kiss to my lips.

"I love you," she says sweetly, batting her lashes as though that will make it all better.

"I can't tell," I pout, which only has her laughing harder.

We miss Maverick's toast because of the lingering whispers behind us that are going on about Tria's announcement. My arms clamp around her waist, and I hold her to me while whispering, "You know I'll get you back for that, don't you?"

She chuckles softly while kissing me again, and this time, I can't help myself from giving in. Her tongue slips between my lips, and my grip tightens for a different reason.

She can drive me out of my damn mind, but I love every wild moment of it.

Music starts playing, forcing us to separate from the kiss that went on much longer than either of us intended, and she stands while pulling me up from the chair.

"Go dance with Rain. I'm going to go dance with your brother," she says while pulling me closer. "She doesn't get to dance with her father, so she should get to share that dance with her best friend."

I smile down at her, and spin her to me before kissing her, thanking her for so many things in that moment. It was certainly a hell of a road to get her to realize that it was her I wanted, but it was definitely worth it.

"I really do love you," I say, kissing her nose while pulling back.

"Obviously. You'd have killed me by now if you didn't."

My laughter comes out as she grins, and she heads over to ask the groom to dance. This gives me a chance to thank Rain for something it took me a while to figure out.

Rain smiles as I proffer my hand, and she takes it while standing up. I pull her to me like she's my own blood, and we dance like the best friends we were always meant to be.

"Thanks," I say, moving her through the crowd that has begun to gather.

"For?"

"For hiring that guy to fuck with Tria that night at the bar. It was clever; I'll give you that."

She snickers while tilting her head. "I have no idea what you're talking about."

Rolling my eyes, I continue the formal waltz, my years of stupid ballroom dancing at my family's parties paying off right now.

"I was too drunk that night to put two and two together, but when I sobered up it all seemed to fall into place. I knew I had seen that guy before, and I finally figured out where. He works for Dane. That can't be a coincidence. And I've seen you talking to him numerous times. You wanted me to lose my mind when he touched Tria, but only after

321

he touched you and I did nothing."

She shrugs, grinning lightly. "When drunk, you never were too perceptive of others fucking with me unless you were right beside me. But with Tria, you're aware of her every move no matter where you are in the room. *If* I had done something like that, I would have factored that in. And *if* I had done that, then I would have told Corbin to get you to back away from her so that this hypothetical plan could go into action. And *if* I had done that, then I would have known that Tria would have done all that was necessary to keep you from going too far. And *if* this was real, I would have warned the guy he'd end up with some sore part on his body, but that I would make sure he was very well compensated. And I would have told the guys to stand down so that she could handle it. And *if* I had done it, I would have known she'd see the truth, and that it would be the breaking point she needed. If not, then I would have had a backup plan."

I grin at her. "That's a lot of *ifs*."

She shrugs one shoulder, then says, "That's because it's a hypothetical situation."

"It was a risky hypothetical plan. I was drunk, and with Tria, I'm touchier than I've ever been with anyone. What if it had pissed her off?"

Her grin is calculated, like she's the mastermind of an elaborate scheme. "Tria is too defensive of you. She wouldn't have done anything if she was worried about someone getting mad at you. So, that would have also gone into that plan. And she would also be vulnerable to your groping attacks."

Laughter falls out of me, and she grins victoriously just as Maverick comes over to steal her away.

"My turn," he announces, kissing her forehead as he pulls her close.

Walking away, my eyes search for my girl. Dane is now dancing with our mother, so Tria is mingling within the crowd somewhere. While searching, I notice Kade Colton. He's alone at the table, looking unapproachable as he drinks wine. If I knew what to say, I'd go over there.

Raya is dancing with her father, and I can almost feel the tension between her and the Colton prince from here. Wren moves to the chair beside Kade, but he seems to be getting ignored as Kade focuses on nothing in particular, numb to the world around him.

Ash is in Tag's lap, kissing him leisurely, and Melanie is holding Trip while he plays with a set of toy keys. Turning again, I find Corbin propped up with his phone in his hand, smiling at the screen like he enjoys whatever he sees. Really don't want to know what that's about.

No Tria. She seems to have gone missing.

As my eyes continue to scour, they land on Dale who is chatting up a pretty redhead, and I laugh when she runs her fingers up his chest. Britt is sitting with Dad, and he's flipping through some of the comic books she brought. She's enjoying things a little late in life, but it's a childish enthusiasm she was robbed of when she was an actual child.

The girl I've been searching for finally catches my attention. She's with Ethan, her cousin, and they're talking off to the side. I start moving toward them, smiling when she gives me a wink. But that smile concerns me. Why is she giving me her best mischievous smile?

"Hey, Kode," Corbin says while coming toward me, grinning like he has something juicy to share.

"Yeah," I grumble, already getting concerned. Between Tria's smile and Corbin's smile, I don't feel so good about what's going on.

"Man, you should have told me," he says, knowing damn well I'm lost.

"Cut the shit. What'd she say?" I groan.

He bursts out laughing, and I cross my arms over my chest, growing impatient.

"I thought it was weird how she announced to the whole damn reception party about what an awesome lover you were, so I asked her about it. She explained it was to build your confidence. I talked to my dad. He said he could get you a prescription for your little problem."

I'm going to kill her.

"What the hell?"

"Early erectile dysfunction isn't common, but it's manageable with the appropriate medicine."

Cursing, my eyes go wild in search for her as my blood pressure rises.

"I don't have a damn problem getting it up, jackass."

His laughter bellows out, and I flip him off while heading toward Ethan who is now chatting up a blonde.

"Where'd she go?" I growl.

Ethan doesn't even bother to mask his grin before nodding toward my house.

I break into a sprint, running toward the back doors, and then my phone buzzes just as I reach the stairs.

True Winner of the War: Now that you're mad, come fuck me like you hate me.

My knees give out at the sight of her text, and I bust my ass on the stairs, spewing a few profanities when I hit too hard. But my stupid grin spreads, and I start searching for her for a whole new reason.

Taking a guess, I head into my old bedroom, and then I stumble to a halt. Damn.

Tria is on my old bed, her body clad in a skimpy lace thing that has me biting my fist to keep from saying something incredibly stupid. She gives me a vixen's smile while crawling across the bed like every damn fantasy there has ever been, and her dark hair falls around her shoulders before she curls her finger, beckoning me over.

"Get my message?" she muses, her smile growing when I finally start kicking out of my shoes.

I'm naked in no time, and I go to lock the door before grabbing her up from the bed and kissing her with all I've got. Damn, she's so perfect for me.

As her legs fasten around my waist, I move her to the wall, pressing her against it as my lips start moving down her neck.

"Yeah, I got it. But I'd rather fuck you like I love you all night."

She grins as my lips find hers again, and I send a silent *thank you* to my brother for stealing Rain's heart so long ago. If he hadn't, I would have never ended up with right Noles girl—the one meant just for me.

The **End.**

ABOUT THE AUTHOR

What does C.M. Owens write? A little bit of everything as long as the central focus is romance.

C.M. Owens is an escapist, and loves to stretch the imagination. Writing is more than a passion – it's a necessity. It's a means of staying sane and happy.

Where do her ideas come from? Usually it's a line in a song that triggers an idea that spawns into a story. Though she came from a family of musicians, she has zero abilities with instruments, she sounds like a strangled cat when she sings, and her dancing is downright embarrassing. Just ask her two children. Her creativity rests solely in the written word. Her family is grateful that she gave up her quest to become a famous singer.

Made in United States
Orlando, FL
21 May 2024

47105739R00183